PRAISE FOR THE RISE

"THE RISE IS A gritty, heart-wrenching, and wildly immersive dystopian saga that grabs you by the throat and drags you through blood-soaked arenas, haunted bunkers, and psychological minefields...What starts as a sci-fi gladiator tale quickly blossoms into a dark, emotional exploration of trauma, resistance, and sacrifice...The Rise left a lasting impact on me. The characters feel deeply authentic, and the stakes are both personal and profound. For readers drawn to darker narratives, flawed protagonists, and antagonists who are disturbingly human, this book is a compelling choice. This is not light or escapist fare, it is a somber, emotionally charged, and battle-worn epic that leaves a mark. And truthfully, that's precisely what makes it unforgettable."

-Literary Titan

THE

RISE

BOOK 3

The Rise

by Brian Penn

Published by

Ink Penn LLC

THE

RISE

BOOK 3

BRIAN PENN

Ink Penn

LLC

For those who are lost, you can always be found. For those who have fallen, you can always rise...

"Those who put themselves in His hands will become perfect, as He is perfect- perfect in love, wisdom, joy, beauty, health, and immortality. The change will not be completed in this life, for death is an important part of the treatment."

- C.S. Lewis

Fan art
by
Jessalynn Adams

CHAPTER ONE

Asher

THE SHAKING OF THE arena was not caused by Apex. It was an act of God. A true dues ex machina. Albeit temporarily; it was an earthquake that took Apex down, not me. Five months ago, I thought Apex would be the end of me. I remember vividly as he scampered towards me and I backpedaled—ricochet in one hand, StunClub in the other. I remember thinking to myself, what good would either one of these do against this savage that is about to trample me?

Then providence intervened. I saw it happen in slow motion. The gasps from the crowd. How quickly their lust for violence turned to fear when it was their own blood at stake. They stampeded over one another. Children and the elderly were left to be trampled on. It was everyone for themselves. A Lazurite condition. Sometimes, a human condition. I would have liked to think we Drecks would have handled it differently. Parts of the grandstand also collapsed. Hundreds more died under the concrete and steel rebar. Small dust clouds emanated from the arena, as if demons were casually puffing on cigars. None of this seemed to bother Apex, a laser-focused killing machine with only me in his sights. He probably thought the tremors underneath his feet were his own making, or that the screams and commotion were praise for him. His eyes were like dark clouds preparing to rain down terror. A half-smirk crossed his wolfish, chiseled face.

He didn't see the metal section of the canopy fall from the sky, landing directly in front of him. He stumbled over it and landed flat on his massive chest. Another four-foot section, probably weighing three hundred pounds, landed on his legs. I heard simultaneous snaps—both his femurs breaking, which sounded like vast branches finally giving way in a windstorm.

As debris rained down around me, I stood frozen. I scanned the arena until I saw Sarai in the Seat of Sultans. Her lips mouthing my name as she and her father were whisked to safety. Everything about her movements and mine seemed sluggish and heavy, as though time itself had become lazy and stagnant. But for everyone else, it was the opposite: the guards barked orders so loudly and so fast that I could not decipher their words. The retreating crowds seemed to disperse quicker than was possible.

I had no urge to run or duck for cover. I even closed my eyes for just a moment. Or was it longer? I had no desire to open them as I stood under our willow. The willow's strands grazed my shoulders as the winds cooled my back and the sun warmed my face. Sarai was there. She was always there. Yet, I could never touch her. As I reached my hands out, she dissolved like smoke in the wind. Like a dream, you couldn't quite control.

I opened my eyes, and my breathing was no longer heavy. My heart rate had slowed. It was a strange feeling to witness the carnage around me without any fear. It's almost as if I expected something like this to happen, as though an angel on my shoulder allowed me to live another day. To breathe another breath. Or maybe it was because I had been here so many times I had learned to control it.

I dropped my weapons, and it wasn't long until I was all alone on the arena floor—except for Apex writhing in pain and grunting unpleasantly, finally brought down by a power greater than his own. Surely, he and

Renatus would see this as bad luck instead of divine intervention. I saw it as a sign. A sign that our many years of hope and faith might finally pay off.

But this trembler that agitated the earth also created a new fault line in Renatus's soul. It had only delayed the inevitable. This wasn't the end of Apex, or the Canonization.

It was just the beginning.

Asher

Would my father still recognize me if he were alive? What about my son? Would Sarai?

I peer up at her. She is perched next to her father in the remodeled Seat of Sultans. I feel old, but her beauty has not waned. Since the earthquake five months ago, the arena has been rebuilt—retrofitted to withstand another earthquake, the Lazurites have been told. It certainly has not affected attendance. They have returned as if it never happened. All I see is weak minds and short memories. The roar of the crowds is like background music to me now—white noise I have grown accustomed to. The same goes for the blood on my hands.

The Lazurite charges me, swinging his StunClub. I step back, my left boot sliding backward in the sand a few feet until it finds purchase in the hardened dirt beneath. I swing the wooden part of my spear and hit him just above his ankles. He flops to the ground, dropping his club. I could end it right now, but that wouldn't be sadistic enough for Renatus and the crowd. They want their money's worth, so to speak. Last time I won in the first three minutes, they just sent out another. Then I was punished. This is supposed to be the main event for the evening. I need to make it last.

"Get up," I whisper to the Lazurite. "Come on, we're not finished yet."

He grabs his club and pulls himself up. All the bravado he displayed during his introduction has dissipated. He is short. Most headliners are taller. His metallic brown hair just reaches his shoulders. He hasn't yet succumbed to the trendy Lazurite buzz cuts, but he isn't fully stuck in the old style either—long flowing hair to his mid back.

The sun is setting, its rays slipping into the open portion of the stadium. For a second, the haziness smothers my view. I can only see his outline, and for a moment, I prefer it that way. A nameless, faceless victim. It makes the inevitable easier.

He swings at me, and I dodge him. The handle of my spear splits his lip.

The Lazurite spits blood. "You're just a dirty Dreck, and nothing will ever change that!"

I hope not.

He scans the crowd with deep-set amber eyes. "Enjoy it, Dreck. They may love you today, but the minute someone better comes along, that's it. It will be the spilling of your blood they root for."

I am not doing it for them. "Perhaps you should worry about your own blood."

He spits before charging me again; his moves are predictable. It's hard to believe he is an elite. I sidestep him again and knock the StunClub from his hands. He turns to retrieve it. I throw my spear in front of him; it sticks into the ground, and his own momentum propels his chest right into the handle, knocking him back down.

He can no longer hide his fear. His shoulders tighten. He blinks rapidly. "Please. I have a family."

I march over and pull the spear out of the dirt. "So do I." I ram it through his chest. No hesitation. I don't like how easy this has become for me. "Sorry," I whisper.

Cheers from the crowd. Death is celebrated.

I am celebrated.

What does that make me?

I hope Sarai isn't watching. I glance up. She isn't. Renatus gives me a nod of approval, gently tapping his hands together, but he seems to be on the edge of boredom. Will this satisfy his bloodlust? I will likely find out later. I finally catch Sarai's eye. All I see is loneliness and sadness, a look that she has lost or is losing me. Renatus has not allowed me to see my wife since the earthquake. Only here, in this coliseum of death, does he allow us to see each other—so he can force her to watch what I am becoming. Renatus has a way of killing you without killing you.

Six Lazurite elites march into the stadium to escort me out. As they near, I raise my hand to scratch the back of my head. A little too fast for their liking, as all six of them flinch, then raise their weapons in a defensive position. Elites fear me. I fear me. Who am I? Am I the new Legion?

I have killed so many Lazurites in this arena that I have lost count. While Apex heals, I am Renatus's new gladiator. And apparently a crowd favorite. My heart is becoming cold. For a moment, it is warmed by the adoration of the crowd. This is what Renatus wants. He wants those in my position to feel loved. It's pure manipulation to do his bidding. Yet, it is powerful. Especially when you're kept in isolation. Things begin to blur when the only kind words or reverence comes from your enemy. Zion wants to ensnare me. Renatus wants to break me. But I have been here before, and I must fight not to let that happen again.

My thoughts wander to Cephas, Jude, and Kenan. My army. My friends. Are they still alive? Or are Sarai and I all alone? Are we the last of The Defiance? Have we already lost the war? Is this my life now? Will I never again experience my uncle's gruff mentoring or my friend Jude's sardonic jokes? I looked forward to watching Kenan grow into a strong leader. Perhaps I would have one day become a mentor myself.

I examine the dead Lazurite being dragged from the arena and feel nothing. Killing is something I never thought I would become acclimated to. What would Cephas do in my shoes? His words ring in my head: *fighting for freedom is noble, but those who are celebrated for killing for sport have been given a fraudulent honor.*

But then I justify it by telling myself each man I am forced to kill brings me one step closer to my son and my wife.

As I stare at my crimson-stained hands, I can't help but wonder if maybe it's the other way around.

Asher

Being a gladiator for Renatus does have perks. I am escorted to his palatial gym. It is replete with an entire array of weights, machines, a lap pool, ice baths, sauna, you name it. Apex is in the corner, still rehabbing his legs. His quads pulsate, and his veins cord as he squats an ungodly amount of weight.

"Rematch coming soon, little man," he tells me with a smile.

I grab a ricochet off the weapon's wall and hurl it at a moving metal target. Ping. It returns to me. I am older, but with all this training, I have become more accurate and nimbler than ever. At least, I feel that way. The irony does not escape me, that I am working out and training next to Apex. My enemy, the man I will face sooner or later. In fact, I see him so often in here that our conversations border on banter now. Sometimes, I must remind myself where I am and who I am talking to.

"Yeah, because last time was a *quaking* good time," I say sarcastically, referring to the earthquake that caused his injuries. Then, channeling my

inner dad jokes, I say, "Leg still bothering you, huh? Just *shake* it off, man."
I was a lot better at sarcasm ten years ago.

He hurls a hundred-pound plate at me as if it were a Frisbee.

I duck, and it smashes through the window behind me, taking out a Lazurite guard.

"Nice shot."

He simply grunts as he leg presses five thousand pounds with ease.

"How long was the match?" he asks, sweat streaming from his forehead.

"Nine minutes. Had to stall, make your boss happy."

"Who was it?"

I shake my head. "I don't pay attention to the names anymore. Just some elite."

"Hah, that term 'elite' is thrown around rather loosely these days. They're not what they were ten years ago. Protocol has made them soft. Don't be too proud of yourself, Asher."

"I don't take pride in killing. I leave that up to you."

He reveals his long, chalky teeth, which remind me of piano keys. "I like you, Asher; it will be a shame to crush you."

I fling the ricochet again. "Will you hurry up and get better? The anticipation is killing me."

I have a feeling Renatus is getting impatient as well. He wants his killer back. He could easily have had Apex killed and restored with a LifeCell, but he refused. Apex wants nothing to do with protocol. He reminds me often that he is a PureCell. That if he dies in battle and actually loses, he doesn't deserve to be brought back. I found something I can admire about him—probably the only thing.

But he would be a great ally, just as his brother Legion was.

"You're a smart guy; why are you here, Apex? I can't imagine you like being Renatus's pawn?"

"In case you haven't noticed, I follow my own will."

I foolishly think I can turn him—perhaps let him believe he can be supreme Sultan, and once Renatus is out of the way, he would be a problem for another day. "But you can have what Renatus has—to rule all of Zion. It wouldn't be hard for you to vanquish him and his elites. The rest of them would follow you, as would my people. You could use your talents for something other than the entertainment for those who think they are above you."

His jaw clenches. His teeth make a grating sound like two rocks rubbing together. "What makes you think I want that, little man?"

"You realize Renatus and his Lazurites view you as a performer, nothing more. In fact, they think of you as a dumb brute."

"You're entitled to your point of view, Dreck."

"What do you want, then?"

He rubs his round chin. "I like to ravage and slaughter. And I like to get paid for it. I am not my brother. Legion's mind was frail, his heart tender. Besides, it's my name, not Renatus's, they chant when I enter the arena. I am using Renatus. It's not the other way around."

"If you say so."

Another hundred-pound plate comes flying at me. I duck, and this time, it shatters the vanity mirrors against the back wall.

"Do you think for a moment that they will still cheer you on if you ever happen to lose or stumble? Would Renatus still hold you in high regard if he couldn't profit off you? Once you no longer serve his purposes, he will put you out to pasture. You must know this."

"I don't worry about that, Asher. I don't stumble. And I don't lose."

"There's a first time for everything. Your brother once thought as you did."

"Like I said, my brother was weak. Besides, if ever the day comes that someone like you can defeat me, I will put myself out to pasture."

His hellish, perverse eyes tell me I am a buckethead to think he would join us. Then I smile to myself; who else would call Legion frail and tender-hearted? I miss him. I miss my friend.

Before I finish my workout, an elite marches in. "Asher, Renatus wants to see you."

Apex stands. "After he finishes his workout."

"But, sir, Renatus will not be kept waiting."

"AFTER!" Apex's voice reverberates off the walls.

The elite takes a step back. His legs wobble a little. He nods.

I turn to Apex. "Gonna miss me or something?"

"No, I just want you in prime shape, so you'll last at least three minutes with me when the time comes."

Asher

Four elites usher me into Renatus's newly built palace. It isn't as grand as the one at Pt. Reyes, but Renatus wanted one closer to the arena. The aroma of vanilla and cedarwood wafts from the freshly installed Calacatta marble floors. From the corner of my eye, I catch the sparkle of the gold leaf crown molding. A maid passes me by. Her hair is short, her arms thin and wiry. She is essentially a slave. She gives me a look. First sadness. Then, one of hope. Her eyes betray her thoughts: *save us, Asher.*

Everywhere I go, I am under such pressure. The burden... no... the *obligation* to liberate Zion. First, it was a dream. Then, the dream turned into my uncle's outlandish plan. Now, it's an expectation. *Asher the Liberator* is one of my monikers, after all.

But how? How can I save anyone?

I am trapped here. My uncle is gone, and my army is dead. The Defiance has been all but eradicated. I have been reduced to a gladiator. A killer. An entertainer. Biding my time. But for what? I don't see a way forward.

I am brought into the dining hall, where Renatus sits at the massive table made from a slab of claro walnut. I am not a connoisseur of fine things like Calacatta marble and claro walnut. The only reason I know this is that Renatus tells me almost every time I'm here.

"You're late," Renatus states, sipping an expensive wine from Napa Valley, no doubt.

"I was training. With Apex."

He raises an eyebrow. "Training together now, are we?"

I shrug. "In the same room is all."

He has a servant pour me a glass of red wine, and he leans in. "You know, Apex is not Legion. You cannot flip him. His loyalty is to me—to Zion. Besides, he loves his job too much."

I don't say it, but I think to myself, *Apex's loyalty is to Apex.* I take him off the scent. "Apex doesn't want to join me. He wants to destroy me."

He answers as if my death is a foregone conclusion. "In due time."

Dinner is served—black cod. In my opinion, it is the best-tasting fish in the sea. Another perk of being a gladiator of Zion. What isn't a perk is watching Renatus eat. The smacking of his lips. The licking of the fingers. He even drools at times. His fingers leave grease marks on his wine glass.

"Your fight tonight was fast, wasn't it, mate?" His tone a bit agitated.

I reply, "He was weak for an elite. If you want a longer match, bring me someone stronger. This is Zion after all, isn't it?"

"I have always appreciated your honesty, Asher. When you're not pretending to be someone else." He is referring to when I was sculpted to look like Amos.

The servants bring us port and Blackberry Crisp—Renatus's favorite. We eat dessert in an awkward silence for the next five minutes. Renatus's bouts with paranoia and delusion are becoming more frequent, but tonight, he has been calm. Tranquil even. This isn't the first time he has invited me in for dinner after winning a match. But something about tonight seems different.

And as usual, I'm right.

He stands and notices some blackberry on his tight gray shirt. He casually wipes it off, leaving a purple smear across his chest.

"Let's go for a walk."

I follow him out of the rear entrance, and we enter the garden. The juxtaposition of the rare and beautiful flowers in the background with Renatus's wicked, unnatural and sometimes outlandish gestures, dull the garden's allure. He stops to smell the Purple Passionflowers and Darwin's Slippers, which look like orange and maroon penguins.

He turns to me. "I often wonder what makes these flowers beautiful—their appeal to the eyes or the fact that they are so rare?"

"I'd go with the first. If something is beautiful, who cares how many of them there are?"

"I disagree, Asher; it is the things that are unique that make them attractive. I'm not being vain here, but take my blue eyes, for example. Did you know only eight percent of the population has blue eyes? It makes you wonder if that's what makes them preferable."

"I like brown eyes."

"Yes, I know." He is referring to his daughter Sarai.

"We here to look at your garden?"

He peers down and squeezes the bridge of his nose. "You know what else is rare, delicate, and utterly beautiful? Our *wounded* sons."

I tense up at the thought of what he might do to my son Silas. Being his gladiator has delayed the inevitable, and I fear his patience for resurrecting his own son has run out.

"It's time, Asher."

My heart pounds against my chest, and I begin to sweat. "No, no, listen, you don't need to do this. We—"

"My wounded prince has been gone for too long. I miss my son. I am not the same without him. Ask my wife. Ask Sarai."

I plead with him. "What about your new Canonization? What about me and Apex? If you do this to my son, I will not fight; you will have to kill me."

"You will fight. You will fight, or Sarai dies."

"Your own daughter?"

"She ceased being my daughter the moment she became a Dreck."

"And your grandson? You would murder your grandson?"

He plucks one of the Purple Passionflowers. "Not ideal, I know, but he is half Dreck. My son Eleazar is a hundred percent Lazurite and a prince of Zion. He is destined to return."

And he truly believes it. That's what makes him so scary. I plead with him. "You don't have to do this."

Renatus plucks another rare flower, then tosses it to the ground. He has cheated death and God so many times that he no longer appreciates things that are delicate and scarce. His timbre is placid. "What other choice do I have, Asher? Like all good things, a sacrifice is always involved."

I rack my brain and devise a lie that will buy me more time. "I'll find you one, another wounded one."

He shakes his head. "I have scoured this country for years with no luck. What makes you think that with your limited resources, you can accomplish what I couldn't?"

"I might know where to find one. Look, give me three months. You need at least that much time to finish building your new Canonization, not to mention Apex isn't fully healed yet. This way, you can have your son *and* grandson."

"You really think I would let you go?"

"You're holding my wife. I will return to her as I always do. What do you have to lose? If I return empty-handed, you still have my son, and I still have to fight in this year's Canonization."

He is deep in thought. "If you don't come back in three months, Sarai dies. And I burn her body, so protocol won't ever be possible."

"It's a deal then." I can't believe I have convinced him; a new sliver of hope has emerged. I now have options. They are limited, but they are options. "I ask for one more thing."

"You have become too brash. I might change my mind," he says, annoyed.

"I want to see Sarai before I leave."

"I'll allow it."

Again, I'm shocked. He must be in a good mood. That worries me. "Thank you, sir."

Then, he flashes a toothless maniacal smile. "Such a quick battle tonight was, I feel so, so unfulfilled."

I know where this is going. And it's not the first time. I creep toward him with my hands in the air. He unsheathes an eight-inch knife and holds it up. I press my neck up against it. His bloodlust is insatiable. Sweat beads on his forehead. The reflection of the garden lights flicker and dance off the blade as his hands shake in eager anticipation. He is so often a spectator to death that now and then, he likes to get his hands dirty.

"Get it over with," I tell him.

His breathing becomes heavy and labored. "The crowds may love you, Asher, but I don't have to."

And with the zeal of a sadistic executioner, he stabs my chest. Blood trickles onto the blade's handle, percolates for a moment at the end before splattering onto his boots. I fall to one knee, not looking forward to the resurrection pains I will feel tonight, or the guilt of having once again reaped another's LifeCell.

Chapter Two

Cephas

THEY HAVE MANAGED TO stretch four months of slurry into five. But now it looks like they will starve to death in Eden. Cephas doesn't look like Cephas, but is now more like his deceased friend Jude. He shuffles his gaunt body to a sealed casket in the corner of the concrete room. Inside is Jude. A lone tear traverses his sunken cheekbones, riding the tiny ridges of his scarred face.

He touches the casket and whispers, "Why'd you have to go and do it? If you weren't such a buckethead, you would be here now. I didn't deserve it." His stomach growls. "Or maybe you're the lucky one." He shivers from the biting chill that has engulfed this underground bunker. He longs for the sun and the wind, for the warm breeze and the sound of rustling leaves. All this place offers is the echo of his own somber voice.

Adam trudges in. "Cephas?"

"Any luck?"

"No, we got one of the computers back up but couldn't access the main blast door."

Cephas grunts. "Where's Kenan when you need him?"

Adam is confused. "What's that?"

"Nothing, talking to myself."

For months, they have tried everything, from digging their way out, to restoring the computer systems to find a way out of Eden. But now it looks like they will starve to death in this underground bunker meant to restore humanity in the event of an apocalypse. Ironic. Cephas was always a closet optimist. Underneath that surly cantankerous shell, he always had hope. Saw every setback as an opportunity. And he was a visionary. He saw the big picture, made grandiose plans, and enacted them. But a body can't live off of hope and dreams alone. Even his faith was tested like never before.

Eve comes in with Cephas's chief engineer, Daniel. They both look at Adam as if to say, *"Did you ask him?"* Adam shakes his head.

Cephas swings around and can read the looks on each of their pale, dirty faces. "Just come out with it already," he snarls.

Daniel clears his throat. It's apparent he is intimidated by Cephas: "Sir, I don't need to tell you. In a few days, we will starve to death. But the Ark room has enough protein slurry to feed us for at least another year." Daniel is referring to the room that has a hundred people (fifty males and fifty females) in a cryogenic state, in the event that they need to repopulate the earth.

"Dammit! I told you already, I will not kill a hundred people so we can live another year in this miserable tomb!" Cephas barks. "Instead of worrying about that, find a way out of here."

Eve chimes in, "We are not suggesting we take all of their sustenance, just enough for us to survive a bit longer until we can figure out a way to get us *all* out of here."

Cephas is in a surly mood. Not only is he hungry and cold, but he could use a drink right about now. "Figure something else out. We are not killing those people so we can survive a few more days."

"We have tried everything!" Adam snaps back.

Daniel sheepishly adds, "We did find a massive chest of gold bullion. It looks like Boaz and his Lazurite friends missed it."

Cephas laughs, his tone sarcastic. "Great. Perhaps we can go to the market and use it to buy some food. Oh, and while you're there, grab me some whiskey."

Adam approaches. "Cephas, we are running out of time."

Cephas grabs Adam's torn collar. "Maybe that's it then. Maybe we die here. Perhaps this is our end."

Eve pushes Cephas away from Adam. "That's it? You're just going to give up? Thought you were their leader? Maybe in your world, being a leader doesn't mean what it used to. But Adam and I are Marines. We don't give up." She turns to Adam and Daniel. "I'm now taking command. For all I care, Cephas can go drink in a corner and mourn the loss of his friend like he is the only one ever to lose someone."

Cephas is surprised by her strength. He forgets that Adam and Eve are not just scientists, but Marines. They have also been using the gym religiously—Cephas has not. "Perhaps you would like to be put back under ice?"

"I would like to see you try."

Cephas is about to respond, but then, like it was suddenly planted in his brain, an idea hits him, "The cryo chambers in the Ark room—what runs them?"

"Why?" Eve asks, still perturbed.

"Just tell me what runs them."

"Each one is equipped with its own generator that keeps each chamber frozen," answers Adam.

Cephas knows little about physics, but he remembers hearing about what happens when you freeze steel. "So we have a hundred units?"

"Yes."

Hope is beginning to chisel through Cephas's rough exterior. "Look, I'm no expert here. You guys are the scientists and engineers, but what would happen if we redirected the cooling mechanisms produced by the generators from the cryo chambers to the main door?"

Eve says, "You mean try to damage its structural integrity by freezing it?"

"Yes, then we might have a chance to bust through it," Cephas replies.

Adam, Eve, and Daniel huddle in a circle and literally put their heads together. From Cephas's vantage point, it looks as if their foreheads are almost touching, as if they could gain each other's knowledge that way. Cephas is annoyed at their whispers of "it could work" and their head-scratching, almost as if he weren't deemed smart enough to be part of the conversation, even though it was his idea.

"Speak up, will ya?" barks Cephas.

Daniel clears his throat. "I think there's a chance. If exposed long enough, it could make the steel door brittle enough for us to break through with the primitive tools we have here."

Eve chimes in, "Just one problem: the thawing-out process was meant to be gradual. If we immediately remove their cooling units, there is a chance everyone in cryo could die."

"Why don't we wake them first, then use their cooling source?" Cephas suggests.

Eve shakes her head. "It doesn't work that way; the coolant evaporates during the thawing process."

Cephas takes a long and labored breath. "They're your friends; you make the call."

Cephas

Cephas, Adam, Eve, and Daniel agreed to use ninety of the cryogenic generators on the door and leave ten with the chambers in the ark room. That way, they could rotate the ten every twenty minutes to the hundred respective chambers. Hopefully, this will slow the thaw and not injure any occupants.

The room is eerie, Cephas thinks as he surveys the frozen humans in what has been their home for over a hundred years. He wonders who they were and what compelled them to volunteer for such a thing. Was it out of pure sacrifice? Or adventure, perhaps? Or perhaps they were forced? Maybe they wanted to escape their current situation. Maybe it was a way to numb themselves for eternity—literally. Right now, he could relate. If they were hoping to be awakened to a better world, sadly, they will be disappointed. Isn't each generation supposed to learn from the last one and do better?

As he gets older, Cephas seems to philosophize more than he used to. A young man looks forward. An old one looks back.

He turns to Adam. "You think ninety will be enough for the door?"

"One way to find out," Adam replies.

Cephas has always asked direct questions and has hated indirect answers, but for now, he ignores Adam's reply. Besides, how could anyone know for sure? The other eight who had sailed with them to Eden have joined them in the Ark room. Cephas addresses them.

"We will monitor the door; you will be responsible for rotating the generators from chamber to chamber." He turns to Adam. "Are we ready?"

Adam nods. They begin the process of disconnecting each coolant generator from the ninety chambers. Each time they do so, a warning alarm blares. Cephas says a silent prayer that they don't kill any of them in the process.

After an hour of this, they relocate the ninety generators to face the massive steel door at the entrance to Eden. Cephas and company turn each one back on. Like massive air conditioners, they spit their frigid air towards the door. Cephas can only shake his head at how ridiculous this looks. "A Dreck plan for sure," he murmurs to himself.

Adam, with tongue in cheek, says, "These Drecks sound like wonderful people."

"Sure beats being a Lazurite; you have seen firsthand what they are capable of."

Eve peers around. "Makes me wonder what all this was for?"

"What's that?" Cephas asks.

"Eden. To rebuild and restore humanity. If we keep insisting on destroying ourselves, what's the point?"

Cephas huffs. "The problem these days isn't eradicating ourselves. It's living forever. A fool's paradise."

"Is that such a bad thing?" Daniel interjects.

What a buckethead, thinks Cephas. He never liked Daniel, always thought of him as more of a Lazurite than a Dreck. But he is here because he is one of their best engineers. So Cephas tolerates him.

"Life is hard enough. Who would want to do this forever?" Cephas spits.

Daniel replies, "I wouldn't mind it."

Cephas places his hand on Daniel's shoulder and smiles. "I don't think anyone wants *you* to live forever."

Adam and Eve muffle a laugh. Cephas thinks to himself that if Jude were here, he would appreciate the comment, but for now, he'll take Adam and Eve's complimentary chuckle. It's the first time he has heard laughter in months.

Daniel shakes his head. "I'm going to go check on the Ark room."

"Settle in, it's going to be awhile," says Cephas.

Eve pulls out a book and sits in the corner.

"What are ya reading?" Adam asks.

"Orwell. *1984*."

"Appropriate," Cephas adds.

Another few hours pass and Eve closes her book. "Done. Need to find another one."

Adam says, "That was quick. What did you think of the ending?"

"Don't know, didn't read the last chapter."

"What? Why not?"

She shrugs. "I never finish the last chapter."

Cephas asks, "How could you not finish the last chapter? What's the point in reading the book?"

Eve smiles. "That way I'm not disappointed. I can write the ending in my head the way I want it."

Adam shakes his head. "Too bad life wasn't that way."

After fifteen hours of watching, reading, and banter, the door is completely frosted over. Cephas touches the frigid steel with his dirty fingers. He peers over at the pile of sledgehammers, pick axes, shovels, and other tools they have brought along.

"How much longer?" he asks Adam.

"Hard to say."

Before Cephas can suggest they test it now, Daniel bursts in, out of breath.

"They are starting to come out of cryo!"

"And?"

Daniel shakes his head. "So far, four are dead. A few more are waking up, and so far, they are okay."

"Damn," Cephas growls. "Reattach the generators to the chambers before we lose any more."

"We won't get another shot at this," Adam interjects.

"I won't be responsible for losing any more lives. This isn't working. We gave it a shot."

Eve steps up. "Let's test it now, then. Hurry, everyone, grab a hammer." She doesn't wait for Cephas's approval. Eden is her and Adam's domain. They were put in charge many years ago, long before Cephas was born.

Wanting to be unburdened, Cephas is more than happy to let her take the wheel, at least for now.

The four of them each grab a sledgehammer and bang against the frozen door. The sound of the hammers, pounding against the steel doors and reverberating through the bunker, is almost too much for their ears to take.

"Harder!" Cephas roars.

Chunks of ice fall off the door, but its integrity holds.

Eve grunts as she swings with all her might. "It's not working."

Swing after swing, Cephas has become enraged. He thinks of Jude and again wonders how they got here. A place that was meant for society's rebirth has become their tomb. They have enough seeds in here to replant the earth, yet they are going to starve to death. Eden was supposed to save them, but instead, it will be their demise. His life is one big irony. First, his wife. Then his brother. Then Jude. Everyone he ever loved is now gone. And without the spoils Eden has to offer, soon Asher and The Defiance will also perish.

The four of them, huffing and sweating, stop swinging, their arms burning.

Adam wipes his brow. "It was worth a shot. Bring the generators back."

But from somewhere in the depths of his sadness and wallowing, Cephas has found a new resolve. A restored strength. He turns to them and spits, "I helped bring down an entire wall. I will break through this door!"

Like a bull, he charges the door with one final, robust swing. The steel end of the sledgehammer busts through the frozen steel door, leaving a six-inch gap. Cracks immediately spiderweb around it.

"You're through!" Adam hoots.

The rest of them join in until they have made a hole big enough for them to fit through.

"That's good enough. Get your people back on ice!" Cephas orders them.

As fresh air hits Cephas's face for the first time in five months, he finally feels like he can breathe. The amber rays of sunlight are like a beacon of hope.

But now he has to immediately solve another problem. Is their boat still there? And if so, how will he fit all these people coming out of cryo?

Assuming they survive.

Cephas

"You think your boat is still there?" Eve asks.

"No," Cephas answers plainly, trudging through the forest as they make their way back towards the sea. His knees ache, and the cold is not helping matters.

Adam frowns. "Then what are we doing?"

"Maybe we'll get lucky."

As they get closer to the coast, Adam and Eve squint as they take in the majestic ocean views of Sitka, Alaska. Their eyes haven't seen the sunshine in over a hundred years. The crisp air bites their lungs, causing them to cough. Eve takes it in. "I forgot what I was missing."

Cephas says, "When we get to the mainland, you may change your mind."

"Assuming we get to the mainland," Eve corrects him.

Adam gets in lockstep with Cephas. "Is America really in another civil war?"

"If we haven't already lost, yes."

Eve says, "I had a lot of different scenarios in my head for which we might have been awoken; this certainly wasn't one of them."

"When you see what the world has become, you might want to go back under the ice," Cephas tells them bluntly. *It might not be such a bad thing,* he thinks. As he loses more things and people, he starts to lose faith. Right now, he can only think about having a bottle of Renatus's finest. Ironic that he spent years destroying pallets of the stuff; now, he would do almost anything for a sip. With Jude gone, Asher is the last of his family, and who knows if he is even alive? Cephas's heart has become sullen, and it has been months since he last prayed. He can feel himself slowly descending into his old ways. He has lost his eternal mindset.

They finally emerge from the forest and approach the battered and dilapidated pier.

Nothing.

The ocean is throwing a fit, hurling waves at the rocky shoreline. Cephas's mind is doing the same.

"It's not here." Cephas's tone indicates he expected this.

"You think Boaz took it?" Eve inquires.

Cephas shakes his head. "Sitkans."

"Who?"

"Natives, for lack of a better term. They ambushed us when we first arrived. In exchange for safe passage, we promised them either gold from Eden, or our boat."

"We have gold, let's find them," Adam states.

A voice from behind them says, "No need." It is the Sitkan with the red beard who stopped them months ago on their way into Eden. He is pointing a shotgun at them. He manages to speak while spraying brown tobacco at his feet. "Gold, you say?"

"I told you I would return with gold. Where's my ship?"

Red Beard laughs. "That was a long time ago. We figured you for dead."

"We had a bit of a setback."

"Lazurites?"

"Yes."

Red Beard says, "We saw their submarine arrive shortly after you."

"And why didn't you accost them as you did us?"

Red Beard shrugs. "They were better armed than you."

"You have my ship or not?" Cephas spits.

"Yeah, old man, we have your ship."

"Where? I don't see it."

Red Beard spits again, half of it nesting in his beard. "Other side of the island. Where's the gold?"

"We will bring it to you."

Cephas huddles with Adam and Eve, out of earshot of Red Beard. "Go back and grab the chest, along with anyone else who wants to help you carry it."

Eve is skeptical. "How can we trust him?"

"We can't. But I don't see another choice, do you?"

Six hours later, they arrive at the Sitkans' camp carrying the chest of gold that Boaz had missed inside Eden. They find the camp to look like a village from the 1800s. There are log houses, communal fire pits, storage sheds, barns, and chicken coops. About forty or fifty people mill about, dressed in dirty rags and with knotted hair. They eye Cephas and his crew with guarded wariness.

"This way." Red Beard points toward one of the larger fire pits, where elk quarters are being roasted over an open flame. A man with a bushy beard and long hair slices a piece of raw meat from the elk and tries a bite. Red Beard introduces them. "This is Jethro, leader of our tribe. Jethro, these are the Inlanders whose boat we have."

Jethro eyes the chest. "You found Eden, yes?"

Cephas steps forward and sizes up Jethro, who reminds him of a Viking. "Yes."

Jethro spits, "Under my nose this entire time, and it was Inlanders who found it. In all honesty, I didn't think it existed. You Lazurite or Dreck?"

Cephas points his hands inward towards his own ragged clothing and emaciated body. "Do you even need to ask?"

"Good point." Jethro motions towards the chest of gold. "Was the contents of Eden a lie? If not, where is the rest of it?"

"Lazurites. They stole everything inside and left us for dead. This is all that is left."

Jethro pulls on his beard. "Oh, Lazurites, the forever people. Were there nukes there also?"

"Yes."

He shakes his head. "Why do you think Eden is so coveted?"

"Not sure what you mean?"

"Riches beyond measure, along with a destruction beyond comprehension. That is the human condition. Seems not a lot has changed on the mainland."

"It's worse," Cephas states bluntly.

"You a book reader, Dreck?"

"Most of them have been burned where I come from." Cephas points to Eve. "But she is. Well, sort of."

Jethro flips the large piece of meat. "The famous Russian author, Anton Chekhov, once said, '*Death is terrifying, but it would be even more terrifying to find out that you are going to live forever and never die.*'"

Cephas smiles. "So we are of the same mind."

"That is to be seen. What do you want, Inlander?"

"My boat."

"Ah, yes. Your boat for Eden's gold, or what's left of it."

Cephas motions to Red Beard. "Your man over there made me a promise."

"And we keep our promises."

Cephas eyes two larger ships coming into the harbor, the decks full of salmon. "How about I make you a promise? My boat isn't big enough to take all of us home. You lend me one of your larger vessels, and I will return it to you with its belly stuffed full of gold."

Jethro laughs. "So you and your tiny band of Drecks are going to defeat the Lazurites and bring me their spoils? That is quite the promise, Inlander."

"I will, or die trying. Actually, I have a better idea. Why don't you come with us? You would be a good addition to my army."

Jethro's tone slides into sarcasm. "What army? I don't see any army."

"I will find one. As another famous author once said, '*Those who expect to reap the blessings of freedom, must, like men, undergo the fatigues of supporting it.*' I will find a willing army. There are still people on the mainland willing to fight."

"Thomas Paine. You are read. You Drecks are ambitious and a little crazy; I like that. Tell you what, you can have one of my larger boats. But it isn't gold I want. I have no need for it. To me, the contents inside Eden, whether it be gold or nuclear weapons, lead to the same thing. Ruin. Gold leads to wars. Gold turns friends into enemies. Gold won't make the sunset more beautiful or force Chinook to bite my hook. Nor does it make the stars dazzle brighter or the Eagle more majestic. I'll tell you what I do want, Inlander: tear down the wall and return here a victor. Then my people can go home."

Even though Jethro is long-winded, Cephas takes an instant liking to him. He stretches out his hand. "Deal."

Cephas

Six of Eden's "Popsicles" perish while coming out of Cryo sleep. Cephas will have to mourn that fact another time. Now he must focus on the ninety-six that did make it. He marches past their hairless, pasty, gaunt bodies. Adam, Eve, and a few others tend to their needs. It will be a few days until they can walk, and Cephas sighs at the logistical nightmare of getting them all to the ship. There are only so many wheelchairs, and he knows for sure that because of his bad knees, he probably won't be carrying anybody.

Cephas pulls Adam aside. "They can't walk yet. How will we get them to the ship?"

"We wait," Adam says.

"We don't have time. We have to return to The Defiance, assuming there is still a Defiance to return to."

Adam is calm, but direct: "We have been here five months. A few more days isn't going to matter."

Cephas squints his bloodshot eyes as Adam returns to providing blankets to the newly unfrozen. He overhears their questions and confusion: "What is happening? Was there a nuclear war? Why are we awake? Who is that?" and on and on.

Eve approaches Cephas. "I think it's time we tell them what's going on."

Cephas is in no mood. "Can't you?"

"It's best if it comes from you. Besides, Adam and I are still brushing up on the past hundred years. And try not to grumble."

Cephas won't admit it, but he's beginning to like Eve's wit and sometimes sharp tongue, which appeared soon after she got her bearings.

Cephas trudges into the center of the room and holds up his hands. "Okay, everyone, listen up. I know you have a lot of questions. I know you have been under for over a hundred years. I know you want to know why you have been melted, for lack of a better term."

"Has there been a nuclear holocaust?" one of them asks.

"No."

"A war?"

"Yes. America has—"

Cephas is interrupted again. "What kind of war?"

Cephas peers over at Eve as if to say, '*Can I grumble now?*'

Eve raises her voice. "Please let him finish, then we will answer all your questions."

"America is no longer America, at least not—"

"Was it the Soviets?" another interrupts.

Cephas throws up his hands. "We can do this later if you like?"

"Let the man speak," another Popsicle cries out.

Cephas spends the next hour telling them about The Wall. The Drecks and Lazurites. Protocol and the horrors behind how it works. Renatus and The Canonization. Zion West, Zion East, and The Middle. About Asher, Sarai, and The Defiance. When he finishes, there is sober silence, many mouths left agape in shock. Numb once again, but this time, not from the cryogenic cylinders.

"All this time, I thought I would be awoken because of a holocaust, that we would need to start over," one of them states to no one in particular.

"You're welcome to go back under ice," Cephas jokes. "I surely wouldn't blame you."

One of them attempts his own joke. "We go under for a hundred years, and this is what humanity decides to do."

"Are you surprised?" says a woman in the back, her voice cold and raspy.

"So now what? What do we do now?" another asks.

"We go back. All of us. And we win this war once and for all. We return America to what it was before you went under."

"Does this Defiance of yours have an army?" a man in the front asks.

Cephas peers at the ceiling and closes his eyes. "I hope so."

Sarai

I am a prisoner in my own home. I am free to move about, even leave the compound now and then, but always under the watchful eye of my father's elites. I have not seen Asher in five months. No. That is not true. I see him battle in the arena. But is that really him? Is that Asher the Great? Asher, the leader of the Defiance? Asher, the patient father, the loving husband? Or is he what I see of him now—another of my father's creations? A bloodthirsty gladiator like Apex or Legion before him? Has Zion once again ensnared him with praise and power? He is once again adorned by the Lazurites, all while being showered with the amenities that come with being a gladiator. Ironic that my father, who was never a father to me, had a way of becoming a father figure to those he deemed useful to Zion.

My sparkling dress is blood-red with white stripes. Why am I wearing a dress? So I can dine with my father while we pretend to be a family? Soon, I will eat with Renatus and be forced to smile, compelled to pretend I am enjoying his company. He holds Asher and my son Silas in his grip. My mother, Joanna, has willingly returned, not for my father, but for me. I don't know how much longer I can keep up this charade. My pity party is short-lived when I think about what Asher is going through. He has to put his life on the line almost every day, and some days he dies. Literally.

I gaze into the mirror and imagine that I don the dress for Asher. Not that he cares for that sort of thing. But still. I close my eyes and see us dining underneath the stars on fresh perch that we caught and gutted. No chef necessary. Just us. Then, I picture myself spending the next twenty minutes convincing him to dance. He only steps on my toes twice as we cut a rug to what surely would be an old '80s rock ballad. I can feel his thick, calloused fingers intertwined with mine. He makes a show of dipping me while mockingly raising his other hand towards the sky. What he lacks in grace, he makes up for with sardonic whimsy. But that was the old Asher, before my father withered his spirit.

I open my eyes, search the dressers, and see all my old clothes have been replaced with these pompous Lazurite threads. I miss my Van Halen T-shirt. I can't remember the last time I wore something comfortable. Everything is fake here, in what my father is dubbing "New Zion." When death means nothing, what is true? What is real? There are no tears here. Not real ones. I stare at my room; it is clean, too clean. I miss the dirt. I miss being a Dreck. I miss Asher. I miss him stepping on my toes while parodying the arrogance of the Lazurites.

I have made up my mind. I am not wearing this dress. I enter my walk-in closet and peruse the rack for something more comfortable and less ornate. The choices are limited. Zion is all about appearances, a facade that must be upheld if one wants to fool the populace. Then I hear my name. It has been so long that I hardly recognize the voice.

"Sarai." It's Asher.

I scamper out of the closet and see him up close for the first time in what feels like forever. He looks gaunt, weathered, and ragged. I can tell he has recently gone through protocol again, having done it twice myself. I can see it in his eyes; taking another soul does something to yours.

At the moment, I have no words. I run to his arms. We hold each other for what seems like an hour. Both of us are crying, perhaps the only real tears in New Zion.

I finally pull back from his strong, secure grasp. "How? What are you doing here? Does my... does my father know?"

He kisses me before answering. "Yes, I am here with his permission."

I am perplexed. "Why? How? Did he change his mind? And how is Silas? Have you seen him?"

He gets down on his knees and brings me with him. His brambly, scarred hands cup my face and stroke my hair. "Listen to me, Sarai. I have not seen Silas. But I have good news. He is letting me leave."

"What? Why? And what about Silas? I don't—"

He shuts me up with another kiss before telling me, "That's just it, Sarai. I told him I could find another wounded one for your brother. He said that if I succeeded, he would spare Silas; he would no longer need his LifeCell."

"How? I mean, where?"

"Look, I lied. I have no idea. Besides, we can't willingly take the life of an innocent, even if it's for our own son."

I ask, "So you're buying time then?"

"Yes. He has given me three months. It will take at least that long for him to finish his new Canonization. I am hoping I can figure out a plan, a way out of this. Perhaps raise another army."

"And if you don't return?"

His voice is raspy. He sounds sick. "Then Silas isn't the only one I lose."

He stands and looks out the window, watching the Pines bustle in the wind. "Something isn't right, Sarai."

"What do you mean?"

"I don't know, I don't feel right, I don't feel like myself."

He is being hard on himself. "Under the circumstances, who would?"

"No, this is different. I... I have dreams, thoughts, memories that don't feel like mine. Or maybe they are, but for some reason, I just can't remember doing them."

"Your body is taxed, mentally and physically, and protocol doesn't help."

"When I'm in the arena, it's almost... almost as if I *like* being a gladiator."

I try to rationalize what he is saying; it's the only way I can make sense of it. I have to believe he is the man I once knew, not the man Renatus is molding him to be. "You're only doing what you have to do to survive, to keep your son alive."

He quickly changes focus. "You'll need to stay strong while I'm gone. Keep the charade up with your father, but at the same time, I may call upon your help when the time is right."

I don't want to be separated again. I feel so useless here. "I wish I could go with you."

"So do I."

"Where will you go first?"

"I don't know yet, I haven't had time to think—"

"I do."

He looks at me with tired eyes. "Where?"

"Cephas. He is alive."

"What? How do you know? I thought—"

"I have friends in my father's cabinet sympathetic to me and our cause. He escaped Eden two days ago."

I see hope in his eyes. He kisses me again. "I'll be back for you. I'll be back to end this once and for all. I promise."

And as it always is with us, I once again watch him leave.

Kenan

The situation for Kenan and his army is just as dire as it is for Cephas. They still had water in the underground bunker at NORAD, but their food supplies are almost gone. Kenan has done his best to encourage his soldiers and keep their spirits up.

But, everyone can see the writing on the wall: starve to death or face the radiation outside. It's time to make a choice. A choice Kenan has been dreading for months. He checks in with two of his technicians, who are hard at work tinkering with the old communication equipment.

"Any... any... any luck?" As he begins to lose hope, his stutter slithers to the surface. For him, it has always been a confidence issue. And right now, his confidence in himself, in their survival, is low.

Without looking up, the technician answers, "No, sir, I don't believe any of this is salvageable."

Kenan bites his lower lip. "Just keep... keep at it."

"Yes, sir."

Kenan hears one of their stomachs growl as he leaves, and wonders if that sound is the beginning of the end. It is the sound that usually precedes chaos and mutiny. Everyone has been on half-rations for three weeks while trying to get the communications back up. He strolls past the entertainment room, where a group of his men watch Full Metal Jacket on a worn-out VHS tape for probably the thousandth time. Just last week, there was a fistfight over which movies they would watch. Not only are they hungry, they are also bored—an unwanted recipe in an already combustible situation.

And then it happens. Kenan has feared this for months now.

"What the hell is this!?" a husky soldier yells, holding up an empty MRE wrapper.

"Where did you find that?" another asks.

"It was in Fred's pillowcase!" He then holds the pillowcase upside down and shakes it; a dozen more wrappers float to the ground.

The brawny soldier grabs Fred by the collar and slams him against the wall. "He's been stealing rations!"

"That's not mine!" Fred responds.

"Liar! Someone do a count."

Fred pushes the soldier off of him, who then draws his plasma gun.

"You gonna shoot me over a few stale MREs?" Fred asks, stone-faced.

"No, I'm gonna shoot you because you're a liar with no honor."

Fred inches closer. "You don't have the sand to pull the trigger."

"Don't shoot him unless you have proof!" another yells, charging him.

Before the soldier holding the gun knows what is happening, he is tackled to the ground, and four more join in. It only takes a matter of seconds until ten more join the melee. Then twenty. Fists fly, as do chairs and an occasional table.

"Stop this!" Kenan yells as a full-blown riot materializes right in front of him. He repeats the command to no avail. His hands begin to shake as he is engulfed by self-doubt. *You must lead your men, Kenan.* He hears Asher's voice ringing in his head.

He takes a deep breath and steels himself. "That's enough!" he yells and jumps right into the fray. He is immediately and inadvertently hit in the head, causing him to fall backward into the metal lockers—blood streams from a cut on the back of his head. A second later, he dodges a folding chair. Is this just his men at the end of their rope? Or do they truly not respect him as their leader? He is temporarily paralyzed by indecision. *Maybe I'm not a leader? Perhaps I'm kidding myself? Maybe NORAD was a bad choice? Perhaps I have led my army into a tomb where we slowly starve to death? If we don't kill each other first.* But he can't disappoint Asher, himself, or his army. *I must do something. I have to stop this.*

Before he can reenter the ruckus, he is halted by a woman with long dark hair, narrow eyes, and sharp features. She is standing on top of a table. Her commanding voice roars, "Enough of this! Are we Lazurites, or are we Drecks?!"

It doesn't matter; she is ignored as the brawl continues to mushroom. Kenan recognizes her as Helah. During their battles, she was a warrior through and through. She couldn't have been any older than twenty-five, but she had an aura of hardened maturity about her. She is tall, dark-skinned, and radiates leadership. She fires her plasma gun just above the fracas and into the metal lockers, causing a loud vibration that reverberates off the walls.

The fists stop flying for a moment as they look up at her. She is holding a white and yellow radiation suit.

"Stop being idiots for just one second, and look what I found!" Helah tells them through gritted teeth.

Kenan wipes the blood from his head and jumps up on the table next to her. "A radiation suit. Where did... where did—"

"It was under a mattress on one of the unused cots in the room below us." She doesn't have the patience for him to finish his stutter.

The soldiers cheer and smile. "We can venture outside and find help," one said.

But Kenan is a Dreck now. And since he is Dreck, he now has Dreck luck.

He inspects the suit more closely, finding multiple tears throughout—some small, some big. He quickly takes the suit and heads for a corner away from prying eyes. He doesn't want the men to know the suit is compromised; they have finally been fed a dose of hope. He doesn't want the situation to deteriorate further than it already has.

Helah edges near him. "I'll go."

Kenan peers around, then whispers, "This suit has tears. It won't protect you fully."

She shrugs. "So we'll tape it up or something."

"I can't let you."

"We have to try. We are gonna die here anyway."

Asher's words invade his head once more. *First on the battlefield, last to leave. To lead your army is to serve your army.*

Kenan buries his stutter. He matches Helah's look of resolve: "I'll go."

She protests, "But sir, you are their leader. They need you here. You can't risk it." She pulls up her sleeve to reveal her Pelican tattoo, identical to Cephas's—the symbol of the Defiance. "Let me go."

"I appreciate your bravery, but you're right. I am their leader, and that's exactly why I must go. I will leave at first light." He peers around the room. "Besides, I think you'll do a fine job being in charge while I'm gone."

Four hours later, Kenan lies in bed, thinking about how bad it is outside. Did Renatus nuke other Reservations? Is Asher still alive? Did Cephas and Jude find Eden? Perhaps they have already won the war, and all they need to do now is escape. He manages to fall asleep on that last thought.

At four-thirty the next morning, Kenan wakes up to find that the radiation suit he had stuffed underneath his cot, is gone.

And so is Helah.

Chapter Three

Asher

I T IS ALMOST DAWN. In the distance, I watch as HeliDrones drop multiple EMPs. The flashes against the sooty sky are bright and powerful. I am glad I *borrowed* a gas-powered Mustang over an electric vehicle. I pull my Pony to the side and jump out to survey the landscape.

It has been a while.

Reservation 9.

I am flooded with memories, both good and bad. I can't believe how much has happened in the past ten years. It seems like yesterday, I was working for Boaz as a RefuseRat. I went from being a slave to Boaz to a prince of Zion, and now back to a slave to Renatus. Dreck life.

If I go any further East, I risk the fallout zone from the nukes Renatus dropped on Kenan and my army. I will head just south of Reservation 9 in hopes that Cephas has returned to one of his many bunkers. The first three I checked were empty and have been long abandoned.

I jump back into my vehicle and start the engine. The sound of American-made horsepower never gets old. Shortly after, I am stung by another headache—that's four in the past week. Along with the pain, I experience something new—something frightening. It's hard to explain, but it's like I'm feeling someone else's emotions. I can tell they're not mine, that they are counterfeit. I also hear voices:

A child murmuring for his mother.

A man crying out for his family.

The sound of a HeliDrone's rotors slicing through the air.

Then I inexplicably smell the sweet, grassy aroma of corn.

What is happening to me? Is protocol making me crazy? Schizophrenic? I squeeze my head with one hand and force myself to think of Sarai. Fishing on our tin can of a boat. A lazy spring afternoon. Her smile. Her laugh as she out-fishes me. Finally, the fragrance of jasmine and lavender overpowers the honeyed scent of corn.

THUMP.

My Mustang veers to the right. I hit a rock, blowing out my passenger front tire. I become instantly heated. It is a rage I am having trouble containing. I pound the dash with my fist while shouting curse words in a way my uncle used to and my father never did. I clutch the steering wheel as if I can snap it in half. My white knuckles look as if they will burst through the skin.

Prayer and deep breaths. This is not me. This is protocol. Or is that an excuse? I have to believe this isn't who I am. That protocol has changed me, but I can change back. If this is who I am, then who would I be to Sarai if I'm no longer the man she fell in love with? How could I look my son in the eyes and tell him I tried to change the world, but instead, it changed me?

After stewing for another five minutes, I pull my last spare from the back and change the tire. I chuckle for a moment at my mini-tantrum and hop back in. I am glad Sarai isn't here to see my little outbursts.

After another hour of driving, I watch the sunrise. My stomach snarls. I grab my last ham sandwich from a bag on the passenger seat. Renatus was kind enough to let me raid the palace kitchen before I left. It behooves him to help, if I succeed in what he *thinks* I'm trying to accomplish. But of course I am not looking for another *wounded* one. I'm looking for Cephas and Jude. I am hoping they have returned to Installation Five. It was one of his main bunkers on the outskirts of Reservation 9 for many years. I am hoping he has returned with the spoils of Eden.

When I arrive, it is just after dawn. It is still familiar. The red barn is now a burnt husk, barely standing from the fire set by the Lazurite army. To the left, under a canopy of pine trees, are a dozen hydrogen-powered trucks. A few horses tethered to a tree graze on the grass behind them. I spent much of my childhood here. I helped dig out the dirt that created this bunker. And it wasn't by choice. I was sculpted here. I officially joined The Defiance here. Now, I can only hope there is some Defiance left.

Someone is here. I back up and park behind a grove of pines. I slowly exit my car, switching on my ricochet. The faint hum of the electric current is soothing in a strange way. I make my way towards the trucks for a closer look. They are Lazurite standard issue. My heart rate goes up a notch. The horse's saddles are painted red and white, colors usually donned by the elites' horses. Was Cephas ambushed? Have the Lazurites attacked this compound again? I unhook my ricochet from my waist and remove my plasma gun from its holster. I hear a rustle behind me. I turn to shoot.

"Didn't expect to see you back here, Nephew."

It's Cephas.

He has a Magnum 44 in one hand and a bottle of Demon Tonic in the other.

Actually, a half bottle. He holds it up. "Want some?"

I shake my head.

He takes another swig. He is obviously plastered. "Suit yourself."

"I almost shot you, Uncle." I scrutinize his bottle, his wobbling, "Perhaps I should have."

With his hand on his knees, he lets out a belly laugh. A laugh I know all too well, unfortunately. A past I would like to forget. A past I had forgiven.

"Where is everyone else?" I ask, my tone rigid as I try to suppress my ire.

"You mean Adam and Eve? Or the Popsicles?"

"Popsicles? What are you talking about, Uncle?"

He snorts. "You have missed so much, Nephew."

I finally ask, "What's with the Tonic? What happened, Cephas?"

He stumbles towards the horses, his hands waving drunkenly in the air as if what he has to say has gravitas. "The Tonic? Why should it go to waste?"

I shake my head and can't believe he is back on the sauce. "You are talking nonsense. Who are Adam and Eve? And where is Jude?"

He hops onto one of the horses and sticks his cleft chin high in the air, his back rigid and straight. He mocks like a soldier or a great adventurer ready to embark on a long journey. "This way, nephew, I will show you."

His horse doesn't get ten feet before he falls off it, landing on his side with a thud. He laughs in a drunken stupor.

I am too pissed to help him up. Instead, I watch as he slowly pulls himself up, like a toddler learning to walk.

"Follow me!"

"What happened at Eden?"

He stumbles but doesn't entirely fall. "Eden... Eden... Eden." Each time he repeats the word, I hear the rage simmer in his voice.

"What happened, Cephas? Were there nukes? Gold?"

"Eden... Eden... Eden."

"Answer me, Uncle!"

His eyes widen, his smile maniacal. "You wanna know what happened at Eden? Yes, there was gold. Yes, there were nukes. But they didn't make it. They are gone. All gone. Everything is gone."

I have had enough; I fling my ricochet at his bottle of Tonic, shattering it. It flies back to my wrist. I twirl it around my finger a few times like a cowboy from an old Western movie, and reattach it to my side.

He is left holding only the top two inches of the bottle. "What the hell was that for?"

"You know what that's for, Uncle. I don't understand. After all these years, why?"

He grimaces, his crimson cheeks crawling up toward his eyelashes. His eyes water. "I couldn't do it sober; I'm sorry, Asher, I just couldn't."

"Do what?"

"Jude. His funeral is in an hour."

Sarai

The ocean is tranquil today. I am not. My father forced me to go with him on his fishing yacht in another attempt to pretend we were a happy family. He went into the cabin about half an hour ago. I fish for salmon, which is usually my thing, but it isn't the same when you are forced to go with company you don't like.

But every time I cast a line, it reminds me of Asher. We spent many blissful afternoons fishing on his makeshift boat. And his proposal was imaginative yet ill-advised. Such are many of the actions taken by Drecks. I wonder how Asher is faring. I still can't believe my father let him go. He is either getting crazy or desperate. From the noises emanating from the cabin, it must be the former.

"Eleazar! Eleazar!" I hear my father yell my dead brother's name.

I put my pole down and slowly trudge into the cabin. Then I spot my father. He is holding a framed picture of my brother, Eleazar. His eyes are crazed. His tone is raving. "Of course, Eleazar! Of course, we can go fishing. You should have said something earlier."

"Father, who are you talking to?" I ask, but instantly regret it.

"Your brother, dear, your brother. He wants to go fishing."

He brushes by me, almost knocking me over. "Fishing, we will go!"

He laughs loudly and manically as he heads to the boat's back deck. I watch as he sets the picture on a chair and grabs the fishing pole. "All right, my prince. Are you ready to catch a big one?" He casts the pole, and the lure splashes into the serene waters. He sits near the picture, acting like it's his actual son beside him.

I stand behind him but keep my distance. Protocol is making him crazy and more volatile. Suddenly, there is a tug on his pole. He pulls it back and reels, "We got one, Eleazar! We got one!" He fights the fish, wild-eyed. "What do you think, son? We going to get this one in?" He looks over at me, a smile plastered on his face. "We've got one, daughter. Your brother and I we got one! Do you see this?"

I don't know what to say or do. I back against the railing on the other side, unsure what he might do next. This is the worst I have seen him. I feared him before, but right now, he is a force without form.

As if taking a cue from Renatus's chaotic behavior, the boat begins to rock back and forth as the ocean awakens. The wind blows a salty mist toward my face, and I close my eyes. How is this my life? To be the daughter of an evil man, watching him descend into madness as he holds everything dear to me captive. And Asher, who seems gone, even when he's not. Is this his future from being forced to The Mountain so many times? All I can do is watch my world drown. I have never felt so helpless.

Then, a rogue wave hits the side of the yacht. The boat tilts toward my father, and the picture of Eleazar flies off the chair and splashes into the ocean.

"Eleazar! No!" Renatus screams. To my shock, he throws down his fishing pole and jumps into the raging sea after the picture. As the boat rocks back and forth, I slide to the railing and peer over. My father's bald head bobs up and down in the ocean. He still calls his son's name, swimming and diving under the water. The scene is so surreal, I wonder if I'm dreaming.

My first instinct is to yell his name and try to talk sense into him. Even throw him a life ring.

But then, I look at the Lazurite captain manning the yacht. He doesn't notice his Sultan is in the water. Neither do the two elites still in the cabin. I am without my scourge, but maybe I could take them out, as well as the captain? Essentially, leaving my father out here to drown. They would never find his body. He could never be resurrected again. It could end this war.

The irony is not lost on me. The same waters that took his son would also swallow him up.

He frantically kicks and slaps his arms, still yelling for his son. "Eleazar! Where are you? I'm coming, my prince!"

But what if I'm unsuccessful? Who knows what the punishment would be? It's not me I'm worried about; it's Silas. Would Renatus take it out on him? On my mother?

But I'm too late, anyway. I have thought about it for too long.

"Sir!" an elite yells as he throws Renatus a life ring.

The floating life ring seems to bring my father back to his senses, back into reality. He grabs it, and they pull him up onto the boat.

"You okay, my Sultan?" his elite asks.

Renatus removes his shirt and squeezes the water from it; he gives his guard a look like it's a stupid question. "Of course. I just thought a swim might be refreshing."

Was this my chance? Did I miss a golden opportunity to save my son and end this war? What would his elites and generals do if he were actually to die? He believes he will live forever and, therefore, hasn't seen a need to name an eventual successor. Do his followers believe in what Zion stands for? Or do they follow him out of fear?

Renatus peers at his fishing pole on the ground and then up at me. "What happened?"

I'm still stunned by what just occurred. "Um, you dropped your pole."

He shrugs, picks it up, and casts his line back into the sea as if nothing happened. A chill travels down my spine as I realize just how far gone my father is.

Asher

I spend the next hour force-feeding Cephas coffee and water. He is beginning to sober up. He tells me about Eden, what was there, Adam and Eve, the hundred in Cryo, how they escaped, and how Jude died.

"That snake Boaz, when I see him again…" Cephas shakes his head, thinking about revenge.

"You will," I reassure him. "And The Wall. How did you get through and make it to Res 9?"

"There are a few places still open, or at least there were; my spies tell me it's fully erected again."

I smile. "Spent years trying to get out, and here we are sneaking back in. Let's just hope it's not for good."

"I didn't know where else to go. My compounds are here, and so are my men and weapons." Cephas takes another sip of coffee. "And you? I heard you've become a great gladiator of Zion."

"This is true." Then I flinch and squint as a sharp pain pierces my forehead.

"You okay, Nephew?"

"I don't know. Protocol, I think."

Cephas rubs his temples. "You're not the only one with a headache."

Still mad at his drinking, I dig at him. "You're going to compare your hangover to protocol?"

"Good point." He raises a bushy eyebrow, his tongue in cheek. "Protocol? Maybe you weren't such a great gladiator after all?"

I shake my head. "No, I never lost. It's what happened after. Renatus's hate for me is still strong, so he got to relish in killing me more than once."

Cephas is now concerned. "How many times?"

"I don't... I don't know. Twenty, maybe thirty? I lost track."

"And how did you escape?"

"I didn't. He let me go."

"Let you go?"

"I promised him I would return with a wounded LifeCell for his son."

"And?"

"Of course, it's a lie."

Cephas is starting to get his wits about him. "A brilliant idea, but I'm surprised he believed you."

"Not sure he did, but he holds all the cards. If I don't return in three months to be a part of his new Canonization to dedicate his New Zion, then he will kill Sarai."

"How a man can murder his own daughter and grandchild is beyond me."

"His wickedness grows by the day," I tell him.

"And what about you?" he asks, referring to what protocol is known to do to a person. To what it may have done to me. I don't want to answer; maybe it's because if I say it out loud, I will be forced to admit something I don't want to see, or that it might come true if it hasn't already.

"Are you asking about me to take the focus off of you? What's with the Tonic, Cephas?"

His teeth grit. I can see a glint of shame in his eyes. "When they killed Jude, I just lost it. It broke me, Nephew."

"Should I be worried?"

He laughs in his vintage fatherly style that I know so well. "You're all grown up, aren't ya?"

"Don't change the subject."

He places his hand on my shoulder and smiles. "Truly, it has been one of the great pleasures in my life watching you become the man your father knew you could be."

I ask again. "Cephas, should I be worried?"

Before he can reply, Eve enters. She has a book in her hand. Her voice is solemn, angelic. "It's time."

Cephas downs the rest of his coffee. I follow him outside until we reach an opening between the pines. Next to a freshly dug grave is a casket holding Jude's body.

I still can't believe he is gone. Adam and Eve hold hands on the other side of the casket. Most of the "Popsicles," as Cephas called them, are also gathered about. It's ironic; they too don similar clothes from the 1980s. It's hard to believe that's how old they are. I guess this was the option for immortality before protocol existed—to just freeze themselves.

I hear Cephas take a deep breath, steel himself, and trudge towards the casket. I worry that he is hooked on the Tonic again and won't be able to stop. I have suffered loss, but he has lost more. Where is his breaking point? Has he hit it? Where is mine? I am teetering towards an abyss. It's hard to keep my mind straight. My thoughts clear. The burden placed upon me is overwhelming. Save Sarai. Save Silas. Save The Defiance. Save America. Lately, I feel like I can't even save myself.

Cephas loudly clears his throat. In his gruff manner, he makes no introductions, no explanation of why we are here, even though it is obvious he just gets right to it.

"Jude wasn't just a friend. He was my brother. I will miss many things about him. His kind soul. His sardonic sense of humor and his acid tongue. The way he could eat like an elephant and still weigh next to nothing. He was my softer side and kept me grounded. Kept me laughing. He was a friend when I did not deserve one. He forgave me when it wasn't merited. He followed me on one crazy quest after another. No questions asked. I couldn't have led without him. When I was wrong, he let me know. He was one of a kind." Cephas peers at the casket. "You will be missed."

Cephas opens his tattered bible and reads, "From John Chapter ten: *My sheep hear my voice, and I know them, and they follow me. I give them eternal life, and they will never perish, and no one will snatch them out of my hand. My Father, who has given them to me, is greater than all, and no one is able to snatch them out of the Father's hand.*"

Cephas closes his bible, clears his throat, and his stubby index finger mops up a few tears from his coarse, wrinkled cheeks. "Jude has been called home. His soul has risen into the Father's hand and been given eternal life, the way it was meant to be, up in heaven, not here on earth."

Cephas turns and lightly touches the casket. "I will see you again, my brother. Sooner probably than later."

I watch as his casket is lowered into the earth. Each one of us takes turns piling dirt on top of him, including the "Popsicles" from Eden. I wonder what they are thinking. How did things get this bad? How did we as a society go so awry, treating human life as a commodity?

I take my turn scooping dirt onto Jude's casket. His body is buried, but his soul risen. If he were a Lazurite elite in New Zion, neither would have happened. While we mourn him, I can picture his skinny legs tap-dancing in heaven, telling jokes to the angels. Cephas returns to my side and places his paw on my back. His eyes are crisp. Steadfast. "I'm done with the Tonic, Asher; it's time to get to work."

I want to believe him, but considering his past, I just don't know.

Later that evening, we sit around a campfire. Food is scarce, so we munch on MREs and OatBars. EMP blasts light up the horizon in the distance.

"Sure beats protein slurry," Cephas announces. Adam, Eve, and a few others nod in agreement.

Adam turns to Asher. "On the trip back, Cephas told us a lot about you."

"Don't believe a word of it," I respond, tongue-in-cheek.

"Says you had surgery to look like the enemy so you could enter a fighting competition, to join their army, and marry your fiancée, who happens to be the daughter of the leader of Zion?"

"Yes, that's part of it."

"And this second-life protocol? How does it work exactly?" Eve inquires.

I take another bite of my bland bar. "I don't understand the science behind it exactly, but essentially, you steal the LifeCell from one human being and insert it into another. Not only are they resurrected, but it slows the aging process."

"Killing the donor?" asks Adam.

"Yes."

Adam shakes his head. "For as long as I can remember, people have been searching for that magic pill, that fountain of youth, wanting to live forever. It seems you people finally figured it out. Not a lot of good it's done, has it?"

"You're preaching to the choir here," says Cephas. "We were against it from the beginning."

"Does the person have to be alive when their LifeCell is reaped?" Eve asks.

"As far as our scientists can tell, a LifeCell will last up to twelve hours after its host dies," Cephas replies.

Eve stares at the crackling fire. "What's your plan here?"

I turn to Cephas. "Was wondering the same thing, Uncle. With Kenan and our army gone, what is our play?"

Cephas stands and points to the hundred people milling about, most of them from Eden, "This is the start of our army."

Eve scoffs. "A hundred against thousands?"

"You said yourself that they are the best your generation had to offer. Scientists, doctors, engineers, all with military training. Besides, we will recruit more."

"We only have three months until I must return. Until the new Canonization," I remind him.

"I have faith."

Eve says, "You call that a plan?"

I peer at her with a sideways smile. "You don't know my uncle."

And just as if he planned it, two Dreck guards emerge from the forest. They are helping a woman walk. She is dressed in torn rags.

The first guard approaches Cephas. "Sir, she says her name is Helah. She was a lieutenant in Kenan's army. She has an urgent message for you."

I stand and rush towards her, along with Cephas. She is breathing heavily; she has cuts and sores on her arms, and half her hair has fallen out. She falls to one knee.

"Get a medic!" I yell. It's obvious she is dying from radiation poisoning.

"Kenan... Kenan... Kenan," she murmurs. The word can barely escape her lips.

"And someone get some water!" I add.

Cephas holds her head. "Kenan, Kenan, what? What about Kenan?"

She is coughing up blood. Cephas wipes her face with a rag. "Kenan, he is alive."

"Alive, how?"

Eve brings water. Helah places her cracked and bleeding lips on the cup and gingerly takes a sip.

"We escaped the nukes."

"How Helah? Where is Kenan and his army?"

She starts into another coughing fit.

"NOR..." She is wheezing now.

"Where, Helah, tell me where?"

"NORAD. They are at NORAD."

Her eyes close.

Sarai

It's like watching a ravenous wolf eat. My father snaps and breaks up the King Crab's legs with his bare, greasy hands. Crab pieces fly across the table, and one lands in my expensive wine.

"More crab, dear?" Renatus asks me.

My appetite has waned. I simply shake my head. How can he converse with me like everything is normal? Has he forgotten that the only reason I'm here being cordial is that he holds my son's life in his hands? He even says the word *dear* affectionately. In fact, since the incident on the yacht when he jumped into the sea, he has been calm, or at the very least, more relaxed. Maybe in his warped, delusional mind, he thinks that having my mother and me here makes us truly a family again.

He then turns to my mother. "How about you, Joanna? More?"

"I'll have a bit more," she says, her tone soft. Ever since she returned, she has been passive. Subservient. Perhaps it's for Silas's sake? Or mine? Or has she fallen under his spell again? Or is it Zion itself? Lured into its net once more. Asher and I were once ensnared by its opulence. Its promise of a better life. The wool covering the facade of Zion is thick. And before you know it, you are a slave to Zion's abundance. It owns you. You don't own it. But once your eyes are opened, there is no going back.

I hope that is the case for my mother.

Renatus turns to his CA (Canonization Architect), Jokim. "I want it to be big, I want it to be expansive, I want it to stretch for miles and miles, I want different challenges with different landscapes, I don't want it contained to just one arena."

Jokim shows him blueprints and pictures. "This is what we have done so far, my Sultan."

His eyes flicker with a hint of delight. "Good. And we are on schedule?"

"If I get that extra crew as promised, then yes."

"You'll get it. And remind them how important this is. It must be more than a spectacle. This will put the initial stamp on New Zion, and it will set the tone for my next millennial rule."

He doesn't think in decades or even centuries about his lifetime; he thinks in units of a thousand. I can't imagine the mindset and God complex someone must have to think this way. It's like déjà vu. Asher is away, trying to figure out how to save us, while I'm being forced to break bread with the enemy while pretending to like it.

Jokim reaches across the table and snatches the bottle of wine. The chandelier lights reflect off the gold and diamonds embedded in his skin. His hair is like liquid gold. His ears stretch towards his shoulders from the massive diamonds attached to his lobes. Even his eyes are gold. The glitter of his gilded body is surely to mask the depravity of his spirit. He embodies what it was to be a Lazurite: to have your earthly body exist forever while your soul rots. His petite hands grab a silk napkin that he uses to blot his lips. Unlike my father, at least his table manners are tolerable.

Renatus turns to me. "Three months away. Excited?"

"No, Father."

"It's no secret, my daughter, that you aren't a fan of the Canonization."

Really?

He makes a show of dropping a crab leg onto his plate. "Do you know why we do this?"

"A populace entertained is a distracted populace," I answer.

He admits it, "Somewhat. But to rule people, to rule a nation, you have to exhibit power and prosperity. Creativity. A poor and weak nation could not put on a Canonization in the way I will." He cracks another crab leg. "But also, it sends a message, for anyone who would become my enemy or an enemy of Zion. No, New Zion. They must know that at any time, it can be them or their children battling it out for Zion's glory."

Punishment disguised as a game. He is brilliant as he is wicked.

"Is it for Zion's glory or yours?"

My mother looks at me as if to say, *"Stop being so antagonistic."*

"They are the same, dear."

He sees himself as not just the leader of Zion, but as Zion himself. Immortal.

Then, out of the corner of my eye, I see him walk by. Hagar, my trainer, my friend, my confidant. Now, he is also my messenger. He shoots me a quick glance and continues on.

I clear my throat. "I think I'm going to turn in for the evening."

Renatus ignores my comment, as he is once again absorbed by the blueprints for his new Canonization for his New Zion. Slap *"New"* onto something, and the shallow masses automatically assume better.

I slip out of the palatial dining room, jaunt through the kitchen past a horde of chefs, and then onto the back patio.

Hagar sips water and stares up at the yellow moon. At fifty-five, he still has the physique of a gladiator. Not a single strand of gray has yet permeated his long, curly black hair. He looks behind me to be certain I wasn't followed.

"I have had contact."

My heart speeds up. "Asher?"

"Yes. He needs something. Radiation suits."

I wasn't expecting that. "Radiation suits? What for?"

"For Kenan and his army," he whispers.

"They are still alive?"

"Yes, they are trapped inside NORAD. They need the suits to evacuate the fallout zone."

"How many?"

"Around five hundred."

I shake my head. "How?"

"If you can get into the system, you can search the weapons and storage depots. See if you can find one close to Reservation 9."

I hug him. "Thanks, Hagar."

"Be careful, Sarai."

"You too."

I watch him leave, and for the first time in a while, I feel a shred of hope. Asher will have a seed of an army, but that is all he needs to build on to start a movement to recruit more.

I take a deep breath of ocean air and retreat to my quarters. Finally, I feel useful.

Shortly after, a knock on my door. "It's your mother."

"Come in."

I sit at my desk; she sits on the corner of my bed. "Not hungry tonight, dear?"

"My son is imprisoned. I am held hostage here. And once again, I am separated from Asher. So, no, I don't really have an appetite."

She sighs. "I have tried to reason with him, but he is too far gone, I'm afraid."

"What are you doing here, Mother?"

"Talking to you."

"No, what are you doing here in Zion, at the palace? Why did you come back?"

She stands, places her hand on my shoulder. "For you. For Silas."

"But you too are a prisoner."

"I would rather be a prisoner with you and my grandson than out there all alone. Besides, I can help you."

Help me? Has Renatus sent her in here to spy on me? Can she be trusted? She did just save my life. And it's true, she doesn't have to be here. I am not sure if I can confide in her. I am not sure if I can trust her. But I don't have a choice. Besides, she doesn't need to be privy to the big picture. I just need her help with one thing.

I clear my throat. "Mother. I could use your help, actually."

"Name it."

"And I can trust you?"

"Of course. My eyes have been opened, dear." She winks. "I guess I'm one of those dreadful Drecks now."

I never knew she had a sense of humor. "The password to father's computer."

She smiles. "That's an easy one."

After telling me, she heads toward the door, "Be careful, daughter. Your father may be going crazy, but he isn't stupid." I nod and watch her leave.

It's three in the morning when my alarm goes off. Renatus only sleeps four or five hours a night, so it has to be now. I put on a robe and exit my room into the wide hallways. An elite marches by as I hide around the corner, waiting for him to pass. I tiptoe to the end of the hall and reach the grand stairway. It is wide enough for a tank with massive pillars on each side. I hurry to the top and turn right, walking until I reach my father's locked office door. There is a keypad next to it. His maid, who is sympathetic to me and my cause, has given me the four-digit code, which I enter. The door clicks open.

I slither into the office, slowly close the door behind me, and switch on the light. The furniture is expensive. The bookshelf is curated with dozens of books he hasn't read. There are at least five or six pictures of Eleazar. None of me.

His computer sits on top of The Resolute Desk. Yes, the one from The Oval Office. He procured it during his time at The White House.

I switch on the monitor and am ready to enter the password. Let's see if my mother is correct. When it comes to his children and which one he loves, my father is nothing if not consistent. I type in *Eleazar*. His computer unlocks, and I am in. On the screen is a map that updates in real-time. There is a wealth of information here, including troop movements and Drone patrols. With the mouse, I hover over the many green squares representing weapons and storage depots. I click on four or five that are adjacent to Reservation 9 until I find one whose manifest list includes radiation suits. Seven hundred and fifty are currently in inventory. It is Depot #231.

Then, CLICK. The door opens. I shut off the computer monitor and crouch behind the desk. I can see my father's red slippers, scattered with gold flecks, slog into the room.

He mutters to himself, "Did I leave the light on?"

He walks towards the front of the desk as I squeeze tighter underneath it. Does this man ever sleep? Luckily, he grabs a notepad from a desk drawer and trudges out, turning off the light as he leaves.

Like a child, I am left trembling in the dark.

Asher

I sent a Runner thirty miles west of here to the nearest underground Internet cafe not yet hit by Renatus's EMPs. The drops are becoming progressively worse. He figures that without power, he can root out the last of us.

And he is right.

Without electricity, food must be fresh; water must be boiled. Nineteenth-century style communications and organization. Not to mention the heat and the cold. Speaking of water, I drink another glass (warm) in an effort to avert another headache. My dreams (nightmares) are intensifying, becoming more vivid. More real. Sometimes, it's hard to tell what are dreams and what are memories. Things are becoming blended and almost confusing. It is a struggle to suppress my appetite for violence. I almost miss the arena. At first, I was playing the role of gladiator, but it didn't take long for me to become one. I begin to crave the approval of the crowds. It was the only victory I had. The only thing I could control. But, of course, that is an illusion. I controlled nothing. Protocol has warped me. How could something as wanton and nefarious as protocol not? My mind is like a cloud of battling emotions and principles. Turbulent thoughts swirl together in a disoriented state. Cephas says I need to pray more. Take my thoughts captive. He is right, but he doesn't fully understand what is happening to my brain.

I squint as a brisk breeze bullies my face towards the ground, where I watch decaying leaves dance around my boots. My Runner, Stephen, pulls up in one of the stolen Jeeps and approaches. He is wiry, like Jude. His veins stick out like bloated worms. His hair is stubble, and he has sunken cheeks.

"Depot 231, eighty miles south of here," he shouts.

"How many?"

"Seven hundred and fifty."

I ask, "And security?"

"She didn't say."

"Thank you, Stephen."

Before he turns to leave, he stops, hesitant. I can tell he wants to ask me a question.

"What is it, soldier?"

"Kenan. We were friends. Do you really think they are still alive?"

I don't know for sure. But he doesn't need to know that. "I do."

"And this war, you think we can win?"

I have been asking myself the same thing. But I don't hesitate. I feign assurance. "I do."

He leaves with more confidence than he had a minute ago. I have to keep up the facade of the confident, calm, and all-knowing leader. If he or any of my men knew what was really going on in my head, they would run for the hills.

The communication went like this: if I needed to talk to Sarai, Stephen would email one of Hagar's men, who would then tell Hagar, and he would pass the message on to Sarai. It would come back to me in reverse order. All this, assuming we could find a working cafe with a working signal.

I march towards Cephas, who is taking a weapons inventory.

"Seven hundred and fifty radiation suits, eighty miles south."

"How do you want to play it?"

"Let's go light and quick, a team of eight. A jeep and the wrecker." I am referring to the truck with the massive wrecking ball attached to the back. We found it broken down and abandoned ten miles south of here. Adam's people were able to get it running again.

"You think that's enough?" Cephas is weary, his tone doubtful.

"Renatus has close to five hundred depots scattered across this country; how heavily armed can each one be?"

He spits, "No reconnaissance?"

"There's no time." Who knows how much longer Kenan and his army have?

He crows, "Sounds like a Dreck mission."

I smile. "Would you have it any other way?"

He stands, knees creaking. He looks left, then right, cracking his neck. His hands tremble slightly. "I'll check the fuel."

I hesitate to speak the following words, but I must. "Maybe you should sit this one out."

"What are you talking about?"

He sees me glance at his shaky hands. "Look, I'm fine, Nephew." He knows what I'm thinking. "I'm shaking because I'm off the Tonic." I stare at him, not sure what to believe. He stares back, long and hard. "I'm going."

Two hours later, we pull the jeep and the wrecker behind a grove of trees about three hundred yards from Depot 231. The rain has turned into a deluge. Thunder peals in the distance, further adding to our cover. The raindrops pelt our exoarmor with such force that it's like the clouds have sneezed. Adam and Eve asked to tag along. Why not? They are ex-military.

Cephas peers through the binoculars. "One on the roof, two out front."

The depot, fifty feet long and thirty feet wide, is made of thick concrete and has a massive steel door. The three guards shiver miserably in the rain and look completely uninterested in their job; they are obviously not elites.

"This should be easy," I spout with confidence.

"That's usually about the time everything falls apart," Adam chimes in.

Cephas turns to him. "You'll fit in just fine."

I turn on my exoarmor-penetrating Gen2 plasma gun. "I'll take the one on the roof. Cephas and Adam take the two out front." I turn to Eve and the four other Drecks who volunteered to come. "The rest of you check the back."

Eve rips off her exoarmor and shakes the rain from her cropped brown hair. "I'll take the front."

"What are you doing?" Cephas barks at her.

"I am assuming their weapons are also Gen2. This armor will just slow me down. Besides, I'm a marine, remember?"

I like her spunk. Reminds me of my wife.

Adam sighs, "I guess I'm going around back."

Thinking of Sarai, I grab his shoulder and smile. "I know how you feel. Sometimes, you just have to roll with it."

I slosh my way to a large pine overlooking the Depot. I don't have a direct shot at the guard on the roof. Two trees partially block my line of sight. I unlatch my ricochet from my belt and fling it around the outside tree. It curves around it, then to the left, hitting the guard in the neck.

Just as he rolls off the roof and almost lands on the two guards below him, Cephas and Eve take the two of them out. Actually, Eve took them both out before Cephas could even fire. Cephas is getting slower with age. That, or Eve is extremely quick. Let's go with that. That Eve is swift and agile. I see Adam and the four Drecks round the corner from the back and give me the all-clear sign.

Easy.

Maybe too easy. But then again, it's about time something was easy. I can tell by the look on Cephas's face that he also thinks this is too simple. Uncomplicated is not very Dreck-like.

"Grab the Wrecker," I say to Cephas.

He lumbers past me, then stops for a moment. I try to hide my concern about the fact that he didn't manage to get one shot off before Eve got two. But he can read me like a book.

"Not a word," he growls. Raindrops surf the crags in his face until finally beading onto his beard like sprinkles on a cupcake.

I can only throw up my hands and smile. I wonder how he is faring without the Tonic. He is grumpier than usual, but so far, he has been true to his word.

Cephas pulls himself into the operating cage perched on the back of the pickup truck. Adam hops into the front and pulls the truck parallel to the Depot, about thirty feet away. Cephas mans the controls of the giant metal wrecking ball. He swings the cage from left to right. The metal ball attached to the heavy chain is gaining momentum. He shifts his cage from left to right until the massive ball slams into the side of the Depot. It smashes right through the thick concrete. Chunks fly overhead. Dust rains down.

With a smile, he gives it another go; he looks happier than a butcher's dog. After three swings, the hole in the depot is more than big enough for us to enter. Cephas hops down and sidles next to me, still grinning.

"Feeling better?" I ask.

"One hundred percent."

Renatus

Renatus strolls the hallways of his new underground protocol complex. The security is greater than at the Mountain. It is built underneath his compound, meaning the only way in is from the inside, and that itself would require the biometrics of only a select few. The only outside access is the portholes that open only when a HarvestDrone delivers its payload. In fact one is happening now.

He watches with morbid curiosity as the porthole to his left opens. The HarvestDrone hovers above it while connecting its long tubular hose to the open porthole. An unconscious man, dressed in 1980s attire (a Dreck), is sucked from the hose and into a cylinder full of the pink gel. There, he will lie in a suspended state until his LifeCell is harvested.

Renatus is proud of himself and his well-oiled machine, which trades one life for another. He walks to the end of the hall where Eleazar floats in the same pink substance. He places his sweaty palm on the glass cylinder and closes his eyes. Tears roll down his smooth face. That angers him. He sees it as a weakness.

"Soon, my wounded one. Soon."

He wipes the tears from his cheeks and peers around to be sure no one is watching. Next to him is Asher and Sarai's son Silas. He floats in his cylinder with outstretched hands, almost as if perpetually trying to receive a hug. Renatus looks from one cylinder to the other. His son, then his grandson. *One button*, he thought. It would only take a push of this button to bring his son back to life. He places his palm near it; the temptation to push it is great. But a small part of him still doesn't want to lose his grandson. *Maybe Asher will deliver?* And he could have both. Perhaps then his daughter will love him again? Maybe it will restore his marriage? He thinks about the death of his sister and his parents. And how he was helpless to do anything about it. But protocol. Protocol could have saved them. Saved the world. That is all he wanted he tells himself. To be a savior. Yet, this was a delusion. He doesn't want to be a savior, he wants to be worshiped like one. Soon, he will save his son.

But could he kill his grandson to do so? He would undoubtedly lose Sarai forever. Joanna would never forgive him. This is a rare moment where he actually feels conflicted about what he has done and what he will continue to do.

But it is a fleeting moment. *Pure and simple weakness.* Whatever demons and angels battled upon his shoulders, the demons always win. *It doesn't matter what my wife and daughter think. They don't see the big picture. They don't know my burdens. My responsibility. I was purposed for this. I was destined to lead Zion. Nothing extraordinary or everlasting happens without sacrifice. Sarai and Joanna will one day realize this. They will see what I see. Zion was ordained to be eternal. And so am I.*

He heads towards the exit just as the demon swats the angel from his bony shoulder. He turns around and marches with purpose to the console between the two cylinders. He raises his palm, readying to slam it against the button that will activate protocol and bring his son back. His arm shakes, his teeth are gritted. Sweat drips from his forehead onto the clean, cold, sterile floor.

"Damn!" he relents.

Soon. I have waited this long. Just a bit longer.

Later that evening, he sits at his desk with a glass of Scotch. His CA, Jokim, sits across from him.

"Still on schedule?" Renatus's tone suggests it's more of a *yes or else* confirmation than a question.

"Yes, my Sultan," Jokim replies. He then points to the blueprints. "I think you will be quite happy with what we have planned here. This will be larger and grander than anything we have ever done. It will be talked about for ages."

Renatus smiles in delight. Then his eyes narrow. "I hope so, for your sake." Soon, he will have his son. Soon, he will have a new Canonization for a New Zion. The Defiance will be eradicated. A new era of peace and prosperity. *One of many eras I will live to see.* It always brings him great excitement that he would be around for centuries to come. To not only see but be a part of history from here on out.

I am history.

"And what of Apex? How is he healing?"

"Marvelously. He will be ready, my Sultan. And to say the least, he is very eager."

Renatus waves him off. "That will be all."

After gathering his papers and a quick bow, Jokim leaves, just as Boaz enters the room. Jokim gives him a sideways stare as if to say, *"Good luck."*

"You wanted to see me, my sultan?"

Renatus's tone is a bit maniacal. "Boaz. Boaz. The man with the maps. King of contraband. Americana aficionado. Peddler of arms. Trafficker of secrets. My patrols have sent word that Cephas has escaped Eden."

Boaz stutters, "Impossible, I—"

Renatus cuts him off. "It was you who convinced my elites to leave them at Eden alive. So it is you who will be held responsible."

"But my sultan—"

Before he can finish, Renatus shoots him with his plasma gun. Boaz backpedals into a bookshelf before crashing to the ground, a look of shock on his face.

A guard runs through the door. "Sir, are you okay?"

Renatus waves towards Boaz as if he is a dead ant. "Get him out of here. Actually, prep him for protocol. I might still need him."

"Yes, sir." The guard drags Boaz's limp body out of the room.

Renatus swirls his Scotch, watching the golden brown liquid almost crest the top of his glass. He clenches his eyes shut as a plethora of different thoughts and voices churn in his mind. He tries to drown them out with a sip of Scotch, then turns on his computer monitor and types in his password: "Eleazar." He clicks on a program called "Keystroke Tracker."

On the screen, he watches a recorded session of everything Sarai did the other night, specifically the map she opened and how she clicked into Depot #231.

Renatus breathes through his teeth, trying to figure out if the traitor is his daughter or not. *Would she really risk her son's life? Or is it more likely I have a mole in my chain of command, someone sympathetic to The Defiance and their cause?* He shuts off his monitor and, with a gulp, downs the last of his Scotch.

Asher

It doesn't take long for the rain to tamp down the dust from Cephas's robust wrecking display. We march into the Depot with weapons drawn. We are greeted by a surprised and visibly shaken guard with his hands up. The scene inside must have been terrifying as the massive steel ball smashed through the walls.

"Put your gun down!" Cephas grunts.

The guard obliges.

"Where are the radiation suits?" I ask.

He stutters, "In the... in the crates near the back."

In front of me is a HeliDrone; its wings and propellers on the right side have been smashed by the wrecking ball. I wish I knew this was part of the inventory. I turn to Cephas. "We could have used this if you weren't so enthusiastic with the Wrecker."

"Get over it, Nephew; it was worth it."

Seeing the rare smile on his face, I guess it was. We spend the next thirty minutes loading the radiation suits into the jeep and storage compartments inside the Wrecker. I only hope we can reach Kenan before they starve to death.

Then I hear it.

The unmistakable whir of HeliDrone rotors. Two of them are heading straight for us. Then, from our flanks, fifty or more Lazurite soldiers emerge from the forest.

It's an ambush.

"We've been flanked!" I yell.

"Get inside!" orders Cephas.

The eight of us stream into the Depot. The two HeliDrones hover directly overhead.

"This building won't hold up long against those Drones," I say.

I peer out of one of the massive holes in the Depot and see the Lazurite commander stop. He makes sure there are a few soldiers between us and him. "Come out with your hands up, and you don't need to die today."

We have heard that line before. They have no intention of letting us out of here alive.

Cephas barks, "We've been sold out!"

"There's no way out of here. We have to give ourselves up," Adam suggests.

"It's a death sentence either way," Cephas responds.

"We're not going without a fight." It's Eve. She sprints past me and jumps onto the broken wing of the HeliDrone. She opens the hatch and slides into the cockpit.

"What are you doing?" I ask her. "This thing can't fly."

"It can move, can't it?" she growls as she inspects the controls.

Adam pleads, "You're gonna get yourself killed, Eve."

She ignores him. "When I tell you, open the front door. Then get to the Wrecker."

"I like her." Cephas spits.

I know what she's thinking, and it's our best chance. The fact that I didn't see it or suggest it makes me wonder what has been happening to my brain lately: conflicting thoughts, random ideas. I am still hearing voices and smelling the scent of corn, of all things. I am no longer feeling fit to lead. But who can I tell at this point in the war? Cephas maybe. But he'll just tell me I'm imagining it. I can tell Sarai, but things are hard enough on her. All I would be doing is lowering her morale. Besides, people expect me to lead. They expect me to live up to my many monikers. Asher the Liberator. Asher, the Defier of Zion. Even my weapon of choice is a symbol of freedom. Defiance. What would my army do if word got out that I was crazy?

I order Adam to man the door while we ready our weapons.

"You want the Wrecker or the Jeep?" I ask Cephas.

"What do you think?" he snorts.

Then, the Lazurite commander's whiny voice chirps: "This is your last warning. Come out with your hands up, or ready yourself to incur the wrath of New Zion."

New Zion? Sounds like Old Zion to me.

Eve fires up the HeliDrone. Only the left two rotors spin, as the wrecking ball has crushed the right two. "Open the door!" she yells.

Adam doesn't like this at all. "Eve, are you sure?"

"Open it, Adam."

Adam flips the switch, and the massive metal door slides up. The Lazurite commander looks befuddled as he sees a hobbled HeliDrone bounce off the ground, straight toward him and his army.

"Dreck!" he screeches. In true Lazurite fashion, the cowardly commander pushes his soldiers in front of him while he dives out of harm's way.

Because the drone only has two working rotors on the same side, it begins to spin. Like a fast-moving top bouncing off the ground, it spirals into the heart of the platoon. Lazurites fly indiscriminately like seeds from a crushed orange. We all stand in awe at the crazy scene unfolding before us, crazy even by Dreck standards. We may be from different generations, separated by a hundred years, but it pleases me to see that we share the same fighting spirit. We call it courage; others might deem it pure lunacy.

For a moment, I forget about our part. "Now!"

While the Lazurites try to scatter away from Eve's rotating drone, four Drecks and I make our way to the Jeep. At the same time, Adam pulls himself into the driver's seat of the Wrecker truck, while Cephas jumps into the control cage mounted on the back. Plasma bombs drop around us from the HeliDrones above. Not wanting to leave without Eve, we drive in semi-circles, dodging plasma blasts.

One of the drones comes in lower for a better shot. I point to it, then to the wrecking ball, but Cephas is already on it. He brings the arm up and down until the wrecking ball builds momentum. He then releases the lock on the chain, and the ball swings upwards, smashing into the low-hovering drone. Crippled, it crash-lands into a gaggle of fleeing Lazurites, only a few yards away from Eve's drone.

She gives us a look. Yeah. Like we're the crazy ones.

I wave her over. She jumps out just as another plasma bomb destroys her drone. Cephas's truck drives in circles, causing his wrecking ball to form a protective barrier, pummeling any Lazurites in our wake. Cephas, all smiles, bounces in his control cage like he is riding a bull. I think he would have been perfectly content having a career manning big machinery. Or explosives, perhaps. But, like it or not, he was called to a bigger purpose. As was I.

"Head east! Towards the trees!" I order.

Cephas is the first to go. My jeep is more agile, so I swing towards Eve, who jumps up and grabs the rear railing. Her strong arms pull her into the back as plasma blasts fly overhead.

"You okay?" I ask her.

"Fine." But blood is streaming from the side of her head. She touches it with her fingers and then smears it under her eyes like she is applying war paint. "Why do you ask?"

I smile. Jude would have liked her. Within thirty seconds, we are under the cover of trees, protected from the last HeliDrone.

"So much for your contact inside. How did they know we were coming?" Eve snarls, wiping more blood from her forehead.

"I don't know."

How did Renatus know? Was Sarai caught red-handed? Is she okay? Or has Hagar been compromised?

Or is it my Runner?

Chapter Four

Asher

OUR JEEPS TRAVERSE THE charred and barren landscape of the fall-out zone. An eerie gray vapor emanates from the ground, almost as if it's still burning. The soil wheezes from the man-made poison. The earth hisses at us as we drive by. The thickness of the radiation suit is causing me to sweat. My mask is partially fogged, which is welcome because it obscures the calamity I see in front of me.

Our convoy consists of twelve jeeps and seven hundred and fifty radiation suits. We will have to make more than one trip to evacuate everyone. Assuming they are all still alive.

To my left, on what used to be a busy highway, is an array of scorched cars. The occupants are ashen molds of their former selves, their hair seared, and skin parched. In the backseat of a minivan are two car seats; still strapped inside are tiny, shadowy, sooty figures. One of them still has a pacifier where its mouth used to be.

I peer over at Cephas, who is shaking his head. Who could do such a thing? A line I never thought Renatus would cross. An evil I thought I would never see. Senseless. Protocol has more than corrupted his mind.

What has it done to mine?

Then I see it.

My Weeping Willow. Where Sarai and I were married. *Our* Weeping Willow. Its singed strands twist in the wind. Some of them fall and disintegrate before hitting the ground. Its bark is blackened, as if it survived a fire or lightning strike. It looks like a shadowy shell of what it once was. Is that what Sarai and I are now? But it still stands. Somehow, while all the other trees around it have been knocked down or burnt to the ground, it inexplicably still stands.

As does Sarai and me. As we always will. Together or not, we fight the same fight; we always have. A physical and metaphorical wall has always been between us, always separating us. The universe conspires to keep us detached, only letting us be us when we are apart. Yet, we still operate as one; we always have. Love is the bridge that fills the gap. Like the willow, our love may be scorched, attacked, and burnt by our enemies, by life, by this war, but we have not yet fallen.

Cephas pats my shoulder and points to the willow. "It will grow back." But that future is difficult to see.

Then, without warning, the pain has returned—like a mountain climber inside my head, trying to escape using an icepick. I close my eyes and grip my head in an effort to quell the pain.

Then, instead of voices and smells, I'm assailed by memories that I'm not sure are mine:

A child I have never seen before with a fever.

A funeral for this same child.

A HeliDrone pilot dropping plasma bombs on my own army.

A farmer tending to endless rows of corn.

A man being dragged away from his family by Lazurite elites.

Who are these people? Are these repressed memories from my childhood? Maybe protocol is making me schizophrenic? The child I see in my memories is the same one crying out for his mother. The farmer tending the corn is what I have been smelling.

Then a terrifying thought hits me. What if these memories and feelings are from the many LifeCells that now dwell inside me?

I should mention it to Cephas and Sarai, but the thought of it is too chilling for me to comprehend at the moment. They have a war to focus on. Instead, I think back to our lake. Our boat. Sarai's bucket full of fish, while I continually bait her hook. It's like a dream that feels real, yet I know I'm dreaming. Thoughts of her are the only thing that can pluck my mind away from whatever is happening inside my brain. She has always been my refuge.

I finally open my eyes when I hear Cephas yell, "We're here!"

We approach the tunnel that burrows inside the mountain. I read the sign: 'CHEYENNE MOUNTAIN COMPLEX'.

NORAD.

We disembark from the jeeps and approach the steel door leading into the mountain.

"It's unlocked." Cephas's voice is muffled through the radiation suit.

Weapons drawn, we move cautiously inside the building. Its dermis is made of steel and concrete. The necessity for a place such as this, such as Eden, such as The Fort Worth Armory, tells me that strife and division have always existed. Perhaps The Wall was inevitable—expected and maybe even welcomed by some? And once it's gone, something will surely replace it. And when Renatus is finally dead, undeniably, another dictator will rise in his stead. Conflict and control are predictable human conditions.

But the fight must go on. We can never stop. Even if we lose, that's the one thing they can never take from us. Our will. Our indomitable spirit.

"Freeze!" a man yells as we turn a corner. He is holding a plasma rifle. His hair is long, his beard ragged. He is so thin that I don't recognize him at first.

"Who... who are you?" he yells, his hands shaking.

I recognize the voice, the stutter. It is Kenan—at least, I think it is. He is an emaciated husk of his former self. But why doesn't he recognize us? Then I forget—the radiation suits, of course. I remove my helmet. "Kenan, it's me, Asher."

Kenan drops to one knee, his shaking hands releasing his weapon. The plasma rifle clinks to the floor. Tears of relief spill from him. He must have been strong for his men this entire time, and now the emotional floodgates have opened. I can sympathize with him. Being a leader sometimes means keeping your tears private. "It's you? It's really you?"

I grab underneath his arm and help him up. "Yes, it's me, Asher."

"So she found you? Helah, she found you?"

"Yes."

He swivels his head back and forth. "Where is she? Is she here?"

I grip his shoulder. "She didn't, she didn't make it."

His eyes clench shut. "It was me who was supposed to go; I was the one who—" He shakes his head. "She was, she was brave. Braver than I."

"Yes, she was very brave."

Cephas also removes his helmet. "Kenan, your men. How many are still alive?"

"All of them."

I draw him close. "And they are alive because of you, because of your courage. Your bravery. Your choice to bring them here. Don't ever let anyone question your leadership."

"And the rad suits?"

"We have them."

"And food?"

I hold up an OatBar. "Your favorite."

Cephas is getting impatient. I can tell he doesn't like being near the radiation, even with the suit on. "Let's unload the suits and start the evacuation."

But what Kenan tells me next is a game-changer.

"We found something, Asher, something left behind when this place was looted."

He rips into the OatBar, all the while leaving me hanging.

"Spit it out, Kenan."

"Follow me. Best I show you."

My men and I follow Kenan down the stairs and into the cold bunker. His soldiers' countenances immediately change when Cephas and I march in. We can hear them whisper our names. Some solute us. Others hug us. We hand out OatBars and rad suits.

Kenan leads us down another set of stairs and into a small room. On a table in the middle rests what looks like an oversized metal suitcase.

"What is it?" Cephas asks.

"A ten-kiloton nuclear suitcase."

I stare.

"Yeah, we were as shocked as you."

Cephas asks the pertinent question, "Is it operable?"

Kenan shrugs. "No idea. None of my platoon are scientists or engineers. At least not nuclear."

This is precisely the good news we needed. I smile. "Good thing I know where to find some."

Asher

It takes three days to evacuate everyone from the fallout zone. Now, we have returned to the bunker. Unfortunately, I have been told that the nuclear suitcase is currently inoperable. Fortunately, I have a batch of nuclear scientists from Eden looking at it.

Adam approaches me.

"They tell me the uranium is still good, but the detonator has a problem."

I ask, "Can they fix it?"

"We'll see."

"I was hoping for better news."

"As a scientist and a marine, I don't sugarcoat things."

"I appreciate that about you, Adam. Do what you can."

He clears his throat, a look of judgment on his face.

"What is it, Adam?"

"What are you planning on doing with it? The nuke?"

I reassure him, "I don't intend on using it unless I have to. For now, it's an insurance policy."

That doesn't satisfy him. "Because if we use this, we are no better than them."

I am offended that he would think I would be so casual about considering using such a weapon. "Just get it working."

"We'll do our best."

I grimace as the piercing in my head has returned.

"You okay, Asher?"

"Fine."

He clears his throat again. "May I suggest another tactic?"

"Go on."

"Perhaps we are looking at this war all wrong."

I rub my temples, my patience waning. "What do you suggest?" I want to tell him I have been fighting this war for almost half of my life, that I have given everything to it. But I hold back.

"You know, some of the scientists and I were talking, and we think we might be able to reverse it."

"Reverse what?" I answer, irked by the pain, not his question.

"Protocol."

My pain instantly disappears. He now has my full attention. "What do you mean, reverse it?"

"Render it unworkable. If we can analyze how it works, perhaps we can come up with an antidote for it. Something we can inject into the blood that can counteract the effects of protocol, effectively rendering it useless. Then there would be no need for LifeCells, no need for harvesting, and Renatus wouldn't have his invincible army."

I shake my head. I can't believe I haven't thought of this before. I realize how shortsighted I have been. I have been so focused on destroying Renatus instead of his source of power. Without protocol, there is no need for The Wall or a war. And no need to harvest my son's LifeCell, for that matter. "You're a Godsend, Adam. Do you have an idea of how that would work?"

"I was thinking perhaps an antibody that would destroy any foreign LifeCells. All we would need is a LifeCell that we could reverse engineer."

"I take that back," I jest. "They aren't so easy to come by."

"Don't their soldiers have them?"

"In an invasion, yes. But typically, they don't just wear them around. For that kind of usage, they are usually reserved for someone important."

"Let's find someone important then."

An hour later, I explain Adam's plan to Cephas. He scratches the deep scars on his craggy cheeks. "It's a long shot."

I smile. "So our usual then."

"I don't know, Asher, it could be a waste of resources. And time, for that matter. We have a nuke now. Let's focus on that and building our army."

"A nuke that isn't operable."

"Not yet. We are already stretched too thin, Nephew."

I say, "Look, the ten from Eden we will utilize are scientists, not soldiers. If we want to win the long game and render protocol dead, this is the way to go. I mean, even if we can kill Renatus, someone else will rise up and implement protocol in his stead. As long as this technology exists, this war will never end."

He stares at me with his aged, wisdom-filled eyes. "This isn't just about Silas?"

"Of course, this is about my son; I would do anything to save him. You know that. But even with him out of the equation, I think this is the right move. You told me that everything happens for a purpose. That God puts people in your path for a reason. I believe that is why Adam is here. That is why we went to Eden in the first place. Not for nukes or gold. But for *them*—for this."

He places his paw on my shoulder. "And my own words once again come back to bite me. Okay, let's do it. Where do we get our LifeCell?"

"Well, as luck would have it, tomorrow Reservation 8 is having a ball for the regional governor there. Surely, the Governor will be wearing one."

"Lucky us. I guess it's a good thing you like to dance, then."

Asher

We arrive at the regional Governor's mansion in the middle of Reservation 8 just before dusk. Our jeep is parked behind a grove of trees. Eve and I are dressed to the nines in full Lazurite elite gear. Red sash and all. I sport a mustache, dark glasses with red frames, and a tall red hat in an attempt to go incognito. Eve's sparkling dress is black and gold. She looks elegant and exquisite. I look ridiculous. I never understood Lazurite fashion. My hat, which is longer than my arm, reeks of pomp. My pants are white, as is my shirt, except it is splattered with red polka dots. I feel like a clown. We were able to procure the outfits on the black market from one of Boaz's competitors. It cost us a pretty penny, but we had no choice.

I point to the balcony on the second floor, on the south side of the mansion. "Eve and I will try to get the Governor alone and onto that balcony." I motion to the two guards right below it, and then to Cephas. "You and Adam take them out when I give you the signal."

Adam smiles. "Got it, Bobo."

"Who?"

"Nothing, a famous clown back in my day. Stupid joke."

I shrug. "Not bad."

Cephas raises his wild thicket, masquerading as an eyebrow. "And how do you plan on getting him alone? Surely the Governor will have security."

Eve just winks at him. "Leave that to me."

I turn to her and plead, "We must take him alive. We have to be sure the LifeCell in his pack is not activated."

She pulls out a syringe filled with a clear liquid.

"You sure that will only knock him out?"

Adam interjects, "Yes. Assuming he doesn't have a heart condition."

Great.

Cephas is growing impatient. "Get going. It's starting."

"How do we look?" I ask Cephas.

"Like Lazurite scum."

"Good."

Eve examines her dress. "I think I look great."

Before we head off to the Ball, Adam grabs Eve's arm. "Be careful, my love."

"Now, what fun would that be?"

As we leave the cover of trees and head towards the estate, I overhear Cephas saying, "Quite the handful, your wife."

In a way she reminds of Sarai, brave and beautiful, but in a manner less humble. As we approach the front doors a guard asks for our names. We reply with the names Kenan added to the guest list last night by hacking into their system.

Inside, the mansion oozes extravagance. Chandeliers are the size of cars. We enter the grand hall replete with marble flooring. A painting of Renatus, thronged with gold trim, defiles the otherwise white, pure wall. The other wall holds a built-in aquarium teeming with rare and exotic fish.

Eve points. "Clarion angelfish, one of my favorites." She catches my look. "We had an aquarium when I was young. You might say my father was a collector."

"I would rather eat them than look at them." That's the difference between Dreck and Lazurite. Due to their overabundance, they can collect what we consider food.

She whispers, "Remember now, you're a Lazurite."

Reluctant Lazurites forced to repopulate the Reservations prance around in swanky clothes, trying to pretend they are still in Zion. Elites surround the Governor, who is trying to swoon a young lady. He is probably fifty, with a receding hairline and dyed golden hair which makes the wispy, frayed locks look more like a mullet. He looks to be average weight for his height, which lessens the chances that he has a heart condition. His hat is a few inches taller than everyone else's. I check mine to be sure I'm not breaking any ridiculous Lazurite custom. The last thing I need is to draw attention to us, for having a hat taller than the Governor's.

A waiter saunters by and hands us each a glass of champagne. We both down them like they are shots to help calm the nerves. Classical music begins to play, as a dozen or so hit the dance floor.

"Dance?" Eve asks me.

I shake my head.

She grabs my hand. "I think we should fit in."

I don't tell her how much I despise dancing, nor do I tell her Sarai is the only woman that I have ever and will ever dance with. Instead I say, "Let's find another drink."

We head towards the bar, where the Governor and one of his wealthy elites approach us.

"I don't believe we have met?" the Governor says to us, while looking directly at Eve.

She answers, "I am Mia, and this is Henry."

"A pleasure. I am Governor Wilson, and my friend here is Sebastian."

I stick out my hand. "It's our pleasure, Governor."

He ignores me and grabs Eve's hand, kissing it. "And where have you emigrated from?"

"Zion East," Eve answers, batting her eyelashes.

"No wonder I haven't seen you before." He looks her up and down. "You I would certainly remember."

Sebastian, with his thinning gray hair and wiry frame, sighs loudly. "And what a dreadful place this is. And to think, I had an ocean view before our forced migration."

The Governor smiles. "Ignore him. He doesn't see the logic in it."

Sebastian went on, "The logic? From the wealth of Zion to living in this dusty Dreck-infested place? Behind The Wall, no less."

"Oh Sebastian, The Wall is temporary. Once we have rooted out the last remnant of Dreck filth, we will be the first Lazurites to inhabit The Middle. Then The Wall will come down, and think of the opportunity. We are pioneers, like those old Westerns. A gold rush of sorts."

Sebastian swipes another drink from the waiter's tray. "Hogwash."

"And what are your thoughts on Renatus's Order 99?"

The Governor is looking at Eve, so I let her answer. "Although we have just arrived, we are quite happy here, Governor."

He turns to me. "And what of your—"

Eve cuts him off. "Brother. Henry is my brother."

The Governor suppresses a narrow smile. "Wonderful."

I finally speak up. "I quite like it here, I—"

He interrupts me. "That's great, Henry. Absolutely wonderful." He turns to Eve. "How about a tour?"

Eve smiles. She is good at this. "Would love that. Perhaps someplace with a view?"

"We must go upstairs, then."

Eve plays the part perfectly. "I was just admiring your Clarion."

"Ah, the most exquisite Angelfish. Beautiful, yet aggressive. Much like yourself."

I have to force myself not to roll my eyes. He grabs her hand and they saunter up the stairs. I am left with a smug-looking Sebastian.

"If you will excuse me, I am in search of a restroom."

Sebastian waves his hand towards the corner and marches off towards the bar.

I make a mental note about Order 99. Perhaps there are enough disgruntled Lazurites here who would consider joining us. But if they are anything like Sebastian, it is probably wishful thinking.

I make my way towards the bathroom, and when no one is paying attention, I beeline up the stairs. I turn the corner towards the room with the balcony.

Guarding the door is an elite.

"Sir, this is a restricted area," he warns me.

"Sorry, I was looking for the restroom."

"It's downstairs and to your left."

As I turn to leave, I grab my ricochet and fling it behind me. It hits him in the chest, sending an electric current throughout his body. He convulses in place for a moment, then drops unconscious to the ground. I sprint over to his catatonic body and quickly stuff him into a nearby closet. I return to the door that Eve and the Governor entered just minutes earlier. I press my ear against the thick wood and hear nothing. What is taking so long? She should have taken him out by now. Then I hear a *THUMP*.

The door handle slowly turns. I ready my ricochet just in case. It is Eve.

"You gonna just stand there or you gonna come in?"

I exhale and march into the room, locking the door behind me. The Governor lies on the floor.

"Is he alive?" I ask.

"Yes, his heart is fine—although broken, probably," she says, tongue in cheek.

"You're kind of a flirt for a married woman."

"Hey, I have been on ice for a hundred years."

"Is he wearing a Pack?"

She lifts up the back of his red dress jacket to reveal the LifePack. I am repulsed that he nonchalantly carries around on his back what used to be someone's life.

I go to the balcony and wave my arms, giving the signal. Hiding behind the Conifers, Cephas and Adam pop up and take out the two guards below us with their Gen2 plasma rifles. They sneak around until they are directly underneath us. Cephas throws up a rope. I catch it and wrap it around the balcony's banister.

"Here." I hand it to Eve while scanning for more guards. I'm sure the guests are wondering where the Governor is by now. Especially his elites. She ties it around his waist and up over his arms. We lift him up and guide him over the railing. I grip the rope in my hands and gradually lower him down towards Cephas and Adam.

Then I hear the wiggle of the doorknob. Even turns and sees it as well. I loosen my grip and let the Governor drop faster than I would like, he almost lands on top of Cephas.

"Buckethead," Cephas growls.

"Governor, are you all right?" an elite asks from the hallway.

I try to match the Governor's high raspy voice. "Fine, thank you."

Eve frowns. Yes, it was a horrible impersonation. Just then, the door is blown open. Two guards burst in, firing at us. Eve pulls out the plasma gun attached to her leg and fires back. I fling my ricochet in their direction for cover.

"Go!" I yell to Eve.

She grabs the rope and slides down just as I tie it to the railing. A plasma blast goes off right next to my hands. I throw my ricochet again while throwing myself over the railing, sliding down the rope as well. By the time I hit the ground, Cephas, Adam, and Eve have made their way to the Conifers, carrying The Governor. I sprint towards them, and without even looking back, I raise my arm. My ricochet returns to the receiver connected to my wrist. I click it to my waist as plasma blasts detonate around me.

I finally reach the cover of the Conifers and jump into the already moving jeep. Adam drives, with Cephas up front. Eve is next to the Governor who is still knocked out.

"I thought that went well," I say with a wry smile, almost soliciting a response from Cephas.

I get one. "Which part? The part where you dropped him on me? Or the part where we almost got shot?"

"Hey, we got the Governor and no one got hurt. Win-win."

"Almost no one." Cephas grabs the absurd hat from the Governor's head, which somehow managed to stay on, and tosses it into the wind.

Asher

"Well, that was quick!" Cephas barks as two HeliDrones appear behind us. He turns to Adam. "Step on it."

"They must have been nearby, already on patrol." I state the obvious. "Or maybe they spotted my giant flying red hat."

"What? Did you think you could kidnap a Governor, and they would just let us go?" Eve spits.

Plasma bombs spew dirt and splinter trees on both our flanks. The drones hover above us. We have partial cover as we hit a dirt road that weaves through the forest. We fire our plasma guns up toward the drones with little effect.

"Look out!" Cephas yells as he spots a giant hole in front of us. Adam swerves the jeep to the right, just missing the hole, clipping a tree on our right side, and knocking off the side mirror.

"Did you check him for a tracker?" Cephas asks, referring to the Governor.

Eve and I glance at each other. "No," we say in unison.

"That's kidnapping 101," Cephas says evenly.

"Sorry, I haven't done it as often as you, Uncle."

Eve and I pat him down and search him for a tracker. We don't find one.

Cephas looks at us. "What if it's internal?"

Another plasma bomb shoots earth and rock into our jeep. "We'll have to worry about that later!"

Then, the dirt road ends. Massive pines block our way.

"Buckle up," Adam says, turning the jeep towards the mountain's edge.

"A bit steep, isn't it?" Cephas says.

Adam ignores him; it's apparent he has driven a jeep in these types of conditions before. Military training, I'm sure. He takes us over the edge until we plod down the side of the mountain. The drones take chase. We bounce up and down so high that I have to hold the Governor down to prevent him from flying out of the jeep. Blasts continue all around us. Adam has to dodge not only bombs but also large rocks. I should have planned for this and brought cover, extra men, and a few more jeeps. But in my defense, I didn't figure a low-level regional Governor overseeing a rotting reservation would be assigned drone security. Maybe he's more important than we thought.

"There! The bridge," I tell Adam. Below us is a short, rather ancient wooden bridge that crosses a wide, fast-flowing river. It looks at least a hundred years old. "If we can get across, we can enter the forest and hide under the cover of trees."

Adam continues to veer left and right, dodging plasma bombs. All the excitement and commotion wakes up the Governor. "What the—"

Whack! Eve punches him in the side of the head. He is out once again. "Was that really necessary?" Adam asks her.

"No," she answers bluntly.

"We could have used a needle," I tell her.

She smiles. "My way was quicker."

It will be a miracle if we make it back with the Governor still in one piece. We finally make it to the bottom of the hill; the bridge is just fifty yards in front of us—the drones are directly overhead. It's going to be close. Adam slams the gas, and the jeep hops onto the rickety wooden bridge. It creaks and groans under the weight of our jeep. It's one lane. We barely fit.

"I hope it holds," Adam states, white-knuckling the wheel.

"This thing is older than we are," Eve adds.

But it may not matter. A drone drops a plasma bomb directly in front of us. It hits the bridge and creates a gaping hole.

Cephas's eyes go wide. "Hit the brakes!"

Adam does, but we are going too fast. We finally come to a complete stop, with half our jeep teetering on the bridge.

Not sure why I whisper, but I feel that even a loud noise will tip us down into the river. "One at a time, slowly crawl into the back. You first, Cephas."

Cephas removes his seatbelt and gingerly begins climbing into the back-seat. The jeep continues to totter.

"Easy now."

But the drone drops another bomb. It hits behind us, and the entire bridge collapses like a house of cards. Our jeep free-falls, then crashes into the rushing white water rapids below us. Our jeep bobs up and down in the rolling river.

"Get out before it sinks!" I order before swallowing a mouthful of icy river water.

"What about the Governor?" Cephas asks.

"I got him! Just go."

"I'll help you," Eve yells over the sound of the river.

But then the jeep flips upside down. Its roll bars slam against rocks in the water, causing it to spin. Before I can unbuckle the Governor, the jeep hits another rock, and I shoot from the backseat, still underwater. Disoriented, I think I am upside down. Then my head hits a rock. So does my leg. I kick and knife my way to the surface, blinking away my blurry vision, only to have my eyes burn. I wipe the salty blood from my forehead before more enters my eyes. I lie flat with my feet up as the rapids take me further downstream, not wanting my foot to get caught on a rock. The water is so frigid it feels like a thousand tiny needles are pricking me.

"Cephas!" I yell. "Eve! Adam!"

But I can't see them. I peer ahead and see the jeep heading straight for a waterfall. If I don't get to the shore, I am next. With all I have, I swing my arms and kick my feet, but the current is too strong. Where is everyone else? Are they still stuck in the jeep? Then I hear my name. Is it from my left or right? Water in my ears and blood still in my eyes, I am still disoriented. Did I get a concussion?

"Asher!" It's Cephas. He, Adam, and Eve stand knee-deep in the small inlet to my right. "This way!"

I scissor as fast as I can until I reach the cove's opening. Adam steps forward, grabs my hand, and pulls me in. Panting, I stand with my hands on my knees. We watch in horror as the jeep rumbles over the waterfall; we can hear it crash below.

"There is no way he survived that," Cephas says, still trying to catch his breath.

I shake my head, blood still streaming from it, "And if the Governor died, then his LifePack was activated, using the LifeCell."

"Let's check to be sure. We can hike down this way," Adam informs us. His timbre is calm. Tone analytical.

Eve looks to the sky. "At least the drones are gone."

Asher

It took us almost an hour to hike down to the waterfall's base. A hundred yards in front of it is the jeep. It washed ashore where the waters finally calmed. Inside is the Governor, drowned. His LifePack is empty.

"All that for nothing," Eve says, then gives me an accusatory look. "We should have had more cover, a spotting team to locate and take out drones."

I am in no mood. "Then perhaps you should have suggested it?"

"You're in charge here, not me. I'm not familiar with this theater of battle or the enemy's tactics. We should have—"

Cephas intercedes, "Enough! This bickering will get us nowhere."

Adam places his hand on her shoulder. "Eve. Please."

She shrugs. "Now what? How do we get a LifeCell now?"

"Sorry, Nephew. We will have to shelve this plan for now and figure out another way to win this thing."

I kick a couple of rocks into the river and grit my teeth. I don't want to shelve this plan. This is how we save my son, end protocol once and for all, and defeat Renatus. In a sense, we can put the genie back in the bottle. Close Pandora's Box.

Adam doesn't want to give up on it either. "We can search for patrols that have elites. Try to ambush them."

Cephas says, "We're out of time."

I cock my head. I hear leaves rustling. A twig snaps. "Did you hear that?"

We ready our weapons.

A voice, high-pitched, shouts, "Put down your weapons!"

I swing around and see a boy, perhaps a teenager. He has red hair and is missing his left ear. His pants are too big, and his shirt is too tight. He wears oversized boots, which are Lazurite standard issue. He points a plasma rifle at me. Behind him are a dozen or so children, all aiming plasma rifles at us.

"Easy now, we're the good guys," I try to reassure him.

"Put them down!" he orders.

I place my gun on the ground and nod for the others to do the same.

Eve shakes her head. "It will be okay," I reassure her. "Just do it." I turn back to the boy. "Who are you?"

"We're Sons of Levi."

Cephas spits, "I know Sons of Levi. You are not them."

"We're starting a new chapter," the boy answers.

"What's your name, son?" I ask.

Before he can answer, a boy, about eleven, with ragged hair and a filthy face, points to my belt and whispers into the redhead's ear. He then points to my ricochet. "You're Asher?"

I nod. Then he points to Cephas. "And you're Cephas."

"Sure am."

He aims his rifle towards the ground. "I'm Lucas." He lifts his ripped sleeve and shows me a scar of The Liberty Bell. It's not a tattoo, but it looks like it has been etched into his skin with a knife. "Like I said, we are Sons of Levi."

I smile at him. "Then we are on the same team." I peer around and see only a dozen or so children. "Where are your parents?"

Lucas has a hard edge about him. "Gone. Harvested or the Dust."

Eve approaches and does her best motherly voice. "You kids out here all alone?"

Lucas answers, "Yeah. We live out here."

"How old are you?" Adam asks.

"Fifteen."

"And how long have you lived out here?"

"A couple of years."

I can't hide my shock. "Where? How?"

"C'mon, I'll show you."

They lead us a couple of miles into the thick forest until we reach their encampment, which looks like something out of a storybook. A dozen little rooms or tree-forts are built up in the surrounding trees. Rope ladders hang down from them. A few fire pits are burning in the middle of them.

Adam smiles. "You guys built all this?"

"Yep."

I peer down at his plasma rifle. "Where did you get the weapons?"

Lucas answers with a feigned bravado. "Where do you think?"

I shake my head; it's like a real-life *Red Dawn*. I stare at the dozen or so kids. Some teenagers. Some as young as nine. "How do you get food?"

"We hunt. We fish. Sometimes, we raid." I like this kid.

"What happened to your ear?"

"Cell-pirates."

I'm beginning to see why he identifies with Sons of Levi. So, I don't ask the question. Instead, I say, "You know, Sons of Levi disbanded and joined The Defiance. You can do the same."

"Why? What's wrong with Sons of Levi?"

"Let's just say we didn't always agree with their methods."

"Maybe if you did, we wouldn't still be fighting this war," Lucas says with hate. He scratches where his ear used to be. "What is the leader of The Defiance doing here anyway?"

"We were looking for something," I answer vaguely.

"Did you find it?"

"Yes, but then lost it."

"Well, what was it? Maybe we can help."

I chuckle. "I doubt that, son. Unless you can conjure up a LifeCell."

He stands with a wide grin and yellow teeth. "Tell you what." He points to my ricochet. "You let me toss a few, and I'll give you a LifeCell."

Minutes later, I climb the rope ladder and enter Lucas's tree fort. He places a blanket on top of his makeshift bed, made of branches and hay, and carefully unfolds it to reveal a LifePack.

"We raided a convoy not too long ago. Got food, weapons, supplies, gold, and this."

"Why did you keep it?" I ask, utterly curious.

"I don't know. For all I know, one of my parents could be in here."

I playfully fluff his red hair. "You, my boy, might have just won this war."

"Good, because I want to come with you and help you fight it."

"Out of the question."

"Why?"

"You're too young."

"I didn't know The Defiance had an age limit. Since when is one too young to fight for freedom? For justice? I can easily say Cephas is too old."

Hard to argue with that. "Don't let him hear you say that. You might lose your other ear. But, like I said, you're too young."

Lucas holds up his plasma rifle and points to the LifeCell. "Do we look like people who can't take care of themselves?"

He has a point, but still. "Look, we will bring you with us. We can feed and house you. There are things you could do to contribute, but you're not going into battle."

"What? Knit socks for the soldiers? Just last week, we took out a twelve-man platoon and two tanks. But if this is your decision, then we will stay here. Thank you very much."

I can tell I won't be able to convince him. He is stubborn. He reminds me of a young Cephas. "Then we will be back to check on you when this war is over."

I turn to leave, then remember he still has my ricochet. I hold out my hand. "Hand it over."

He reluctantly gives it to me. "I was hoping you would forget."

I square his shoulders to mine. "Look, Lucas. You are a warrior, a leader. That is easy to see. I do not doubt that in due time, you will do great things. But now is not your time. Don't waste what you have to offer this world by trying to do it too early. I didn't join The Defiance until I was twenty-five. You're only fifteen. Give it time. Be a kid."

"Heard you were good at speeches, *Asher the Liberator*," he adds with a hint of sarcasm. "But if you would excuse me, I have another raid to plan."

And just when I thought I couldn't be any more surprised, a boy, about ten, pops his head in from the rope ladder. His skin is pigmented, and there are wide gaps between his teeth. Another *wounded* one.

"What are ya guys doing up here, Lucas?"

"Go back down. I'll tell you later," Lucas orders him.

I am taken aback. "Who... who was that?"

Lucas waves off the question, "Timothy, my little brother."

"*Him*. He is why you're here, isn't it?"

Lucas looks surprised. "How did you know?"

"Let's just say I know a thing or two about this."

Lucas peers at the rotten wood that comprises his tree fort, looking sad. "When the raids started happening, and they started taking children, our parents brought us here. They helped us build. They left for more supplies but never came back. They said the raiders were after my brother specifically."

I place my hand on his shoulder. "You're coming with us, Lucas. All of you. Your brother must be protected at all costs."

Asher

"Careful," I hear Adam tell Eve as she and their head scientist use a scalpel and what looks like tweezers in an attempt to extract the LifeCell from the LifePack that Lucas gave us.

Next to the LifePack is a large petri dish filled with the same pink fluid that was already taken from it.

"Careful, nice, and gentle," Adam says again.

With steady and confident hands, Eve extracts the white and blue Life-Cell from the pack, and slowly drops it into the petri dish. The scientist quickly puts a lid on it.

Adam shakes his head. "This doesn't feel right."

"What?" Cephas asks.

"That used to be someone's life."

Cephas stands and cracks his thick neck. "And we are going to use it to save thousands more, hopefully to stop protocol for good. Besides, there is no returning it."

Adam turns to Lucas, who is watching intently. "Thanks for this, kid."

Lucas responds with a reserved smile.

Eve also peers at Lucas. "How old did you say you were?"

"Fifteen."

"You're tall for your age."

"So were my parents."

I see a hint of sorrow in Eve's face; perhaps she does have a softer side. She pulls him close. "Look, if you or your brother need anything, just let us know."

"How about weapons?"

I interject. "No. No weapons."

Lucas shrugs. "Worth a try."

Cephas whispers to me, "What are we going to do with twelve kids?"

"We couldn't just leave them there. They will be safe here. Besides, you like kids, don't you?" I say in a facetious tone.

"And the *wounded* one?"

"What about him?"

"You don't plan on—"

"Of course not! That would make me no better than Renatus. How could you even suggest such a thing?"

Cephas nods. "Sorry, Nephew, you're right. I didn't mean it. You just haven't been yourself lately."

If he had any idea. Truth is, it crossed my mind. Timothy would not only save my son but also Sarai's brother. But those thoughts are the devil talking. Timothy must be kept safe and alive and out of the hands of Renatus. He is now a symbol of this war. A symbol of right and wrong. A symbol of what we humans are capable of. The mere fact that the thought of bringing him to Renatus even crossed my mind tells me that this resurrection power must be destroyed, that it wasn't meant for mankind. We can't wrap our tiny brains around divine power and how to wield it. We weren't made for it. The more advanced our technology, the greater our propensity for evil. We have outsmarted our conscience—buried it deep under intellect, weighed down by greed.

Then, dust rustles inside the bunker, and the lights fizzle out.

Another EMP.

"I can't work without power," the scientist says candidly.

He's right. Without computers and working equipment, we won't be able to successfully reverse-engineer protocol or make that nuke operational.

Cephas rubs his forehead. "We need hardened generators."

Adam adds, "Military grade."

Cephas steps in close; his breath smells of stale coffee. "Asher, this isn't working out. Let's abandon this plan for another time. We can come back to it later. We need to focus our energy and efforts elsewhere."

But deep down, I know this is the right thing to do, that we are on the correct path. I don't know how I know, I just do. Then, the idea hits me. It's a massive risk, but I see no other choice. "I know where to get some."

An hour later, I load gear and food into one of the jeeps.

"Let me come with you," says Cephas.

I reply, "I don't think this will work unless I go alone."

"It's too risky, Nephew; let's do this another way."

"We don't have time. I have to try."

"Then let me go."

"It has to be me, Uncle. You know that."

"How did you get so stubborn?" he says in jest, knowing full well it's from him. "At least your father could be reasoned with." He then throws a sack of gold we got from Lucas in the back. "Take this. Maybe she can be bribed."

"I doubt that."

I jump into the driver's seat and start the jeep's quiet electric engine. As I pull away, Cephas says, "You won't be able to reason with her! Not with your history!"

The "her" he refers to is Neriah. Since her election "win," Renatus banished her to The Middle, as he took the reins of Zion West. And yes, Cephas is correct; this is ill-advised and risky, but it's not just about the generators. It's also about atonement for me. It's about the bombs I sold to The Sons of Levi that accidentally killed her eight-year-old son. It's something I have to do. That I'm supposed to do.

The memories return, along with a piercing pain in my forehead. The anguish, the acrid smoke, the smell of singed flesh, the sobs that torment my dreams. These memories, I know, are real. Far too real. My pearly knuckles clamp down on the steering wheel as I think of Sarai. Of Silas. Of God's love. God's forgiveness. My anger. Of this distorted, backward world that is now our existence.

Why is it that I can't just live peacefully with my son and my wife? Has it been predestined that Sarai and I will forever be apart? Is this our punishment for cheating death?

I relax my grip on the now-damp steering wheel. I have to go back to the moment, to my purpose, which is bigger than me. Bigger than my family. I try to clear my head as I approach Neriah's compound. Four armed guards point their Gen2 plasma rifles at me.

I pull over and slowly slide out of the jeep with my arms up. "I'm unarmed."

They pat me down, then search me. "What is your business with The Prime?"

"I need to speak to her privately."

"And who might you be?"

"Asher. Son of Silas."

One of them laughs. "Right, and I'm Legion. Asher would be a fool to show up here. Go home, stupid Dreck."

Perhaps I was a fool to come here. I am surprised they don't recognize me, but then again, I'm getting older, or maybe my legend has given people a false perception of what they think I should look like. I trudge back to my jeep and grab my ricochet, holding it up for them to see. The four of them prepare to shoot.

"Look, I'm just showing you." I hold it out in front of me. "Here, take it."

The lead guard quickly snatches it from me, his finger on the trigger of his rifle. He studies it. "Just cause you own a ricochet doesn't mean you're Asher."

"You can give it back to me, and we can find out."

A guard in the back nervously approaches his captain. "Sir, I think it's him."

Asher

Four guards escort me into Neriah's compound. It's not your typical Zion compound, adorned with expensive furniture and antique paintings. It is obvious she is no longer a priority or a concern for Renatus. He got what he wanted from her. Only two of her twenty guards are actually elites.

I am ushered into a small yet cozy den. Neriah sits in an oversized chair, sipping tea.

"You can leave us be," she tells her guards, who exit the den and close the door behind them. She takes another sip of tea, her hands steady, her thinning silver hair longer than when I last saw her. She seems calm yet deflated. "I must say, Son of Silas, Father of Silas, Liberator of Zion, Traitor of Zion, or whatever you go by now. You're the last person I thought would show up here."

I clear my throat. "I am here to humbly ask for your help."

Her face forms a frown of pure derision. "Help? Help you? Maybe protocol has made you crazy. Maybe we should call you Asher the Kook. Give me one good reason I shouldn't kill you right now?"

I tell her the truth, the truth from Renatus's vantage point anyway. "I'm on an assignment from Renatus himself."

She taps her teacup. Gone is the motherly cadence she so brilliantly enacted during the debates with my wife. Now, her tone is more cynical. "Yes, which doesn't involve me. Renatus isn't stupid. He anticipated you might use this time to raise an army against him. He told me directly that if you were to come to me, I was to return you to him. In fact, I will be rewarded if I do so."

I'm starting to think this was a bad idea and that, once again, I should have listened to my learned uncle. What I say next is a gamble that could have me killed on the spot. "Speaking of rewards, what about your son? Where is he?"

My words have antagonized her stiff upper lip. Although barely perceptible, they inch towards her nose. "He is still awaiting protocol."

"I don't understand. You won the election. Wasn't that the deal? You work for him, and you get your son back?"

"Once this war is over and The Defiance is gone for good."

"And you believe him?"

She doesn't answer. She taps her teacup even harder, becoming more incensed. "Tell me, Asher, before I send you back to Zion, what do you want? Surely, you didn't come here to talk about my murdered son."

"Listen to me, Neriah. Renatus can't be trusted. You know this, deep down. He will never give you your son; he already has what he wants." I peer down at my scarred hands. "Look, I understand. I do. You would do anything or believe anything to get back a lost child. I'm trying to do that now."

"Then you understand why I'm doing this."

I look into her drab, dark eyes and lean in. "Neriah, I am sorry to tell you this, but your son is gone."

"Liar!" she barks.

"It was during the monthly purge—old LifeCells deemed no good. Donors that have expired, genetic anomalies. Gone. Along with your son. I saw it myself, Neriah."

She hurls her teacup at me; I don't bother ducking it. It bounces off my forehead and shatters on the ground. "YOU ARE A LIAR!"

"I'm sorry, Neriah, I truly am. Think for a moment: why would Renatus hold up his end of the bargain? He has what he wants. That is why you have been expelled from Zion and sent to The Middle. That is why I could have single-handedly taken out your guards. Only two elites? You are the Prime, aren't you? You won the election, yet here you are."

She stands, her hands trembling in rage. "YOU are the reason I'm here. You!"

I take it that she means that I am the reason she is where she is mentally at this very moment, not physically.

I stand as well. She approaches me with a wild gait. Then she completely loses it, bawling and wailing against my chest. "It was you! You sold them the explosives that killed my son! Because of your cowardice. All for profit. How dare you come into my home and speak of my son? And all for what? To kill a few Lazurite patrolmen who would be replaced the very next day? How many families were ruined that day?"

I let her punish me, as this is nothing compared to the punishment I have been doling out to myself over the years because of this. "I know, Neriah. And I'm sorry. I truly am sorry. I wish I could go back and change it. But I can't. And I have to live with it. Every day I think about it."

She wipes her tears. "I still dream it every night. I can still smell the molten flesh of children who never had a chance at life. The shrieks of the heartbroken mothers. The whimpers of the children who didn't die right away. My child was still alive when I peeled him off the dirt. He looked at me as if his eyes were asking, 'Why, Mama? Why?' And that damn soccer ball, charred but somehow still full of air. It rolled by me, leaving a trail of smoke, taunting me that it had somehow survived."

I grab her hand and get down on my knees. "I beg you, Neriah. I beg for your forgiveness. I am not that person anymore."

She places her hand on the top of my head like she wants to crush my skull. "And somehow, Asher, you are still alive; somehow, you just won't die. You are that soccer ball. The mere sight of you makes me sick."

I stand as tears engulf my reddening eyes. "We can end this, Neriah. We can end this war so that this never happens to anyone's child again. We can make it right. I can't do it without you, without your help."

She stares at me. No. She stares through me as if I don't exist, or don't deserve to exist. "What was his name?"

And suddenly I realize that I don't know. I never knew.

"My son. What was his name?"

I should know this. I should have asked. "I... I don't know, Neriah. I am sorry, but I don't know."

"Ethan. His name was Ethan. Do you know the meaning of the name?"

I do. "Enduring, strong. Permanent."

She shakes her head. "Enduring. Permanent. The irony."

"Maybe his permanency isn't on earth, but in heaven. Maybe he was meant to endure through you. Through your legacy."

I pause for a moment, then try to lighten the mood. "If it makes you feel any better, Asher means *happiness*. Not a lot of that going on."

She puts her arms down to her sides. I can see her softening. Maybe this is what she needed, what we both needed.

I continue to plead with her. "We can end the abomination that is protocol. We can take down The Wall for good. It's time to put a stop to this generational suffering. The children deserve better."

She turns and trudges away from me. She considers herself in a mirror hanging in the corner. She touches her face as if it's a stranger's. She swivels back towards me. I can almost see the sorrow and scorn drain from her face. Now, a look of resolve and clarity. A reset.

"What is it that you need?"

"Generators. Hardened generators. And any soldiers still loyal to you. I can pay for it. I brought gold."

"I don't want your gold."

She picks up the pieces of the smashed teacup and arranges the sharp shards neatly on top of a glass table, almost as if they are the broken pieces of her life.

"Now that I have forgiven you, tell me, will your wife forgive me?"

CHAPTER FIVE

Asher

THANKS TO NERIAH'S HARDENED generators, the power has been back on for almost two weeks. In that time, we have been hit twice by EMPs. So far, they have held up. I'm starting to think the drops aren't random, that Renatus knows we are close by.

As I stroll through the narrow hallway, four ex-Lazurite soldiers bump into me.

"Excuse us, sir."

The bunker is overcrowded since five hundred of Neriah's soldiers have arrived. It is a good problem to have. Tomorrow, three hundred will be moving to a location just east of here. Cephas, trying to keep up behind me, turns his wide frame so the soldiers can pass.

He whispers, "Can we trust them?"

The truth is, I have considered that Neriah might be lying, setting me up. But something inside me tells me that she is being genuine. Perhaps it's a shared bond between parents whose children are under Renatus's thumb. Besides, once again our options are limited, our path to victory narrow. "We can't afford not to."

"And a few weeks ago, they were Lazurites, loyal to Renatus."

"And so was my third army who fought and died for us at Donner Lake, in case you forgot," I remind him.

"And Neriah? How do we know she's not playing us?"

I stop and peer into my uncle's hardened eyes. "I just know."

"That's not an answer," he replies.

"What are you always telling me, Uncle? That I need to take more things on faith. This is one of them."

A gruff bark emanates from his mouth. "Stop using my own words against me."

I smile. "But they are such a good weapon. Besides, I saw it in her eyes."

"Well, now I'm reassured."

We round the corner and down another flight of stairs, until we reach a locked metal door. I place my thumbprint on the scanner, and the door opens. We enter the room lined with concrete and lead, a bunker within a bunker. For the past two weeks, Adam, Eve, and a gaggle of scientists have been studying the LifeCell we received from Lucas, in hopes of reverse-engineering protocol. Along with that, the nuclear scientists have also been working on the nuclear suitcase we found at NORAD. So far, no luck with the nuke, but Adam says he has news about the LifeCell.

A bank of computers rests against the back wall. Beakers, microscopes, and other tools of their trade are lined up on clean white tables. Adam is analyzing what looks like a DNA strand on one of the monitors. Eve is behind him, reading a book.

"What's up, boys?" Eve asks. Rock music blares from an antique boom box in the corner. Cephas switches it off.

"I was listening to that," Eve says.

"Don't care," Cephas barks back. They, too, have become fast friends. Cephas is only sarcastic with people he likes. With Jude gone, it seems Eve is filling in nicely. "Besides, it looks to me like you're reading."

"I can multi-task."

Cephas peers at her book and quips, knowing full well that she doesn't read book endings. "Atlas Shrugged, huh? You'll love the ending."

Enthralled at whatever he is looking at on the monitor, Adam turns in his chair. "Asher. Cephas. I'm glad you're here. We have found something."

Eve turns the music back up. Cephas rolls his eyes. She turns it back off. "Kidding. You sure have good hearing for your age."

"Shut it."

Adam, deadpan, says, "You through?"

We sit in two cold folding chairs next to him. He points to the computer screen. "We have isolated a protein molecule inside the DNA of the Life-Cell that we believe, if deactivated, would render protocol useless."

I ask, "And how do we deactivate it?"

"That we're not sure of," Adam replies bluntly.

Cephas scoffs, "So what is the news exactly?"

"Look, if we can figure out exactly how the Lazurites extract a LifeCell and what is used to keep it alive, then we would have the necessary information on how to deactivate it."

"And how long might that take?"

"With more computing power and men, maybe six months."

Cephas shakes his head. "We don't have six months." He turns to me. "I think this little gambit of yours is a waste of time. I know you're thinking end game, but we should be focusing our energy on raising an army, how exactly to attack Zion, and getting that nuke operable. We can take another look at ending protocol in the future."

"We may not have a future," I argue. But maybe he's right. Maybe I'm too focused on using this as a way to save my son.

Eve casually strolls behind us. "Or we do what you Drecks do best."

"Which is? Cause there are not a lot of things we Drecks do well," Cephas jokes.

"Instead of spending the next six months figuring this out on our own, we kidnap the person who knows it already."

"Mammon," Cephas whispers.

"Who?"

"Mammon was the head scientist in charge of protocol; if anyone has the knowledge you need, it will be him."

Eve asks, "So we kidnap this Mammon character. How do we find him?"

"You don't," I sigh. "He's dead. Renatus had him killed just for this reason. He wanted to be the only one with the complete picture of how protocol works."

"There goes that idea," Cephas spits.

Adam finally pulls himself away from the computer and clears his throat. "Maybe not."

"What do you mean?" I ask.

"There's something else we found. After thoroughly analyzing the Life-Cell, we believe resurrection isn't the only thing it does. We think thoughts, memories, and even feelings can be transferred into one's DNA."

Cephas perks up. "So, in a way, you are forever linked to whoever the LifeCell was harvested from?"

"Yes, in a way. You might even inherit some of their characteristics and traits."

Cephas rubs his chin. "You suggesting that whoever has Mammon's LifeCell may have the information about protocol we need?"

"Yes, it's quite possible."

Cephas looks at me. "That could work. Sarai could dig through the records and find that out, couldn't she?"

I'm too stunned to answer.

"Of course, you would need to send a new Runner; we can't trust the last one didn't sell us out."

Adam is like an excited kid with a new toy. "It is fascinating, really. I never thought..."

But his words are drowned out by my spinning mind. That explains the memories that aren't mine. The child. The funeral. The Pilot. The

Farmer. They are forever a part of me now. And so is my father. Is that where my goodness comes from? Is it enough to conquer the evil and anger that has seeped in? Is this what a schizophrenic feels like? Is this why Renatus is so crazy? Will I ever be me? Or just an amalgamation of those put inside me? What is in store for my soul? I have so many LifeCells that I feel as if someone has injected me with a foreign substance that my body now rejects. The headaches. The nightmares. The guilt. One man's consciousness is more than enough for anyone to deal with. How am I supposed to fuse all of them without losing myself in the process?

I am nobody.

I am everyone.

Sarai

I like the pool cold. It keeps me awake. Refreshed. It attacks my senses, my central nervous system. As I turn for my hundredth lap in my father's Olympic-sized pool, I realize how freeing the water is. My sadness suffocates—the water masks my tears. As I swim under the surface, I feel insulated from this cruel world, even if it's just for a moment. My braided hair makes a lump underneath my swim cap. I considered cutting it off, but I know how much Asher likes it. Not that it matters; I never see him, and may never see him again. Destiny has once again conspired to keep us apart.

A splash.

A muscle-hewn body streaks under the water like a torpedo. His head breaches, water trickling from his curly raven hair. It is Hagar.

"Thought I would get some exercise."

We synchronize our laps so our heads and ears are out of the water at the same time. This is how we communicate—the sound of water splashing covers our whispers. Like everywhere here, we are being watched and listened to. There is no privacy in Zion, no trust, only tyranny. Building a wall and calling those on the other side prisoners has created an illusion that being on this side is freedom. Creating a distraction such as The Canonization—excuse me,—the *New* Canonization, and letting people bet on the winners, makes one think they have choices. There is no sovereignty in Zion; it's a mirage. Renatus has told the people here that they are freer, smarter, and better off than the Drecks, for so long that they have begun to believe it. They have been programmed to believe that cleanliness and order equate to freedom and virtue. That is why my father keeps the streets so clean and the grass manicured. Why all of our trash is dumped into The Middle. We may not be encapsulated by a wall, but we are in prison. A *clean* prison. But a prison still. A mental jail.

"Asher has made contact," Hagar tells me before inhaling a breath and putting his head back under.

We reach the wall and spin around for another lap. "He needs to find someone."

"Who?" I ask in between breaths, my arms finally getting tired.

"Mammon."

"Mammon is dead. My father killed him."

Hagar spits a mouthful of water. "Not Mammon per se, but his LifeCell. They need to know who reaped his LifeCell."

"Why?"

"I don't know."

"My father changed his computer password, and I'm unsure how to find that information."

"The archives," he tells me.

That's right. My father duplicated everything digital onto paper. He didn't trust that an EMP would wipe out everything one day.

"Where?"

"Underneath the arena."

"How do we get in?" I ask.

"I have a plan."

Three hours later, we stand in the arena, donning full battle armor, including helmets, to hide our identities. I have my scourge, Hagar, his StunClub. We are just two elites sparring, as far as anyone else is concerned. I whip my scourge at Hagar's feet. He hops over it, does a tuck, and rolls towards me, swinging his StunClub. I dive out of the way and roll to my feet behind him.

"You're like a cat," Hagar tells me. It is encouraging to know that I still have my chops.

I regard the massive arena and think of Asher, how he almost died here, how he still might die here. I wonder how much more we can take. The separation. The war. Our son, frozen behind glass, who at any moment could be murdered for his LifeCell. It is too much for me to take, too much for anybody.

I don't realize it, but I have stopped sparring. Stopped moving. My eyes are closed.

"Sarai? You okay?" Hagar is now worried.

"Yes, I—"

"You don't have to lie. I know it's hard."

"You're right. I'm not okay. I haven't been okay for a long time."

"Let me help you make this right. Let's go get Asher what it is he needs."

I tell myself to take one step at a time, one foot in front of the other. I need to focus on the next task, the next ten minutes, or I'll fall apart. I can do this. Whatever the reason is for Asher needing what is in the archives, it must be important. If it weren't, he wouldn't have asked. He wouldn't risk my life over something trivial.

Hagar snaps me back into the moment. "It's time."

We exit the arena and enter one of the many underground tunnels. There are numbered doors to our left and right.

"Number fifteen," Hagar tells me.

We turn a corner, and as we approach door number fifteen, it is the only one with a guard in front of it. His exoarmor is the same color as ours, and he also dons a helmet. A surveillance camera is perched on the wall across from the door. As we approach the door, we nod at the guard, who nods in return. Then, in one fluid motion, I toss my sweat towel up. It lands on the surveillance camera, blocking our view just as Hagar taps the guard on the back of his neck with his stun club. The guard convulses for a moment, then drops to the ground unconscious. I grab his hand and place it against the biometric scanner near the door, and it opens.

"Go, he'll be out for probably an hour," Hagar tells me.

I enter the archives room, pulling the guard in with me, just as Hagar shuts the door and pulls the sweat rag from the camera. He'll pretend to be the unconscious guard and wait for me while I search the archives. I pass by filing cabinet after filing cabinet, record after record of all of the previous year's Canonizations: who won, who died, how they died. My father likes to document his barbarism in specific detail.

I finally reach the cabinets labeled "Protocol." I find the one for the year Mammon died. Then, I flip through the files alphabetically until I get his name. Just before I pull out the file, someone yells, "Don't move!"

I slowly turn to see the guard Hagar knocked out pointing his plasma gun at me. We took his rifle but not his gun!

"You think you can stun me and get away with it? Take off your helmet!"

I reach both of my hands up like I'm about to remove my helmet, but with my right hand, I reach behind my back and grab the handle to my scourge. With my thumb, I click it on.

"Now!" he yells.

With my left hand, I remove my helmet. He is taken aback.

"Well, well, if it isn't the sultana. Your father will be very interested in what you're doing down here. Traitor."

Before he can think about the rewards he might receive from my father, I simultaneously throw my helmet at him and snap my scourge at his wrist. It knocks the gun from his hand, and it slides to his left.

Without hesitation, he dives for it. I whip my scourge, and it wraps around his ankle. But I'm not fast enough. He swipes the gun and fires at me just as I duck. The blast hits the cabinet containing Mammon's file. Before he can fire off another shot, I slide behind him, wrapping my scourge around his neck and pull. His feet kick the ground as the electric current surges through him. After a few more seconds, he is finally choked out.

I take off his helmet and peer into his lifeless eyes. Did he have a family? It's not his fault. He was just doing his job. But I had no choice. Damn this war. Damn my father.

But I have another problem.

I quickly turn my attention to the cabinet, still smoking from the plasma blast. I reach in and grab the folder with Mammon's name on it. There is a hole in the middle of it, and the tattered edges are burned.

Of course there is.

I open it and scan the document. Luckily, the harvest information is in the lower right corner. Then I see the person who appropriated Mammon's LifeCell.

Boaz.

Boaz? Really?

I don't know what this means or why Asher wants to know, but I can only hope it brings us one step closer to ending this war.

To getting my son back.

Asher

"Boaz?" I look to my Runner, perplexed. "Are you sure it said Boaz?"

"Yes, sir, positive."

I turn to Cephas. "Boaz, the man with the maps, now has the secret to protocol in his head."

Cephas rubs the deep fissures in his face. "Boaz? Does Renatus really trust him enough to have given him Mammon's LifeCell?"

Adam says, "You're assuming he knows what we do, that memories can be passed to one another through the LifeCell."

"Good point."

Cephas's eyes narrow. "Perhaps, perhaps not. Renatus's scientists are top-notch. If we know, he probably does, too."

"Maybe, but many of them are dead, including Mammon."

Ironically, an unscrupulous man like Boaz has led us to The Fort Worth Amory and then to Eden, and now he could help us bring down Renatus and protocol with it. None of it was by his choice, of course. "Sounds strange, but Boaz could be the gift that keeps on giving."

Cephas cracks his knobby knuckles, his nostrils flaring. "If you have forgotten, Nephew, that *gift* is why Jude is dead."

I understand his resistance to using Boaz, but his anger clouds his judgment. "Then we use him to be certain that Jude didn't die in vain."

Always the scientist, Adam analyzes the situation. "A useful idiot is still useful."

Cephas adds, "Boaz is smarter than he seems. And he is only out for himself."

"Which we can use to our benefit. His number one priority, other than profit, is self-preservation."

Eve sighs, "All this overthinking is killing me. So we kidnap this Boaz character. How hard can it be?"

I say, "Well, we would have to get over The Wall for one. Then we penetrate Renatus's heavily fortified compound and snatch Boaz from there, who is surely guarded around the clock."

"Not possible," Cephas mutters.

Cephas hasn't liked this plan from the start, and I don't blame him. And perhaps he's right, but then I have a thought.

I say, "Unless."

Cephas frowns, "Unless... unless what? I know that look, Asher."

I can't believe I am considering doing it again. "Unless I pose as Amos."

"We've done that song and dance before."

"And it worked before."

"What the heck are you guys talking about?" Eve inquires.

Cephas grunts, "It's a long story."

"Look, Sarai can tell us when Amos is there. And when he is, we take him, and I replace him, just long enough to snag Boaz."

Cephas replies, "And what if this gambit doesn't work? And you're captured? Where does that leave The Defiance? And what then of Sarai? And your son?"

"You know if we are to win this war, it won't be without risk. Isn't the mere fact of being a Dreck a hazard?"

Cephas looks into my eyes, my marrow as if he is a scientist peering into a microscope. "It's a massive risk, and I worry that it is not you talking, but someone else inside your head doing your thinking for you."

Maybe it *is* protocol—one of the many LifeCells that have annexed part of my brain, my consciousness. Is it the Pilot? The Farmer? Perhaps they were reckless or foolhardy? Or is it my father?

"Perhaps it's Silas?" I suggest to him.

Eve shakes her head. "Too much family history with you two, clouding your judgment. Are we gonna do this thing or not?"

We ignore her for the moment.

"I mean, c'mon, from all your inside jokes about being Drecks and whatnot, this sort of plan is perfect for us, isn't it?"

I smile at Cephas, whose gaze hasn't left mine. "She's got a point there, Uncle."

"And how do we get over the Wall this time? It is fully activated," Cephas asks, still skeptical.

"Surely they will let General Amos and his brigade of Lazurites through." I can't believe I am posing as Amos again.

Cephas taps his chin. "But if Amos is in Zion West, and someone at the border knows about it, the ruse is up."

Good point. I think for a moment. "Neriah could get us in."

Cephas paces the room. I can almost hear his knees creak, the gears grinding in his head. "I still don't trust her."

"We have electrical power because of her."

"Maybe she is a spy for Renatus. For the record, I'm against this idea. But you have earned the right to make this decision. Call the ball."

"You guys always take this long to make a decision?" Eve derides us. She then turns to Cephas and places her hand on his shoulder. "And you, big guy, you have trust issues."

"If you pull this off, who's to say this Boaz will talk?" Adam asks.

"He'll talk," Cephas replies firmly.

Seeing that Boaz is responsible for Jude's death, I'll have to be certain Cephas isn't too firm once Boaz is in custody.

Eve claps her hands. "So, all set then?"

"One last thing, Nephew. Maybe you have forgotten the incident with the Jeep and the backhoe, the oil that burned Amos's face," Cephas reminds me.

"Then I do the same."

"There isn't enough time to sculpt you."

"Then you'll have to burn me."

Adam looks horrified. "You Drecks are crazy."

Eve pulls a Zippo lighter from her pocket. "Let's get started."

Asher

Why is it always me? First bloodletted, then sculpted. And after that, the suffering of protocol more times than I can count. Now, acid poured onto my face. We found an updated picture of Amos on Zoogle to be certain the burns matched. The salve my scientists concocted healed the wound overnight, so that it won't look fresh. As we head towards The Wall in a bumpy military truck, I check the warped skin underneath my eye, just to the right of my nose, in the rear view mirror.

"It's healing nicely," Cephas states, driving the truck.

"Wish we had some tonic before my tormentor back there did the honors," I jest, referring to Eve, who sits next to Neriah in the backseat.

Eve smiles back. "I'm thoroughly impressed what you Drecks will go through to make a plan come together, a crazy one at that."

"That was nothing. You should have seen him volunteer to take down a detachment of HeliDrones with an EMP while flying one, no less!" Cephas banters back. "Or the time he purposely buried himself in an avalanche, or the time—"

Neriah interrupts him with the tone of an annoyed mother. "We are approaching The Wall. Maybe it's time we get a little serious."

I peer at Cephas's garb. He is dressed as a Lazurite elite, full helmet and all. I don the same. "What if at the checkpoint they make us remove our helmets? Perhaps Cephas and I should hide in the back."

Neriah responds, "And what if they check the back? I say they are more likely to do that than have you remove your helmets."

Eve sharpens her dagger and teases, "Decisions, decisions."

"They might recognize me or Cephas, even with our helmets on," I state, noting that the helmets cover our heads and only half our faces.

Neriah sighs. "Okay, pull over."

Cephas stops the truck, and the two of us hop out. I stare at the burgundy sunrise, dotted with purple and orange hues, before loading into the back. Such is my life: moments of beauty and inspiration followed by weeks and months of toil and adversity. But it's those moments that carry me through. It is suffering that forges character, and it is the fire that hardens steel. Without it, would we even recognize those moments?

Are those thoughts mine, or influenced by my father's LifeCell? Will I ever know the difference? As long as it is good and moral, does it even matter? To me, it does. I want to know whether it's me doing what is right or wrong, and that my actions are not a result of what has been artificially put inside me.

My eyes have adjusted to the darkness, and I see we are surrounded by crates full of weapons. A canopy tarp covers us from view. The truck thunders to a start. Eve drives, posing as Neriah's personal guard while Neriah sits shotgun.

Neriah. Even though she has lost everything dear to her, she is willing to sacrifice herself for me, for our cause. Is she being too helpful, too compliant? Is Cephas right? Can she be trusted? Is she delivering us to our doom? Have we willingly boarded the train of demise? Have I overlooked the obvious in my singular focus to save my son and win this war? It's too late now. Perhaps Eve is right; I have to stop overthinking. I no longer have the luxury of time to ponder or be indecisive. The best I can do is rely on faith.

Before we can grab Boaz, we must be certain Amos is incapacitated. The plan is for Sarai to ask him to have dinner and drinks with her. She'll then spike his drink with a concoction my scientists from Eden developed—one that will not only knock him out for a few hours, but also make him completely forget the hours beforehand. She will then signal to us that it is okay for me to pose as Amos while we attempt to snatch Boaz.

Even though it's my plan, I hate everything about it. I hate to think of Sarai flirting with that vulgar and baneful human being. I hate that she can't look at his face without seeing mine. And once again, I hate putting her in danger. But I know she wouldn't have it any other way. She wants to be useful. She needs to be useful. Besides, once again, we haven't much of a choice.

"How will she signal us?" Cephas asks as we bounce around in the back of the truck.

"She said we would know."

I scoot back a bit, as he is much in need of a shower. He stretches out his legs, his rusty knees creaking and cracking. "Getting old isn't for sissies."

"Tell me about it."

He raises an eyebrow. "You're still a young man, relatively speaking."

"In the words of Indiana Jones, 'It's not the years, it's the mileage.'"

Cephas sighs as his next words come from a place of guilt. "And I'm responsible for many of those miles."

I smile back. "Yes, you are, Uncle, yes you are."

Eve yells back at us. "Quiet, you two, we're approaching the checkpoint."

A minute later, the truck lumbers to a stop. We are at a checkpoint just a hundred yards from The Wall. I can hear the Lazurite guard interrogating Neriah.

"State your business."

I tense up, and so does Cephas. If she plans to give us up, this is where she would do it. As planned, Neriah hands the guard her credentials. "Defiance contraband haul."

The guard motions to the back of the truck. "We will have to inspect it." My heart tightens. I grip my ricochet and nod to Cephas. I hear the guard's boots crunch on the gravel as he approaches the back of the truck.

"Wait," Neriah calls out, getting out of the truck.

"Back in the vehicle, lady."

"You know who I am?"

"Yes, ma'am," the guard replies.

"Then you know I have a direct link to Renatus himself. What is back here is classified and for his eyes only."

Cephas and I still haven't taken a breath. I see sweat drip from his forehead and splash onto his hand. My head begins to throb. My hands shake. I feel it coming on—the many lives inside me trying to take over. Trying to hold hostage my thoughts. My humanity. The effects have escalated. It's not just their memories I have, but now it's their feelings as well. It's like they know something is wrong, and they are trying to break free. How much longer will this continue? Will I turn out like Apex or Renatus? Maybe I should leave The Defiance altogether? What good am I to them if I'm crazy? And what about my family?

Cephas notices what is happening to me and mouths the words: *Easy, son.*

Silence for almost a full minute. I shut my eyes and fight with all my power to remain me. I think about specific memories from my childhood. I try to use my real memories and feelings to overpower those inside me. I open my eyes and wonder what is taking so long? Is the guard contemplating? Is he calling reinforcements? A drone strike? Has Neriah told them who we are?

Then:

"Move along."

We exhale as the truck lurches forward. I feel guilty for having doubts about Neriah—she just risked her life for us. I hope we make it the rest of the way to Zion West without further harassment. I hope Sarai can immobilize Amos before we get there. I hope she isn't found out. I hope we can extract what is inside Boaz's head. I hope I can win this battle raging inside me. I hope I can remain me. I hope I can still be worthy to Cephas and my family. But these are just a few of many hopes.

How many am I allowed to have?

Sarai

I feel so nauseated, I think I might retch. But I remind myself, this is for Asher. This is for Silas. This is for The Defiance.

Amos's high-pitched cackle is beyond irritating. It is soft and damp, always followed by two coughs. I sit across from him at the dining room table and try to focus on my crab and salad. His greasy hands crack another crab leg, and he slurps his wine. Are bad table manners a prerequisite to becoming a Lazurite? How I miss market burgers at the bazaar.

Amos clears his throat. "I must say, Sultana, I'm a bit surprised by this invitation, considering our history and all."

"I hope you didn't feel you had to accept just because I'm a Sultana?"

"I said surprised, not disappointed. In fact, pleasantly surprised."

"My father has shown me the error of my ways, General. It was fun playing Dreck for a while. But I now know who I am and where I belong. Here, a Sultana. A Lazurite." I smile and lie. I have been doing that a lot lately.

"Well, lucky you then." His smile smug and presumptuous. I try not to vomit in my mouth. It's all so confusing. His face is the same as my beloved's. It stirs up so many emotions and memories. But all Amos has to do is speak, and I know how great my husband is and what an arrogant, hideous man Amos is.

"And what of Asher?"

"He's a filthy Dreck. I realize that now."

He grins and holds up his empty glass. "More wine."

Hagar rushes over and pours him another glass. He glances at me, letting me know the deed has been done. That the wine has been spiked and that Amos will soon be out, and I won't have to suffer this dinner any longer.

"Not having wine?" he asks.

"I'm a bourbon girl," I respond as Hagar sets a tumbler in front of me.

"Never liked the hard stuff. I think I'll stick with my wine."

I lie, "Well, I can't get enough." Once again, I find myself in a position I hate: lying. Pretending to be someone that I'm not. Being a sneak, a deceiver. A politician. I would rather be on the battlefield with my scourge, standing next to Asher and listening to Cephas bark orders. I'd rather be listening to Legion's primal howl. Jude spitting jokes. I'd rather be watching my husband's ricochet fly through the air like a spinning bird taking out its prey. Black and white, good and evil. To look my enemy in the eyes and know they are my enemy, and they know I am theirs.

Amos glances at Hagar and doesn't bother to hide his annoyance. "Are we going to be chaperoned *all* night?"

I smile seductively and then turn to Hagar. "Leave us."

"Yes, my Sultana."

He slides his hand across the table and grabs mine. I do everything in my power not to grind my teeth, rear back, and punch him in the throat. He is the reason I am here. He is the man who stole Silas from me—the arrogance he must possess to think that I would actually be interested in him. When I'm with Asher, I feel like I can accomplish anything. But sitting here with Amos, I feel dirty. Contaminated. Amos has a way of making you feel subhuman. I pull my hand away and grab my bourbon.

"Drink up."

I down my glass faster than I would have liked, but it is the only way I can tolerate the situation. He watches me with a provocative smile and guzzles his wine.

I bite my lip in an attempt to stifle my nervousness. Then I continue to stroke his ego. "So, a General now? You must get quite a few of these dinner propositions."

"None from a Sultana," he smiles and finishes his wine, followed by that cackle.

"First time for everything." I smile back.

"Ah, so what's next?" he asks as he stands up, causing the flames on the red candles to flicker.

Your face crashing onto your plate. But it's not happening. Did Hagar get the concoction right? I'm not sure how much longer I can put up this facade without him seeing right through me. If he doesn't faint soon, the ruse will be up. I might have to do this manually with my scourge. His plasma rifle is in the corner, but he still has his sidearm. And then... he looks a bit wobbly. He places his hand on the table and slowly sits back down. "I'm not sure I'm bloody feeling so well—"

And then his face does come crashing down onto his plate of cracked crab legs. Hagar, who has been watching us from a back window, rushes in and grabs Amos by the arms. "Where to, Sarai?"

I'm already on the other side of the table, grabbing his feet. "The back garage."

We carry him over to the back door and peer outside, empty. "How strong did you make it?"

Hagar replies, "You have three, maybe four hours."

We carry him across the manicured grass towards the back garage, where his collection of cars is parked. Then, out of the corner of my eye, I see a Lazurite guard turn the corner.

"In the bushes," I whisper.

We drag Amos into a cluster of sticker bushes, receiving multiple cuts in the process. The guard stops for a moment, listening. I ready my scourge. I look to Hagar; words can't describe my appreciation for him and his loyalty. I feel guilty for once again putting him in jeopardy. He has always been my steadfast confidant. A rock. A rare species here in Zion. Then I look at the tiny cuts and scratches on my arm and legs. Asher gone. My son's life is in danger. Pretending to like it here. Pretending to love my father. That is how I feel inside, like I am dying from a thousand tiny lacerations on my soul. It has been going on for way too long. My strength is depleting.

Hagar nudges me back into the moment. "He's coming."

The guard strolls closer to us.

Then I hear my mother's voice. "You mind giving me a hand over here?"

"Of course, ma'am." As she leads the guard in the opposite direction, she turns towards the bushes and gives us a quick glance. That is twice now that she has helped me. No matter what else happens, I am slightly comforted to know that I have my mother back.

We drag Amos into the garage and place him inside one of his shiny electric Ferraris. We even put his seatbelt on as if he planned to drive somewhere.

As we head back towards the door, Hagar stops. "Wait." He rifles through the cabinets, finds a half-drunk bottle of Scotch, and places it on the floor of the driver's seat next to Amos's feet. "That should do it."

But before he closes the door, I say, "One more thing."

And I punch Amos square in the nose. I won't lie; the crunch of his cartilage is music to my ears. Hagar frowns at me as if to say, *Was that really necessary?*

Yes. Yes, it was.

Asher

Hagar gives us the signal, and then Neriah and Eve knock on the back of the truck.

"I'll take the truck to the rendezvous point. See you in a few hours," Cephas tells me.

I crawl out of the back and join Neriah and Eve. It's strange being back in Zion West so soon. I am almost taken aback when I receive a few bows and salutes from Lazurite soldiers. I nearly forgot that I am General Amos. For the tenth time, I touch the new scar on my face. I have to stop doing that. It's not regal, nor is it what Amos does.

Neriah whispers, "Hagar said Boaz is having dinner with Renatus tonight. Maybe we can snatch him when he is en route."

"Let's head near the gardens; he must go through them to get to the dining hall." I turn to Eve. "You have it?" She flashes a needle that we will use to knock Boaz out if need be.

After a few minutes, we arrive at the outskirts of Renatus's palatial garden. I get a pit in my stomach just being here. Renatus has killed me more than once in this very spot. I check my watch; the countdown is on. We will have to apprehend Boaz before his dinner meeting, or we will most likely run out of time before Amos is conscious again.

And then, finally, a stroke of luck. Boaz is shuffling his way through the garden with his small hands resting on his rotund belly. He still looks ridiculous wearing two Rolex watches. The rim of his red tophat is studded with diamonds. His gait is off balance, and he walks with aggravating slowness.

"There," I whisper.

We casually parade through the garden until we are directly before him. He sees me and stops. "General Amos. Out for an evening stroll?"

"Actually, Boaz, I have something to show you."

He tips his hat. "Certainly, General, but dinner awaits."

"Dinner can wait, Boaz. It will be fast. Come with me."

"Show him what?" Our luck is short-lived; behind him is Renatus, with four elites.

I bow. "My Sultan."

"Show him what?" Renatus asks again. "What is so important that would make him late for my dinner invitation?"

I think hard and fast. "Some of my men had discovered a cache of contraband that we found interesting. I thought Boaz might be able to tell us where it came from."

Renatus stares at Neriah, then at me. Does he know? Is the burn mark on my face too fresh? Then he clasps his hands together. "Well, Boaz would certainly be the man for the job. But first, we eat."

It is something we cannot refuse. "Of course, my Sultan." I can only hope this isn't one of Renatus's long-winded nosh sessions. I guess it depends on what mood he is in.

Thirty minutes later, we sit at the elegant dining table. Crystal glasses and China plates. The one thing I have missed from Zion is the food and the wine. Renatus turns to Neriah with a slight scowl. "So, Neriah, to what do we owe the pleasure of this visit?"

She clears her throat. "I wanted to report to you personally on troop movements and Defiance strongholds in my Reservation."

Renatus grabs the bowl of lobster bisque and slurps it down. "And you couldn't have sent someone?"

"To tell you the truth, I also missed it here in Zion."

Renatus takes a bite of raw tuna and licks his fingers. "Is Dreck food not to your liking? Are your accommodations not suitable?" Renatus is goading her; he wants her to complain so he can scold her, or worse.

She doesn't bite. "No complaints, my Sultan."

"Don't get too comfortable here." He takes a sip of his wine. "And what of Asher? Have you seen him?"

I almost choke on my food. Neriah looks directly at him. Renatus is very good at reading people. But Neriah is also a good actor, as we learned during the debate and the election. "No, I have not. Should I be expecting him?"

Renatus waves his hand in the air, like he is shooing away a fly. "I sent him on an important errand. I just want to be certain he is sticking to his word." He peers at me as he finishes the sentence. I start to sweat. I need to calm down. I am Amos.

"If I see him, I'll be sure to let you know."

Then, if things weren't complicated enough, Sarai shows up and sits at the table.

Renatus frowns. "You're late."

"Sorry, Father. I had another headache."

She glances at me, then at Neriah. I can see the surprise and perhaps anger on her face that Neriah is with us. I haven't had a chance to tell her that Neriah is now helping us. Neriah gives Sarai a scornful look. The animosity between the two is palpable.

Renatus picks up on it. "Is this the first time seeing each other since the election?"

Neither answer. Sadistically, Renatus is enjoying this. He rigged the election against his own daughter. My heart goes out to her for what she has suffered, what she is suffering. To be harmed by a stranger is bad enough, but when it's your own family? I can't imagine. I want to reach across the table and hold her hand.

"General Amos, how is your plan coming along to eradicate the Defiance once and for all?"

How do I answer that? I shouldn't have come. This was a stupid plan. As usual, Cephas was right.

But then Sarai saves me. "Come, Father, must we talk war at the dinner table? Wouldn't you rather tell us about your latest plan for the upcoming Canonization?"

Renatus can't and won't pass that up. "Well, Apex is almost healed. The course for my new Canonization, for New Zion, is a bit of a secret, but the one thing I will reveal is the return of Legion."

"You're bringing him back?" I ask, trying not to sound surprised.

Renatus rubs his hands together. "Back from the dead, to face his brother. You know he has always been a fan favorite."

"Wonderful!" Boaz exclaims, with a mouth full of food.

Even though I disagree with the methods, I look forward to seeing my friend again.

Sarai continues to placate her father. "Legion and Apex. That will be quite the show."

"Indeed. And let's not forget about Asher, another fan favorite," Renatus replies, then turns to me. "And what of numbers? Is the Defiance growing or on the decline?"

I am deliberate with my mannerisms to ensure they match Amos's, as well as my inflection. I clear my throat and lie. "Definitely declining. I think Cephas's army has seen the writing on the wall and no longer wants to be on the losing side. In fact, your popularity is growing, not only here but on the other side."

Boaz spots my sucking up and would never miss an opportunity to join in. "And my Sultan, with your upcoming Canonization, your popularity will only swell."

The only things swelling right now are Renatus's ego and Boaz's midsection. My leg nervously shakes, and I raise my glass. "I, for one, cannot wait—to the Canonization!"

Everyone joins me in the toast. "To the Canonization."

"And to Renatus!" Boaz adds.

Even Renatus sports an eye roll at Boaz's sycophantic ways. He turns to me. "Is Asher's ricochet still painted on the crumbling buildings in The Middle? Inside the taverns? How about the slums and bazaars?"

"We paint over them every chance we get," I lie.

Renatus's eyes go placid. "It's a symbol."

"It's false hope, my Sultan, nothing more."

"False or not, hope is dangerous. It can spread like wildfire. It must be snuffed out."

"It will be."

Renatus looks like he has solved the problem. "When Asher dies in the Canonization, that hope, that symbol, will die with him."

Boaz unsuccessfully tries to contain a belch. "He surely will be no match for Apex."

I spy Sarai checking her watch and then glancing at me. It has been almost three hours since they drugged Amos. We are running out of time.

A butler shows up with a tray of desserts.

"Dessert, anyone?" Renatus asks.

I stand. "Looks lovely, but we really must be going. I was hoping Boaz would take a look at this contraband before the evening is over."

But of course, Boaz is not going to miss dessert, so he grabs a chocolate cake from the tray. "What's the rush, General?"

"I really must insist; I have a meeting with my captains afterward," I lie.

Disappointed, Boaz stands while stuffing the rest of the cake into his mouth. I bow, "My Sultan." Then I turn to Sarai. "My Sultana."

Under any other circumstance, she would probably smile at the sight of me bowing to her. I'm sure when this is all over, she'll definitely razz me about it. As we are ready to leave, Renatus clears his throat. "General."

"Yes, my Sultan."

"I want that plan."

"Of course, my Sultan."

He then turns to Neriah. "And Neriah, don't come back here. You're a reservation girl now."

Neriah ignores the sleight, and in Lazurite fashion, slips her arm into mine for me to escort her out. Sarai winces at the gesture. I do as well.

As we file out, Renatus looks troubled, almost as if he knows something isn't right. But I have no time to dwell on it; Amos will be awake any minute now.

Minutes later, we approach the truck. Boaz is almost giddy. "Any Americana in this batch of contraband?"

"Perhaps."

I see Boaz turn and squint. His frown morphs into bewilderment. "What the?"

To our left is the real Amos, stumbling his way through the garden. Before Boaz can raise a stink, Neriah jabs a needle into Boaz's neck. He passes out in my arms.

"I think it's time to go."

Chapter Six

Asher

"WAKE UP!" CEPHAS BELLOWS at Boaz, slapping his face.

"Easy, Cephas," I say, pulling him away. I was worried about what Cephas might do once he saw Boaz.

Boaz's eyes flutter awake. He peers at our underground compound, disoriented. The lights shine brightly in his eyes. "Where am... what happened?"

"You're back with the Drecks in The Middle, you snake!" Cephas growls.

Boaz's confusion quickly turns to fear as Cephas lumbers towards him, then places his meaty hand around Boaz's neck. "You betrayed us! You killed Jude and left us for dead!"

"It was nothing personal, just business," Boaz yips.

Cephas's eyes narrow. "Well, this is personal."

I once again pull Cephas off of him. "Enough, Uncle. Remember why he is here."

Boaz starts to get his bearings. "Why am I here? And how did I get here?" He then has a realization and points at my face. "You, you did it again, didn't you? You posed as Amos?" He then tries to suck up to me. "Clever. I always knew that about you, Asher."

"Is that why you paid me peanuts when I was your mule?"

"I had to eat too," Boaz replies.

"And you did that plenty," Cephas snarls.

I trot towards him, pick him up off the ground, and menacingly place him against the concrete wall. I have to be somewhat rough with him; otherwise, Cephas will. Besides, he won't play ball otherwise. "You are here because you have information we need."

Boaz shakes his head. "I'm not sure what you want this time, but I can assure you, I am all out of maps."

"It's not a map we want," I tap my index finger against his wrinkled forehead. "It's what's in here."

"I'm not sure what you mean."

"Stop lying!" Cephas yells.

Boaz shivers and shrugs. "You'll have to be more specific." He points to his head. "I have quite a bit up here."

"Mammon," is all I say.

Boaz's head flinches back slightly. "Who?"

Cephas interjects, "Don't lie to us. You know who Mammon is."

"You mean the protocol scientist, that Mammon?" Boaz stares at the ground, feigning ignorance.

I place my ricochet underneath his chin and lift his head so we are eye to eye. "No more games, Boaz. We know you have his LifeCell."

Cephas cracks his knuckles. "You are stuck with us, Boaz, until the end of this war. During that time, you can be comfortable or miserable. That is up to you."

Boaz breaks. "Yes, I do. I do have his LifeCell, but what does that have to do with anything?"

"Have you noticed that since your resurrection, you know things you shouldn't? Particularly about protocol and how it works—memories and thoughts that aren't yours?"

Boaz rubs his chin, and the light reflects off his gold rings, "Come to think of it, yes. Yes, I do. Are you saying that I also know what he knows because I have Mammon's LifeCell? Sort of like epigenetic inheritance?"

"What is epigenetic inheritance?" Cephas asks.

Adam responds, "Studies have suggested that experiences and memories can be transferred from the brain into the genome, and therefore, passed to the next generation."

Eve adds, "Further studies have shown that children of holocaust survivors exhibit greater levels of stress disorders than their peers. Or how the offspring of mice feared the smell of cherry blossoms just because their parents were shocked with electricity every time they came in contact with them. Not only their offspring, but their children's offspring. It would be like the puppies of Pavlov's dogs salivating every time you rang a bell."

"So, is that what it is?" Boaz asks.

I begin to pace, tossing my ricochet and catching it. It helps me think. "Yes. In a way. Our Dreck scientists, who aren't as dumb as you think we are, discovered that memories can be passed from one person to another through their LifeCell."

Boaz clears his throat. "And you want me to divulge everything I know about second-life tech?"

"Precisely."

"And what do I get in return?"

Cephas grunts, "You get to live."

"Fair enough then, I'll do my best."

"Your best isn't good enough," Cephas tells him.

Boaz raises his palm. "Look, I just have bits and pieces. Weird memories, some of them dreamlike."

I place a sack on the table. I open it to reveal ten gold bars. "Perhaps this will turn your dreams into reality."

Cephas rolls his eyes at the gesture, and I can't blame him after what Boaz did to Jude.

Boaz nods. "If I concentrate, I can see Mammon's thoughts. I remember him working in the lab. But it comes and goes. I can't control it as much as it controls me."

Cephas looks to me, as I would know. I nod that Boaz is telling the truth. I point to Adam and Eve, whom I have not yet introduced.

"This is Adam and Eve. They will lead the team of scientists whom you will help reverse-engineer protocol."

Boaz's mouth opens, revealing his wide, chalky teeth. "Reverse engineer? You are going to try to render protocol ineffective? Put the genie back in the bottle?"

"Yes."

Boaz shakes his head. "But why? I understand you not wanting Renatus to have it, but think of all you could accomplish with it."

There's no sense in answering him. If he doesn't see that protocol is the reason we are in this war, he never will.

But Eve can't help herself: "We didn't ask for your opinion, just your knowledge." She approaches Boaz, points her dagger at him. "We met at Eden, remember?"

Boaz tries to ease the tension with a bit of humor. "This will all go a lot better if we all can just forget and forgive."

"That depends on you and your memory," Eve warns him.

Minutes later, Cephas, Adam, Eve, and I are huddled in the corner.

Adam asks the obvious question that has been on everyone's mind since we hatched this plan. "After everything Boaz has done, can we trust him?"

"No. But he'll do anything to save his own skin," Cephas answers.

"And remember, he is not loyal to us, but neither is he to Renatus. Boaz is only loyal to one thing. Gold. And thanks to Lucas, we have plenty of it."

Cephas's voice is now solemn. He places his hand on my shoulder. "It's almost time for you to leave, Nephew. What will happen when you return to Renatus empty-handed?"

I shake my head. "I don't know yet. I was thinking I could tell him I have found another wounded one and that he is on his way; perhaps that will buy me some time."

"You Drecks ever plan, or you always fly by the seat of your pants?" Adam chimes in.

Eve says, "What about Timothy?"

"Lucas's brother?" I shake my head. "I will not hand him over to Renatus to be murdered."

"I am not saying that. All I am saying is that you bring him with you to temporarily appease Renatus. Then, when you win the Canonization, and we win the war, everybody will be saved."

"And what if Renatus decides to perform protocol on him immediately? He has no reason to wait. He can have his son and grandson. I can't risk it. If we won and Timothy died, it would be a stain on our victory that would be too great to overcome. If we lose our morals in the process, then there is no victory."

That said, I think about what might happen to Silas when I return without another wounded one. I think about Sarai and her heartbreaks. Her having to pretend to be happy with Renatus, her seeing her son locked away, seeing me show up with Neriah. She knows as well as I do that everybody can change. That everyone deserves a second chance at forgiveness. But lately, it has been hard to find that kind of resolve, that kind of character. Constant war, suffering, and protocol are transforming me into someone I can't stand to be with. Can't stand to look at. It's ironic how much time and effort Sarai and I have put into taking down The

Wall, when it's the wall between us—the wall right in front of us, the wall stopping us, the wall impeding our faith—that needs to be taken down.

I close my eyes, and the pain in my head is acute. The conglomerate of different memories in my mind is becoming a blur. Perhaps that is a good thing? Are they going away? Am I subconsciously forgetting them? Or are they merging into one? Can I still be the husband Sarai fell in love with? The father Silas deserves?

"You okay, Nephew?"

I open my eyes. "It's time for me to leave. It's time for me to return to Zion."

"Are you forgetting something?" Cephas asks.

I stare at him blankly, no longer in the mood to play guessing games.

"Your face, your acid scar. If you return to Zion looking like that, Renatus will know we took Boaz."

It's back to the sculptor for me.

Asher

I was interrogated at the checkpoint for three hours until they finally got hold of Renatus to let me into Zion West. I am apprehensive as four elites escort me towards Renatus's grandiose compound. What will he do now that I have returned with nothing? Will he reap Silas's LifeCell immediately? Will he kill Sarai and me? I wish I had accomplished more in the past three months. Once again, my plan is very Dreckish, with long odds.

I take a deep breath of ocean breeze and steel myself as Renatus approaches. His red sashes flutter in the wind. There is a youthful bounce in his step. He looks the same. He always does. He hasn't aged in years. For each LifeCell taken, the aging process stops or is slowed, at least for a limited time. That is probably why he undergoes protocol even when there is no need to. *Maintenance,* he would call it. Almost as if taking another human life was no more to him than a simple oil change.

I, on the other hand, am feeling old and worn out. The gray hairs are taking over. The lines on my face converge with my scars as though in a crowded intersection.

As Renatus gets closer, he orders his guards to disperse.

"Asher, you have returned." He flashes an expectant smile, furiously rubbing his hands together.

"As promised," I answer.

He looks behind me and then to each side of us, mocking as though he is searching for someone. "And your other promise? The reason I let you leave... I hope you have not broken that?"

"He is on his way," I lie.

He places his face into his hands, then makes a show of dragging his fingers down the length of his face as if trying to wipe away the frustration and disappointment. "Oh, Asher. Oh, Asher. That was not part of the deal. You had three months, yes? Three months to bring me another wounded one. Yet, you show up empty-handed. Tell me, Asher, son of Silas, what have you been up to? Meeting with old friends, perhaps?"

He knows something is not right. I clear my throat. "It took longer than expected. I had people fan out everywhere searching. One was found in Reservation 20," I lie. Well, at least partially. I did find another wounded one. But I have no plans on turning him over.

"So days, then?"

"Weeks."

Renatus's anger is starting to rise. "Weeks? Tell me where he is exactly, and I'll have a drone pick him up."

"It's not that simple, I'm afraid. An ex-member of The Sons of Levi turned mercenary has him, or at least knows of another *wounded* one; he tells me he will have him here in a matter of weeks." I place a bag of gold at his feet. "I have already paid him half. He will expect the rest when he arrives with your prize." I don't like the fact that I have become a good liar, but it is a necessary evil when fighting evil.

He points his finger at me. "Not bloody good enough, Asher. Besides, I cannot trust that you are telling me the truth."

"It's what it is, and it is all I have to offer."

"Then your son shall be prepped for protocol immediately."

"No, please. Just wait. What is a few more weeks? I beg you. You can have your son and grandson."

"NO!" he maniacally screams in my face. Spittle flies from his lips into my eyes.

"If you do this, I won't fight. You'll have to have your new Canonization for a new Zion without me."

"If you don't fight, then Sarai dies with you."

I call his bluff. "Then we both die. But you know, without me, without the Vanquisher of Legion, the reigning champion, your new Canonization will be second-rate."

"I have Apex and Legion. I don't need you," he scoffs.

"Maybe. But Goliath versus Goliath isn't as compelling without a David. And like it or not, I am a crowd favorite."

"Most of Zion hates you for the traitor that you are."

"All the more reason they want to watch me die. Besides, how many bets will you have to cancel if I'm a no-show?" I say convincingly.

He is contemplating. I continue, "What do you have to lose? If your wounded one isn't delivered by the time The Canonization is over, you call kill me and take Silas's LifeCell." I cater to his exhibitionist nature. "I promise to put on a good show."

He scrutinizes me. "You're getting older. Can you still perform?"

"I may be older, but I'm wiser." Then, with a quickness that surprises even Renatus, I unhook my ricochet and fling it at the guard perched near the front gate. As planned, it only knocks his plasma rifle from his hand, leaving him stunned. Renatus has to duck as the ricochet returns to the receiver on my wrist. "And I still have my chops."

He suppresses a grin, eyes me with a slight hint of admiration. With that display, I just spoke his language. "It's not just me you'll have to convince."

"What do you mean?"

"Legion. I have brought him back. Now, he tells me he will not fight his brother or participate at all, for that matter." He shakes his head. "All he does now is sit around and drink tea. What has happened to my mighty Legion? You have broken him, Asher."

"I can do it. I will convince him."

"You have one week until the games begin."

"Done," I tell him. One more thing I hadn't anticipated, one more thing that needs to go right. I need Legion to be my savior once more. I hate to ask more of him, but none of this works without him.

Renatus licks his lips, then pulls a long knife from a sheath on his side. "But, one more thing, Traitor of Zion."

Looks like it is back to The Mountain for me.

Eve

Adam and Eve peer through microscopes and run simulation tests on the bank of computers in their makeshift laboratory on the bottom floor of Cephas's compound. Boaz watches them in the corner while eating day-old bread and sipping newer Coke.

"You have any bisque to go with this stale bread?" Boaz asks, sounding bored.

Eve glares at him. "Someone upstairs will have to go without because we have been nice enough to feed you."

"Any wine?"

Adam ignores his question. "Are you sure this is what is in the fluid to keep the LifeCell alive?"

"That's what my memories tell me," Boaz answers, slurping his drink before lightly belching.

Eve scowls. "I told you, no more burping. Or any other gassy noises, for that matter."

Adam turns back to Boaz. "Can you tell me exactly how the LifeCell is extracted? If so, I believe I can deactivate the protein molecule inside the LifeCell itself."

"I can. That part is not hard," Boaz answers. "But it won't help you with the molecule."

"Why not?" Eve asks.

"I don't know why not; I'm not a scientist. All I know—or not know, but recall from Mammon's memories is that that is not the way to do it."

"Then how?"

"I don't know."

"Think, Boaz. Try to picture it in your mind."

"Nothing is ringing a bell."

"What about a molecule inhibitor?" Eve asks.

"That doesn't sound familiar," Boaz says while getting up and strolling until he is right behind them. He whispers, "Why?"

"Why what?"

"Protocol is the greatest scientific achievement of our time. Why get rid of it?"

Eve frowns at him. "Because it is the reason we have people like Renatus. And you."

Boaz continues to try to persuade them. "Just imagine what you could accomplish if death weren't in the equation. Wrongs could be righted. Innocents who have been murdered or who have died in accidents could be brought back. Children who perished before their time could be reunited with their parents. We shouldn't be worrying ourselves with destroying protocol. We should be embracing it."

Eve counters, "Yet, none of that has happened. Instead, the powerful and wealthy now live because of the deaths of innocents. Invincible armies march through our once free country, spreading tyranny."

Boaz attempts to justify her remarks. "In historical context, protocol is still in its infancy. We must give it time. Work out the kinks, get it in the hands of the right people—people like you, perhaps? Tell you what! Return me to Zion, and Renatus will give you eternal life and riches beyond your dreams."

Eve has had enough. She slams him against the wall. "No more talking. You got that?"

He nods, then shuffles toward the door.

"Where are you going?" asks Eve.

"Thought I would go up top and try to scrounge another Coke, see if the caffeine might jog my memory about the molecule inhibitor."

After he exits the room, Eve turns to Adam. "You think he is going to be of any use?"

"Only if it behooves him, I'm guessing," Adam says.

Before they can return to work, Timothy peeks through the open door. His smile is wide, and the white blotches on his face are more pronounced under the bright fluorescent lights.

Eve smiles at him. "Hey Timmy, can I help you?"

"Looking for my brother. Have you seen Lucas?"

"Can't say that I have."

"Okay. I'm gonna leave now. We're playing hide and seek."

"Have fun, buddy."

Timothy leaves and shuts the door. Eve ponders for a moment. A thought emerges in her brain. One that she doesn't think she has had before. "I think I want kids."

Adam either doesn't hear her or ignores her.

"How about you, Adam? You like kids?"

He clears his throat. "Kids. Sure. For a minute there, I thought you said you wanted kids."

I did.

Adam peers back into the microscope; Eve watches him momentarily, then paces the room. "It's weird, isn't it?"

"What?" Adam replies, eyes still fixated on the LifeCell.

"This whole situation. Being in an icebox for over a century, and now we're in the middle of a war trying to reverse-engineer something that provides eternal life."

Adam is stoic, always the scientist first. "It's quite remarkable, isn't it?"

"And then there's us."

Us. Eve sees that this word causes Adam to look up from his microscope. "And what about us?"

Eve smiles. "We are married and have only known each other for a day. No dating, no wooing, no honeymoon, no ring. I think I kinda got a bad deal, don't you?"

"That's what we signed up for," Adam replies with little emotion.

"I realize that, but you never think about it?"

"Think about what?"

Eve is irritated. "That I'm your wife, and you're my husband."

Eve can tell this conversation is making him uncomfortable.

"I can buy you a ring if you like?"

"It's not that. It's just... never mind."

"Look, Eve. I... relationships were never my thing. I could never figure out people that well, which is probably why I agreed to be put under the ice in the first place. I figured you were the same."

In a way, that is true for Eve. Her parents died when she was five. She was in an orphanage until she was finally adopted at eleven. Her adoptive parents were unkind at best and abusive at worst. At eighteen, she joined the army and became a scientist for the military. Needless to say, people weren't her favorite. Trust wasn't something she was familiar with. But something inside her now longs for closeness. Something personal. Something intimate. She is tired of constantly numbing her emotions. Maybe that is why she couldn't read the ending of a book? She is too afraid of being disappointed, too used to being disappointed, actually.

She sighs. "I guess I kind of am. But now that we are out of the ice box and spending time together, I thought we could start doing married things."

"Like what?"

She flashes a flirtatious smile. "I don't know. I'm gonna go up top, grab a Coke, and think about it."

On her way out, she smacks his butt.

Asher

Waking up from protocol isn't as painful as usual. Perhaps I'm getting used to it. To the pain, that is, not to the idea of protocol. One worse thing is the headaches. My eyes feel like they're going to pop out of my skull. As I walk towards the training center where I am told Legion is, I have a vivid memory, a flashback that isn't mine.

A man working with wood. A hammer whacking a chisel. The buzz of a circular saw. The scratching of a sander. The smell of linseed oil wafting from the wood varnish.

A meticulously made rocking chair.

I must have reaped the LifeCell of a woodworker or furniture maker. I hope this is all I remember of him. I hope he didn't have family or anyone to miss him. I am not sure I can handle memories of him and his children. Thoughts of him being ripped away from his family. Another innocent dead, so I can live.

Then, as if on cue:

He places a child, about seven years old, in the rocking chair—his son. The man pushes the chair and sings what sounds like an old Irish lullaby. His wife proudly looks on.

A happy moment. Perhaps their last happy moment. I try not to let it depress me. I must let it fuel me to win this war, to defeat Renatus and tear down The Wall. To rid the world of protocol forever. I will not be a wasted vessel for their LifeCells that now live inside me. I will not let their sacrifice be in vain. I owe it to them to win, to survive. In a way, it's their legacy I now carry forward, not just my own.

I am looking forward to once again seeing my friend. I pray he can play savior one more time. As I enter the training center, an elite bumps into me and utters "traitor" under his breath. I feel like a policeman placed in jail with the very inmates I arrested. Soon, these people will be lining up to watch me die in their precious games. I feel sorry for them, actually, because the Canonization might possibly be the height of their joy. They have fallen for Renatus's grand distraction. It's not just the games; it's the tall tophats that are nothing short of preposterous. The sashes and long hair. The over-the-top food and decorations. Lazurite fashion and food are meant to keep one's gaze on the external—the superficial. Never looking inward. That is how evil operates in plain sight.

Speaking of The Grand Distraction, I can only imagine what outlandish and perverse brutality Renatus and his Canonization Architect have devised this time. I have heard rumors, but I will not believe them until I see them myself.

Then I see Legion in the corner. He is not training. He is not lifting weights or swinging a StunClub. He sits on a plush leather couch, reading a book and sipping tea. He has a GuillotineRing around his neck to prevent him from escaping. As I approach him, he ignores me.

I hold out my hand. "I can't tell you how good it is to see you again, my friend."

Legion doesn't look up from his book. "The answer is no."

This might be harder than I thought. I sit across from him. "What are you reading?"

He turns a page. "You know I hate small talk."

"You hate all talk," I joke, trying to lighten the mood.

He annoyingly sets his book down and sips his tea. "Why should I fight in Renatus's silly games?"

"Because we can't win without you."

"You won before. Not only did you win without me, you won against me."

"This is different."

"How?"

I stand and twirl my ricochet. It helps me think. "Because if you don't participate, I don't participate."

"Then don't participate," he says plainly.

"If we don't play ball, he kills my son. He kills me. And you."

"We will die anyway. Better now than under the lights entertaining the feebleminded masses."

"And what about Sarai? Silas? They, too, will die."

"A fate no worse than living as a prisoner under Renatus's boot."

"But we can win, Legion."

Legion pours himself another cup of tea. "That's an illusion, Asher. There are no winners here. You think Renatus cares who wins? Even if we win, we lose. As long as the mob is entertained, he has won. What do you think will happen if we pass his trials and somehow defeat Apex? That he will give us a trophy and send us on our way?"

I whisper, "I can't discuss it here, but we have plans. There is more to this than just fighting in the Canonization."

"You were lucky at Donner Lake. You were lucky in the first Canonization. Lucky to beat me. I think your luck has run out, Asher."

Now I'm starting to get irritated at his indifference, his refusal to fight for what is right. "What is wrong with you, man?!"

He stands. The veins and muscles in his neck are bulging so much I think the GuillotineRing might snap in half. "Wrong with me? I am dead, Asher! Do you realize that? I am dead. I shouldn't be here, and neither should you. Nor your wife and child! Anything I do from here on out wasn't meant to be, and that is an abomination."

My tone softens. "Look, I know it's tough. I know it's crazy even to comprehend. But if you give up now, their deaths will be for nothing. Help me prevent this from ever happening again."

A huge tear pools underneath his left eyelid until it traipses down his massive cheekbone and onto the floor. "My 'donor' was a child, Asher. Do you understand?"

"I'm sorry, Legion, I truly am. But it isn't your fault."

"I see him playing in the park, sliding down the rusted slide. Running to his mother's arms. That pure love and innocence is something I have never felt before. It paralyzes me, Asher. Just the thought of what this boy and his parents went through for me to have oxygen in my lungs has frozen my will. Has weakened my resolve." He peers down at his feet. "I am broken."

"Then redeem yourself. Redeem that child by destroying protocol. By saving another child. Silas. My son. Without you, The Defiance has lost. Without you, thousands more children will suffer the same fate. I need you, Legion. You're the reason we won at Donner Lake; it wasn't luck. You're the reason I won the first Canonization. That wasn't you I fought, not the real you. And sitting here giving up isn't the real you either."

Legion wipes the moisture from his eyes and plops back down. He downs the rest of his tea, shakes his head, and points his gnarled finger at me. "Under one condition."

"Anything."

"You never saw me cry."

Cephas

Cephas and Neriah survey the thousands of tents that line the valley floor near their compound. Drecks, Neriah's army, and ex-Lazurites that have sided with Asher start campfires and clean weapons.

"What is our readiness?" Cephas asks, feeling like Washington at Valley Forge.

"Hopefully in a week, maybe more," Neriah replies, her tone hesitant.

"How many?"

"Three thousand."

Cephas grunts. "It's not enough."

"Then we better go check on that nuke of yours."

As they walk through the crowd, their hybrid army eyes them with surprise, some warily. Food is scarce, and many of them don't have shoes.

"Why are we here?" Cephas asks her.

Neriah whispers, "Look at them. Look how they watch us. They aren't sure about this alliance of ours. They don't quite trust it yet. I was hoping that seeing us together would help alleviate some of that."

"Too bad your political career was so short; you would've made a good politician," Cephas jokes.

She elbows him, then stops and picks up a Gen2 plasma rifle from a freshly cleaned and charged stack. "Will you teach me how to shoot one of these?"

"Why?"

"In case you haven't been paying attention, we are about to go to war."

Cephas stops and folds his generous arms. "Have you ever fought in a war? Wielded a weapon? Taken any training of any kind?"

"No," she answers quickly, as if the question is ridiculous.

"Then it's best you stay behind. Help with the planning and all," Cephas half-heartedly tries to convince her.

"I see." Neriah places her hands on her hips. "You know how and why I became indentured to Renatus?"

"Asher told me, yes."

"At first, I would do anything for my son to be brought back. Anything, regardless of the price. And the fact that I got to stick it to Asher was a bonus." She sniffs away a stubborn tear. "But as time passes, I have come to accept it. Do I want him back? Of course. But with protocol? At the cost of another life? No. And neither would he. He was much too sweet. Much too giving." She grabs one of Cephas's hands, inspects his gnarled knuckles and raised calluses. "So you see, Cephas. I may not have the formal training. But my loss, my anguish, has given me the predisposition to fight. It's my cause now, my desire. That has to be worth something, doesn't it?"

Cephas studies her tortured, grief-stricken eyes. "It is worth a heckuva lot."

"Settled then. Now let's go check on this nuke."

After a quick bite, they go to the basement laboratory. Scientists in radiation suits disassemble the nuclear device. Some peer at computers and run tests.

Daniel, the chief nuclear engineer who was with Cephas on Eden, approaches them.

"Any progress?" Cephas inquires.

Daniel removes his glasses and rubs his nose. "Some. But we still haven't figured out how to detonate it."

"We're running out of time," Neriah adds.

"I'm well aware, ma'am. Let us not forget that we are dealing with hundred-year-old technology. I'm doing the best that I can with what I've got."

"You have a week," Cephas tells him.

"A week? This isn't something that can be rushed. That's when mistakes happen." Daniel points to the nuke. "And you don't want to make any mistakes with this thing. Right now, it's like playing with a loaded gun without knowing where the trigger is."

Neriah thinks for a moment. "Take pictures and video."

"What for?"

"If we can't get this thing operable, we can at least pretend it is. Get it out on the web."

Cephas rubs his chin, gives Neriah a proud stare. "Lying. False propaganda. Threats that can't be backed up. I'm telling ya, you would have made a wonderful politician."

She lets a rare smile escape her as they turn to leave. Cephas opens the door for her. "After you." He takes in her smell and thinks that if he were younger, he might ask her on a date when this was all over. *A date? What a silly thing to think about in the middle of a war.* But maybe this was progress for Cephas? He hasn't really thought about another woman since his wife died. There was Linda from his recovery group, but it wasn't long before she fell back into the Dust. Renatus's snares were everywhere. He thinks about his own addiction and how the Tonic still calls for him daily. The stress of this war makes it even worse. He made a promise. A promise to Asher and a promise to God. He holds up his hands; the tremors are beginning to subside. *I will not be lured into Renatus's noose. It won't be him or his Tonic that ends me. I will go on my own terms.*

Maybe after all this, he could put himself out there again? At least he is warming up to the idea—it is something Jude was telling him to do for years. But that means risk—risk losing more people that he cared for. He isn't sure he can handle any more loss.

Once in the hallway, a Dreck soldier approaches them, out of breath, bloody, and sweating. "Sir! He's been captured!"

"Slow down, soldier, and catch your breath. Who?"

The Dreck places his hands on his knees, inhaling oxygen. "It's Kenan, sir; he has been captured."

"How?"

"We were on a patrol, about a hundred of us. We ran into a brigade of Lazurites. It was an ambush. I don't know what happened; they were just waiting for us. They took Kenan, sir."

"Where are the rest of your men?" Neriah asks.

"I'm the only one left."

CHAPTER SEVEN

Asher

I AM HAVING DÉJÀ VU as we are once again paraded into the arena. Hordes of bloodthirsty fans scream and cheer for our introductions to begin. I am nervous as I don't know what to expect. We have been told nothing of this 'New Canonization' for a 'New Zion' as Renatus puts it.

We are in a line—Legion, myself, and seven other Drecks I recognize from The Defiance. They volunteered for this. A chance to fight with me. To fight to end this tyranny. Across from us stand Apex, Amos, and eight other Lazurite elites.

The sound of drums reverberates throughout the arena. Trumpets prime Renatus's entrance to the arena. But any old entrance won't do for Renatus and his massive ego. I pan the crowd and hear gasps as they point their caviar-stained fingers up at the sky. It is just a dot at first. Then it looks like a bird. But as it gets closer, I see Renatus falling from the sky. His arms are outstretched as he becomes ever so close to the ground. The red and white sashes tied to his arms flutter in the wind. It looks like he has wings.

"He's an angel!" a woman from the crowd yells. A demon is more apt. I didn't notice it before, but a red X is painted in the middle of the arena floor.

The crowd becomes deathly silent as Renatus grows so close you can see the sun reflect off his bald head. Of course, he is not wearing a helmet. His grin is so wide I can see the whites of his polished teeth. At the very last moment, he deploys his parachute, his feet hit the middle of the red X, and he is taken to his knees. He immediately jumps up and rips the parachute from his back. He raises his hands to the jubilant cheers of the crowd.

They chant, "Sultan! Sultan! Sultan!"

Always spry, he bounces up and down, in rhythm with their mantra. He's like a kid on Christmas. This is the day he looks forward to all year.

"Welcome back, everyone, to a New Canonization for a New Zion!"

The crowd roars. "Sultan! Sultan! Sultan!"

Renatus raises his hands. "Hold on, hold on. It's not me we are here to celebrate, but all of Zion. New Zion!"

Out of robotic obedience, they change their chant. "New Zion! New Zion! New Zion!"

Renatus smiles, takes a deep breath, and soaks it in. "This year, we are doing things a bit differently. This year, we will be split into two teams of ten." He points to Apex. "The home team will be led by your very own Apex and Amos." As the crowd cheers, Amos's scowl makes it evident that he doesn't want to be here. Now, being a General, he probably thinks this is below him.

"Apex! Apex! Apex!"

He then points to us, his tone playful. "And the visiting team will be led by fan favorites, Legion and Asher."

There is a mix of boos and cheers. Seems we still have some fans.

I quickly count again and notice we have nine to their ten.

I disrespect Renatus under the guise of banter. "Your Sultan, is this going to be a fair fight?"

"Ahh, Asher, Son of Silas, Father of Silas, Traitor to Zion, whatever do you mean?"

"Home team has ten; we only have nine. Or is this *New Zion* math?"

The crowd—or mob, more aptly put—agrees with me with a round of boos.

Renatus shows them his palms. "Oh yes, yes. I almost forgot. Without further ado, I give you another veteran of our great and wonderful games: Kenan the Coward!"

I close my eyes. It can't be. Kenan. How? Was he captured? Did he join on purpose to try to redeem himself from last time? To help me? A massive gate opens, and Kenan is pushed into the arena. He trudges towards us. Like ten years ago, the crowd shouts "Coward!" and throws fruit at him. He stares at his feet until he finally arrives behind me. His left eye is black, and his lips are swollen.

I whisper, "What are you doing here, Kenan? You are needed elsewhere."

His stutter returns, "This... this... this wasn't deliberate."

"What happened?"

"We were ambushed on a patrol."

"Where are the rest of your men?"

He shakes his head, still staring at the ground. "Gone."

Except for the loss of his men, in a way, I'm relieved. Aside from Legion, I have another friend, someone who has been here before. This time, I hope he can last until the end.

"I'm sorry, Asher. I'm sorry I lost the patrol. I'm sorry I'm here."

I try to console him. "It's not your fault. I'm glad you're here. You are going to do just fine."

Renatus mocks him. "There will be no tapping out this time, Kenan."

Renatus smiles at me, then turns back to his audience. "Now that the teams are fair, let's go over some logistics. Before the final showdown right here in this very arena, each team will face off in a set of trials that will test their physical and mental acumen. The first team to have every surviving member finish the trial will be declared the winner. They will be rewarded with fresh weapons, supplies, food, and water. The losing team, however, must choose a member to serve as a..." He thinks for a moment. "As an offering to New Zion."

Offering? Is he saying what I think he is saying?

The crowd is enraptured now, hanging on to his every word. "That's right, my fellow Lazurites. The losing team will choose a member who will then sacrifice their LifeCell to one of you, good folks. There will be a lottery, and tickets will go on sale immediately after we are done here."

There is a standing ovation. Seems this new generation of Lazurites has once again embraced protocol, no matter the costs. And while most people in this stadium cannot afford it, Renatus has found a way to offer it to the masses. Or at least the chance of winning it. But that is all they need. Renatus is smart enough to know that to keep the populace in his control, to keep the mob on his side, all he has to do is offer a sliver of hope. Dangle the carrot. A window into what it is like to be an elite, to be a Lazurite with the power never to die. Not only are they wagering on us, but now they have the chance to own our LifeCells.

Based on their reaction, they eat it up. In a way, it's genius. He has found a way to invite them into maximum participation, and they have shown up in droves.

When the crowd finally settles down, Apex struts by us. "There will be no earthquake to save you this time, Asher." He then turns to Legion. "Brother, welcome back."

Kenan leans over and whispers, "I wonder what is in store for us this year."

"Can't be too difficult. He needs us alive for the final battle," I reply.

Legion grunts, "That, or he'll just bring us back again."

I wonder how many more times I'll have to die for Renatus. For Zion. How much longer until I no longer recognize myself? Until I am no longer me?

As Renatus marches closer to the crowd, I overhear Amos whisper, "Your Sultan, I beg you to reconsider. I am a General. I don't belong here."

But Renatus ignores his pleas. I, too, find it odd that he is here. Perhaps it is Renatus's way of punishing him for being captured? Perhaps every time he sees Amos, he sees me—a perpetual reminder of how he and all of Zion were deceived. Whatever the case, I hope to be rid of him once and for all.

Renatus then spreads his arms wide. "What else is left to say except let the games begin!"

Here we go again.

Asher

We still don't know what the first trial is. This is deliberate. Each team waits on an airfield next to two transport drones. In front of the drone is a large table with various weapons and supplies. Three Lazurite guards instruct us that we are only allowed to choose three. We peruse the items. There are backpacks full of food and water. There is your usual assortment of weapons and other tools.

We all agree on the easy choice first. Each one of us grabs a backpack. It goes without saying that I take a ricochet as my weapon. I watch Kenan take a plasma rifle. Legion grabs a bundle of plasma grenades. I am about to reach for a knife when one of the Lazurite guards whispers from the side of his mouth, "Take the rope."

I hesitate for a moment. Is it a trick? More Lazurite mind games? Then I spot the tiny tattoo of a Pelican on his wrist. He is a Defiance sympathizer. I mouth the words "Thank you" and grab the rope.

Moments later, we are herded into the drone and take off. The ten of us huddle in silence. The nervous tension in the air is palpable. Kenan's legs shake. The other seven Drecks feign bravado. Legion is the only one who is calm, truly at peace.

Maybe I should say something? Legion reads my mind and whispers, "Perhaps a word?"

I clear my throat. "Listen. I know none of you want to be here. Neither do I. What perverse attraction or abominable trial awaits us, I have no idea. I do know that if we stick together and stay calm, we can survive this thing." It is lackluster, but it is all I can muster at the moment.

A Dreck with red hair and a long goatee named Tobias pipes up. "No disrespect, sir, but let's not just survive; let's win this thing."

I squeeze his shoulder. "Thank you for that, soldier. It seems that these days, you guys inspire me instead of the other way around."

Tobias peers around and stares at me with conviction. "Sir, to serve alongside you is the honor of our lives."

"The honor is all mine, soldier."

A Dreck, probably early twenties with a thin mustache, isn't so confident. "And what about Apex? How can he be beaten?"

"One step at a time, soldier. Just worry about passing this first trial. We will cross that bridge when we get there."

Legion adds, "Don't be intimidated by his size alone. Every man has his flaws."

"What is Apex's?" Tobias asks.

"That he is young. Sure, he is fast, strong, and large. But what we lack in that arena, we make up for with wisdom. It wasn't too long ago he was my snot-nosed little brother."

"That's what all old people say," Tobias jokes.

Kenan clears his throat. "Perhaps we should decide now."

"Decide what?" I reply.

"You know, if we lose a trial. Who will it be? I thought we would draw straws or something?" Kenan holds up ten wooden sticks of different lengths.

"Seems fair enough," Legion agrees.

Tobias says, "I agree, but only for the seven of us."

"No way," I say. "I will not let you die for me. Or perhaps you have forgotten how I lead? We will all be drawing straws."

Tobias's voice becomes louder. "Sir, again, I mean no disrespect. But you, Legion, and Kenan are too important to our cause. You—"

I cut him off. "I appreciate that, soldier, but no. End of discussion."

Tobias pleads his case. "Look, if we survive these trials, you are the only ones who could possibly defeat Apex in the arena." He then motions to the other Drecks and smiles. "In fact, none of us wants that responsibility, I can assure you."

Before I can answer, Kenan throws away three sticks. "It's settled then."

"Insubordination already; we're off to a good start."

Even though I disagree with it, I know they are right. Legion and I have to be in that arena. I only hope Kenan can survive the trials.

Our drone lands with a thud. We are here. We exit the drone, and I must cover my eyes from the brilliant sun. In front of us is a thousand-foot-high granite mountain. Looks like we're rock climbing today. My hands aren't as strong as they used to be, but they are still strong enough. As a teen, Cephas had me climb many mountains as part of his reconnaissance teams, searching for Lazurite patrols. Most of my youth was spent either digging or climbing. I still have the calluses to prove it. Every time I complained about it, Cephas would tell me that one day I would thank him.

Once again, he was right.

Viewing bleachers have been set up for the elite few to watch: Renatus and his ilk, dignitaries, and other aristocrats. They tip their silly towering tophats at me as I stroll by. A man with a blood-red goatee eyes my ricochet. "May I touch it?"

I smile, but internally, I mock his question. I unlatch it from my belt and hand it to him. He lets out a feminine yelp; he's as giddy as a schoolgirl. Before handing it back, he rubs it with his silky white gloves. "Thank you, Asher, the Traitor. May you have an honorable death."

I am about to ignore the statement, but I cannot help myself. "You know, you should keep those gloves."

"Whatever for?"

"That way, you can tell everyone those gloves touched the weapon that defeated Apex." I wink before walking off. The other Lazurites have a good chuckle.

Renatus approaches us. "This one is simple, gentleman. First team to have all their surviving members make it to the top and press their button wins." He points to a countdown clock: "You start in five minutes."

Both teams, all twenty of us, approach the rock face and watch the timer countdown. I study the wall. No bolts. We have no carabiners. I'm not sure what good the rope will do me. This will have to be done by hand.

Apex peers over at Legion. "Don't fall, brother. I will not be cheated of your death again."

Legion grits his teeth. I place my hand on his shoulder. "Ignore him, Legion. He is just trying to get into your head."

"Could you?"

I answer him honestly. "No."

The horn blows.

Asher

It is slow going. We have been at it for almost an hour. My hands are starting to sweat. Without chalk for my fingers, this isn't going to be easy. I have gone partway up, then back down several times. Some routes just dead-end. Apex is in the lead; it's almost like he knows the best route. I wouldn't be surprised if Renatus fed him this information beforehand. Legion isn't far behind. They look like two graceful spiders climbing their way up a sticky web. Sure, they are the heaviest, but their fingers are about as strong as my arm.

"Heads up!" I hear Legion yell.

I peer up, squinting into the oppressive sun. I see something fall towards me. It's a rock the size of a basketball. I must hang on with one hand and twist my body to dodge it. I was wondering when something like this would start. Of course, this wouldn't be a Canonization without some barbaric addition. I'm still waiting for the rock to turn into lava. I can hear the crowd below me ooh and ah. A few more fall near Tobias. I look up and can see Lazurite soldiers pushing them off the ledge. They high-five each other and exchange sadistic grins.

I twist back against the wall and grope for a place to stick my fingers. While pulling myself up, I find purchase in the smallest cracks and crevices. Drones hover and take close-up shots of us for all the fans watching at home. My fingers are beginning to chafe and bleed. Whenever my fingers find a cleft or cranny in the flat rock, it's like a small miracle. My arms burn something fierce, and it looks like the veins in my forearms are trying to escape the skin. And my feet, wedged into the undersized climbing shoes, are beginning to cramp.

I am almost halfway up when I realize I am stuck. The sun is unrelenting. I wipe my sweaty hands on my shirt and gaze back down the way I came. I peer back and see that Apex has made it to the top. Legion is not far behind. Apex, who apparently grabbed a rope as well (wonder how he knew), throws it down to his fellow Lazurites. One of them grabs it, and Apex pulls him up. Why didn't I think of that? I could have given it to

Legion. But then again, I didn't think he would reach the top before me. Their agility, given their size, practically defies physics. I am about to go back down and start again, when I have an idea. Fifty feet above, a large rock ledge juts from the mountain.

I climb down a few feet so that I can stand on a ledge and use both my hands. I unhook my ricochet from my belt and tie the rope to one end of it, and then toss it towards the ledge. The ricochet goes up and over the ledge, then back down towards me, causing the rope to catch onto the end of the rocky ledge. Once my ricochet returns, I now have a rope to pull myself up. After a few minutes, I pull myself up to the next ledge, passing a few Lazurites in the process. They kick and try to grab me as I go by.

"Another one!" Tobias warns me. Two more rocks whiz by me, just missing. The sun is bearing down now. Sweaty hands and rock climbing don't mix. I pause to rub my sore hands before they turn into permanent claws.

"Toss me your ricochet," Legion orders. I see what he is getting at. It will be a hard throw to make without the leverage, as I'm only halfway up.

"Here it comes," I respond, hurling it toward him with the attached rope. Not being able to plant my feet, my aim is a tad off. Legion has to lie down and reach his massive hand out. He is just barely able to grab the ricochet. Just as he unties the rope, Apex pulls up another Lazurite from the home team. Legion unties the rope from my ricochet and begins to do the same.

I pat my sweaty hands on my shirt and continue my climb up. Next to me, Tobias hangs onto the rope as Legion pulls him up to the top. My damp fingers find a crevasse, and I pull myself further up. I think I have found a good line. Legion and Apex have pulled everyone up now, except for me and Amos. I hug the wall and move horizontally a bit. I need to make this move to get a bit further to the left, so Legion can toss me down the rope. I need a nice handhold a few feet above my head. I realize I will have to jump for it, and hope my damp grip can hold on.

Further to my left is Amos, who has reached a dead end and is making his way back down.

"Go to your right!" Apex yells at him. Amos is in the same predicament I am, except he needs to move further right to reach Apex's rope. If I can make this next move, I will be way ahead of him, and winning this first challenge should be within our grasp. I take a deep breath and close my eyes for a moment. I steel myself, calm my soul, and attempt to regulate my breathing. I wonder if Sarai is watching. Of course she is. Last time, I was doing it solely for her. This time, it's for our son. For The Defiance.

You can do this, Asher. You can do this. Just imagine you're on the ground.

I open my eyes and use both feet and my right hand to propel myself upwards. In rock climbing terms, this would be the crux, the most challenging part of the climb. For a split second, but what seems like an eternity, I am in the air and completely off the rock wall until my left hand finds the handhold. With one arm, I manage to pull myself up until my right hand also grips the hold.

I exhale. So does Legion. "Here comes the rope."

Moving to my left towards the unfurling rope, I see that that isn't the only thing tumbling towards me.

"Another rock!" Tobias cries out.

Before I can twist out of the way, the corner of the rock smashes into my left hand. I lose my grip and slide down the wall, until I finally land on a tiny ledge.

"You are lucky!" Legion bellows down at me.

Lucky? The knuckles on my left hand have been crushed, my chest and stomach are cut and bleeding from what looks like road rash, and I almost fell to my death. But then again, the rope dangles next to me.

"Grab it!" Legion tells me.

As I do, I notice Amos has made it to Apex's rope. We begin our ascent at almost the same time. I can practically see the sweat, pulsating muscles, and bulging veins of Legion's and Apex's arms as they pull us up. I feel like my grip is about to give out; I hang on with everything I have. It's now a race to the top. With a hundred feet to go, we are neck and neck. Amos looks over and gives me one of his smug, presumptuous Lazurite smirks. He knows Apex is stronger than Legion, and that he and I weigh about the same. On paper, he should win this one. But Legion has dug deep. He is keeping up with his younger, stronger brother.

At the top, about fifty feet behind Legion and Apex, are two cylinders, each with a massive button resting on top. The red one is for them, and the green one is for us. To win the trial, all of your team members must press their respective buttons at the same time.

Twenty feet from the top, I am five feet ahead of Amos. Legion is a machine. His arms and back must be on fire. As long as I hang on, we will win this one. A few seconds later, I am just about at the top. The sun is unyielding and still determined to punish us. Legion is drenched and trying to catch his breath. Like mine, his hands cry blood. He releases a prehistoric howl and then shoots me a slight smile as he knows we have pulled it off. Just as I am pulling myself up, Apex squints at me, then at Legion.

To our shock, he lets go of his rope. "Oops," he feigns, shrugging. I first hear Amos's scream as he tumbles down the mountain. I cringe as I listen to him hit the ground with a thud. Before I can pull myself to my feet, Apex trounces to the finish line, and their entire team presses the red button. I look down and see Amos sprawled out in a pool of blood, undoubtedly dead. I peer down at the man with whom I share a face. That easily could have been me. I wonder if Renatus is okay with Apex killing off his General—the man who brought him my son.

"Wait a minute, he can't do that. That's cheating," Kenan argues.

I shake my head. "Maybe so, but Renatus said: 'First team to have all of your *surviving* members make it to the top and press their button wins.' It looks to me that Amos did not survive."

Tobias peers over the edge, shaken. "He killed him. His own teammate. Just like that. Just to win."

I spit, "Welcome to Lazurite gamesmanship."

Legion is so angry that he picks up a boulder and hurls it against a tree, completely obliterating the trunk. He grabs another, aims it towards Apex, and rears back.

Apex eggs him on, "Do it, brother, do it. We can settle this now."

I talk him down. "Legion, save it for the arena." He exhales and sets the boulder down. He is exhausted. We all are. I can barely make a fist or close my hands. We watch as the home team gathers their spoils—fresh water and food.

Kenan sighs and pulls out the sticks, which act as straws. "I guess it's time to draw."

Asher

We are escorted to our respective cells for the evening. A Lazurite guard shuts my metal door with a clunk. As a team, we finished what little food and water were in our backpacks. We need a win tomorrow. We need to replenish. I can't handle seeing another one of my men drawing the short straw.

Today, it was Peter. He accepted his fate with bravery and dignity. Peter had a wife and four kids, yet he still volunteered because he believed in our cause—believed in me.

It's a heavy burden to bear, to hold one's life in your hands, to know they are willing to risk everything because of your leadership. Your words. Perhaps he had heard a speech of mine and became inspired? Words have power. And consequences. I realize that now more than ever. Peter didn't say the words, but as he was marched off to have his LifeCell reaped, he peered back at me. His eyes told me not to let his death be in vain. To not only win this thing, but to take down Renatus. Zion. The Wall. To set his family free. To destroy protocol once and for all.

Destroy protocol.

I wonder how Adam and Eve are doing and if they were able to obtain the information they need from Boaz. Once again, our plan is elaborate and will take everyone doing their part: Adam and Eve developing a serum that will reverse engineer protocol. My scientists figuring out how to make the nuke operable; Cephas and Neriah defeating the Lazurite army; Legion and I winning the Canonization; Sarai getting the serum to Silas and Eleazar.

Sarai.

My hands yearn for hers. My heart is becoming callous without her. Her fate was once again worse than mine. At least I can die fighting evil. My choices are black and white. She must live with that same evil if there is any chance to save our son. Being hurt by those who are supposed to love you the most. Pretending to like her father. Pretending to be a family, in an environment so toxic that only a heart as pure as hers can fend off Zion's ruinous grasp.

I lie on the surprisingly soft mattress and think about how little life means to Renatus. He threw Amos to the wolves without a second thought. A General. Or perhaps he is planning on bringing him back? That is the problem with Zion's world. Death has no meaning. Morality is non-existent. Anything is permissible.

My head hurts. So do my now-bandaged hands. I have a newfound respect for rock climbers. I close my eyes and am instantly flooded with memories that aren't mine. They are cloudy and filmy, almost like vivid dreams I am just now recalling. Some of the memories are new. Some are the same. I wonder who will get Peter's memories? I should have asked more about him, found out who he was. What were his wife and kids like? What were their names?

I am suddenly hit with another memory. This one is pleasant. I am a child. Perhaps eight, maybe ten years old. He is swinging me around and around by my arms. Circle after circle until we both become dizzy and shrink to the ground. Both laughing. I can't see his eyes. I see my own. It's not my memories. It's his. It's a good reminder that with all these multiple personalities swirling in my head, one of them is my father's. That is where much of my goodness comes from. Is he proud of how I am handling things? Of who I have become? I take solace in the fact that I will see him again one day on the other side. I will ask him these questions, and he will tell me it no longer matters. He will only embrace me with love. That is who he is. On that rare but happy note, I realize how exhausted I am. I wonder what awaits us tomorrow, as my hands and fingers are so sore I can still barely make a fist. Maybe tomorrow will be a mental challenge, so we can give our physical bodies a much-needed rest. Before I can dwell on it further, I am fast asleep.

Three hours later, my cell door clangs open. I jump up for a minute, not remembering where I am.

"Easy, Asher." It is Renatus.

I rub my eyes and almost see the silhouette of a demon as he paces the dark room. "You did well today," he tells me. His voice is soothing, and his demeanor is calm. Luckily for me, he is in a good mood.

"Good? We lost."

"You should have won, but the important thing is you survived."

I can sense he is here to talk. Not wanting him to change his mind about my son, I indulge him. "You okay with how Apex won? With what happened to Amos?"

He waves his hand slowly. He is calm and unusually relaxed. Maybe that should frighten me. "Ahh, Amos. He felt he was above his duty and service to Zion. But the Canonization has a way of bringing one back down to earth, wouldn't you say?"

"He was a General," I remind him.

"In title only, Asher. You, of all people, could see that. Besides, I don't need him anymore. I have a new alliance." He stares at me, waiting for me to ask who.

Out of curiosity, I do.

"With who?"

"With someone your wife is familiar with. An old friend. Czar Percival."

Looks like he did what Sarai could not. We were already outnumbered; now he has Percival and his army on his side.

"So whatever your uncle is planning, it won't work. My army has grown, and yours has shrunken."

I try to sow distrust. "Trust Percival at your peril."

Renatus turns his back on me and stares at the dull concrete wall for a minute. "I have given him what he wants. But I like the way you think. Now you, Asher. You are a General. A leader of men. The *wrong* men in this case, but a leader nonetheless. You and I are a rare breed. How I miss what we had."

I am curious now. "Even though none of it was real?"

"All it takes is a small mind shift to make something real. Change your beliefs, change what you think you know as true."

"I know the truth, and you are wasting your time if you think I will ever serve Zion again."

"I know that, Asher. But I had to try. You see, I want my daughter back. And without you, she will never return to me."

"Maybe you can start by giving her back our son."

"When your replacement arrives, I will."

I stretch my sore fingers, finally able to make a fist. "Sarai will never return to being a Sultana. Doesn't matter what I do. That is one thing I know for sure."

He pats my leg like I am his son. "We'll see. For now, just concentrate on staying alive. Everyone wants to see Apex versus Asher and Legion."

"And if we die?"

"You won't," he states plainly.

Seems he is planning on bringing us back for the final showdown if necessary.

"Is that all? I need my rest for tomorrow's trial."

He smiles. "You certainly do."

"Any chance you want to tell me what it is?"

"If it mattered, I would."

This visit is weird at best. I wonder why he is here. Is he trying to convince Sarai and me to join forces with him? Or is he bored? He is about to leave, then turns back towards me.

"How is Boaz?"

I freeze for a moment. He knows we have him. I say nothing. I knew there was more to this visit.

Renatus's smile is wide, his tone still serene. "He is a gift, you know. Boaz, that is."

"A gift?" is all I manage to say.

"Yes, Asher. He is an offering to the goddess of Athena. And it's quite fitting that he is Greek."

And with that cryptic sentence, he leaves me.

Goddess of Athena? Greek? Maybe this rant was just another psychotic episode. I think back to all the history my mother taught me. The stories she told me. The books she read to me.

Odyssey. Homer.

The gift the Greeks left to the city of Troy was an offering to the goddess Athena.

A Trojan Horse.

Sarai

I hate coming here. I always have. But I have to see my son. My brother. The freshly mopped, frigid concrete floor shimmers from the unduly bright lights above me. I try not to look at the soon-to-be corpses eerily floating in the glass cylinders on both sides of me. I swear that sometimes I can see them looking at me. There must be thousands of them here inside my father's new mountain, with more arriving each day. I zip up my jacket and shiver. I'm unsure if it's cold in here or if it's the frigid aura of impending death that causes me to shudder. Then the smell; I can't quite explain it. It's like a sterile aroma you would smell in a hospital, but with traces of something rotten, like an unwashed body doused with perfume.

As I trudge toward the end of the row, I pass the operations center. Lazurite scientists extract LifeCells from the floating "dead" and inject them into the LifePacks. Resurrection-on-the-go. A Lazurite tenet, if I have ever seen one. One of the scientists peers over at me and smiles. His countenance suggests that he is flipping rat burgers at a bazaar on Reservation 9, as opposed to committing mass murder. They have performed this so often that they probably don't even think about it anymore. Zion propaganda has deemed Drecks subhuman, which makes us easier to murder.

As I turn the corner, I hear the whooshing of rotors. Above the facility is a HarvestDrone making a drop-off. Its long vacuum tube connects to a hole in the roof and deposits its subject. The subject is a poor Dreck who has consumed my father's modified DemonDust. I can see the dirty, catatonic man being sucked down a tube into a back room inside the facility. I peer through the spotless windows and see two scientists pull the Dreck from the tube and carry him over to what looks like a hospital bed. They immediately strap him in before he wakes up. They attach wires to him and monitor his vitals on the numerous computer screens and heads-up displays. Some of them arrive already dead, but their LifeCells are still viable up to twelve hours after perishing. I still can't believe we live in a world where that kind of knowledge exists in my head.

Next, he'll be transferred to the "womb", where his LifeCell will be extracted, so that some wealthy Lazurite can live forever. That or it will be delivered to a LifePack for my father's armies. I shudder at the thought of it—choosing who lives and who dies, sorting human life like mail. They see each body as a commodity to be used and sold. I see mothers and fathers, teachers and carpenters, sons and daughters.

I suddenly feel cool yet hot at the same time. Cold from loneliness and despair. Scorching from anger and injustice. How am I here right now? Trapped by my own father. Estranged from my husband. Separated from my son. Forced to watch Asher and my friends once again risk their lives and suffer through another one of Renatus's frivolous Canonizations. Death for the sake of pure entertainment.

I am so deep in thought that I don't realize I am standing right in front of them—the reason I came in here. Silas and Eleazar, side by side, in their respective cylinders. One is waiting to die. The other is about to be resurrected.

But this isn't just a social visit. I want the guards to get used to me coming around. When they—or perhaps I should say, *if* they figure out the anti-protocol serum, I will need to meet up with Darius and then sneak it inside here. I notice the tiny tubes inserted into the cylinders that feed each of them the necessary nutrients to stay alive, or at least not decompose. I can inject the serum into those tubes, and Silas and Eleazar will be *protocol-resistant,* for lack of a better term. If my father can't resurrect his son, there will be no need for him to harvest Silas's LifeCell. Then, it can be given to all Drecks, and once this war is over, the entire country. I hope and pray that he doesn't kill Silas anyway, out of pure rage. But my choices are limited. This is the best way forward—if not for us, for this country.

"Ah, there you are." I jump at the sound of my father's voice.

"Hello, Father."

He circles the cylinders, rubbing his palms on each one. "I, too, come here to visit. It's a shame that my son, your brother, has been floating in this tube for all these years."

"It's a shame my son is in here with him," I spit.

"If your husband delivers what he has promised, then neither of them will be in here much longer."

I whisper, almost to myself, "Then someone else's child will die for our sons." I turn to him. "Will it ever end? Will *you* ever end?"

"No," he answers plainly. "I am destined."

He really believes that he is a deity whose destiny is to rule and live forever. I want to know why my father is like this. "And you want this? To live forever without your wife, without your grandson, without your daughter?"

"That is your choice, not mine."

The child in me has secretly held out hope that one day, I would have my father back. But I am fooling myself. I can see it clearly now. He is too far gone. Has had protocol too many times. I can only hope that the same doesn't happen to Asher. I am not sure I can handle any more loss.

His fingers stroke Eleazar's cylinder. "I come here and talk to him. He can hear me. My son knows I am here. I let him know that he will soon be with his father. And that neither you, nor Asher, nor The Defiance will make a liar out of me." His face reddens. A vein in his neck twitches, as does his left eye. "Not in front of my son!"

I don't respond, and I wonder if he is on the verge of another episode, as I saw on his fishing yacht.

Suddenly, he is composed. "How about we nosh?" he asks like I'm an old friend.

I cannot be in his presence any longer. I lie, "I must be leaving. I have a training session with Hagar."

He twiddles his fingers in the air. "I am afraid you don't."

I stop in my tracks, too afraid to turn around.

He continues, "You see, Hagar is no longer with us."

I grit my teeth. "What did you do, Father?"

"I did what I would do to any other traitor to Zion."

He has killed Hagar, whom he knows has helped me. And he knows we took Boaz. What else does he know?

As I head for the exit, tears for Hagar stream down my cheeks. He has been with me since I was a child. My confidant, my trainer, my protector, my friend. It is my fault he is dead; I asked too much of him.

"And one more thing, daughter. You are no longer allowed to set foot inside this facility."

CHAPTER EIGHT

Asher

Is Boaz really a Trojan Horse? Why would Renatus say anything if it wasn't true? For what purpose? Did he really anticipate this move? Did he let us take Boaz so he could give Adam and Eve incorrect information about our reverse protocol serum? How did he know? Maybe he found out about Hagar and Sarai and what they found in the archives, regarding Boaz receiving Mammon's LifeCell.

Is Sarai in trouble? Or do we have another mole? What makes my head spin is the possibility that Renatus knew it was me at dinner, posing as Amos. But would he really let me go at that point? Let us take Boaz? It might be far-fetched, but he is nothing if not diabolical. Maybe that is why he forced Amos into The Canonization and let Apex kill him—angry that Amos was so easily tricked and predisposed, while I once again posed as his General.

And what of Czar Percival? Will Cephas and Neriah now have to face his army as well?

I finish telling Legion and Kenan about the latest bad news as we race across the sky in our transport drone towards our next trial.

"So the serum will be useless?" Kenan states the obvious.

"Yes."

Legion rubs his vast chin. "Perhaps we can signal them somehow, let them know during this next trial."

I had already considered that. "I am sure they would edit it out before going live."

Legion says, "There is nothing we can do about it now, Asher. It's not ideal, but we can still beat Renatus without it."

I should have listened to my uncle. If Boaz is truly a Trojan Horse, then working on that serum will turn out to be nothing but a massive waste of time and resources. But I can no longer dwell on it. I have to focus.

"So what's the plan now?" Kenan asks.

"First things first, let's just survive this next trial."

Minutes later, our transport drone lands. We exit the drone just as Apex and his team are landing. Between us sit two dozen turbocharged ElectroCycles.

"Seems a race is in order," I state to no one in particular. "Has anyone *not* ridden one of these before?"

Good news, no hands go up.

Renatus approaches with a spring in his step. His head is freshly shaved. A slight breeze flicks the red sashes tied to his arms. Nothing makes him happier than the Canonization. Behind him, Apex and his team meander over. Renatus stands in the center.

"Gentleman, welcome to day two and your second trial. As you have probably already figured out, today, we will be racing."

"Where to?" Kenan asks.

Renatus's lips part, revealing his porcelain, chalky teeth. "Fury Peak." He points to the top of the mountain behind him. "You will start here and wind your way to the top. The first team to return to where we started wins."

I shake my head. "There are no roads going up to Fury Peak."

He corrects me. "There are now."

I think about the amount of money and manpower used to pave and build a road up and down the mountain—all for the Canonization, all for this one day.

"Good luck, gentleman," Renatus says as he heads to the viewing stands near the finish line.

We spend the next thirty minutes putting on full motorcycle armor, not unlike exoarmor. Our helmets are green. The home team wears red so the audience can tell us apart. My stomach rumbles, and my mouth is dry. We need a win here, if just for sustenance alone.

Apex passes us. "Get ready to draw straws again, boys." He then proceeds to chug an entire gallon of water in front of us, pouring the last drops onto the ground.

Legion's fist clenches. I tap his shoulder. "Ignore him and gather around with everyone else." We form a huddle. "This is a race, yes. But let's not be concerned with speed. If one of us crashes and they don't, that's probably it. We lose. Just focus on making it to the finish line."

I watch Apex put on his oversized helmet and sit on his ElectroCycle. He is so big that it looks like he is on a kid's dirt bike. For once, his size and strength might be to his detriment. Surely, like Legion, his weight will slow him down. But he is heavier than Legion. Finally an advantage assuming they are playing fair and all the bikes are the same. I pull my ElectroCycle to the starting line. There are eighteen of us left—nine on each team.

I turn to my team. "Remember, nice and easy. You don't have to be the first to finish; just don't be the last."

Half a minute later, the light turns red to green, and we are off. The barely audible whine of the electric engines is amplified, as all eighteen red-line it from the get-go. It doesn't take us long to reach the base of Fury Peak. I check my mirror. Just as I suspected. Apex is dead last. Legion is just barely ahead of him. I lean to the right as I take the sharp turn that leads to the narrow road heading up the mountain.

I am third, with two red helmets ahead of me. I am not concerned, as long as one of us doesn't finish last. I lean in, sharp turn after sharp turn. If the context were different, I might say I was enjoying myself. Then, out of nowhere, an explosion in front of me. I turn and narrowly avoid the crater in front of me. What was that? We weren't allowed any weapons on this trial. Then I see it above me. A HeliDrone indiscriminately drops bombs on our freshly paved race track. Of course, I should have seen that coming.

As I turn another corner, we are almost to the top. Ahead of me, another bomb drops. A green helmet swerves to avoid it; in the process, he crashes into a red helmet. They both go tumbling down the mountain to certain death. Was it Kenan? Was it Tobias?

I can't dwell on it. I need to concentrate on what is right in front of me. As I hit the top of Fury Peak, I peer down and see that Apex is still last. Legion is about fifty feet in front of him.

As I start my descent, a red helmet accelerates from behind me. We are now side by side on the narrow, windy road. Before I can let him pass, he swerves into me. I veer to my left, and to avoid a collision, my bike careens up the side of the mountain. I am able to quickly regain control and put my cycle back on the pavement.

I am halfway down the mountain now, and my palms sweat inside my gloves. I have a death grip on my bike. Another explosion, this time behind me. In my mirror, I see one of ours fly through the air before plunging down the mountain. Renatus better back off with those drones if he wants any of us left for the next trial.

Finally, off the mountain, I gun it for the final straightaway. Four have already made it to the finish line—two of them, two of ours. I dodge two more explosions. The drones have not let up. I look back; Apex is still last, and Legion is second to last. *Just finish this final stretch, and we will be home free.*

But being a Dreck has taught me never to celebrate too early. Two more bombs drop behind me. Legion can't maneuver in time; he hits one of the craters and is tossed from his ElectroCycle. Moments later, Apex passes him.

We are going to lose. We can't afford to lose two in a row. We need water and food.

I slow down and let everyone else pass me; it doesn't matter if Legion finishes last. It only takes a few moments for Legion to hop back on his bike and return to the race. But it is too late. He will not catch Apex, who is now only a hundred yards behind me. The finish line is about seventy yards in front of me.

I sigh.

It's time to do something very Asher-like.

I hope Sarai isn't watching.

Just as Apex is about to pass me, I kick my back tire out, crashing into his front. We are both thrown off our bikes. Sparks fly from our helmets and body suits as we slide about twenty yards towards the finish. Our bikes are a tangled, smoky mess behind us.

I pop up. Nothing feels broken. My head hurts, but no concussion. Legion flies by us. It's just Apex and me now. We stare at one another for a quick second, and both realize it will be faster to run to the finish line than to go back for our bikes—assuming they are even rideable at this point. It's now a foot race.

It's a good thing I have a ten-yard head start. I sprint with everything I have. To lose some dead weight, I simultaneously fling off my helmet. Apex does the same, except he throws his at me. I have to jump out of the way, which slows me down for just a second. With every stride of his massive, long legs, he catches up to me. Ten yards away. Then five. We are neck and neck. At the last moment, I dive for the finish line, sliding across it, glad I still don my body armor. I look up at the line judge.

No call.

He consults a small tablet with a video screen. He then calls over another judge. They both examine the footage. I see one of them exchange glances with Renatus. Are we going to get robbed of a win here? The crowd is hushed in anticipation.

"It's Asher and the green team."

I exhale in relief. Finally, some food. Water. And most importantly, we won't have to draw straws.

Apparently, neither will the red team. In a manic fit of rage, Apex punches one of his team members in the head, crushing his skull. He falls limp to the ground.

The Lazurite was still wearing his helmet.

Adam

"Are you sure it's a molecule inhibitor?" Adam asks.

Boaz sits on his spinning chair and twirls like a third grader. "Yes. The memory hit me like a ton of bricks at 3 AM last night. Not that I was sleeping in those awful things you call a mattress."

Eve peers through the microscope. "It looks like it's working."

Boaz folds his arms triumphantly. "Of course, it's working! That is how protocol works."

Adam smiles. "So we have done it. We have created a reverse protocol serum."

Boaz spits, "And I still don't know why you would give up a chance at a second life?"

They ignore him. Eve turns to Adam. "Problem is, we can't test it."

"At least not until someone dies," Adam responds. "Until then, we'll just have to trust Boaz." They still have the LifeCell that Lucas stole.

"I trust a bear not eating me while being slathered in honey more than I trust Boaz."

Adam speaks as if Boaz is not in the room. "You think he's lying?"

Eve contemplates, "I didn't say that. I think he helped us out of fear for his life, not because of his scruples or trustworthiness."

Adam adds, "And let's not forget the gold."

Boaz stands. "I'll pretend not to be offended." He heads towards the door.

"Where are you going?" Eve asks.

"It's time for my nap. You got your serum. What else do you need me for?"

Adam waves him off.

"A nap doesn't sound like a bad idea. Be back in a couple of hours, and I'll help you produce more," Eve says, referring to the serum.

"Great. The sooner we can hand it off to Darius, the sooner he can get it to Sarai." Before she leaves, he says, "Eve, we did it. We actually did it."

"I knew you could."

"We. We did it."

She smiles. "Maybe, but let's be honest, I mostly scared the information out of a Boaz. You did all the hard work." Before she exits, she grabs her book from the corner table.

"Nap or reading?" Adam smiles.

"I can multi-task."

Adam points to her book. "Try finishing it for once. You might be surprised."

After she slips out, Adam immediately gets to work. This is the moment he's been waiting for. He grabs a small round table from the back room and unfolds the legs. He spreads a ratty blue towel over it as a makeshift tablecloth. Next, he places two candles and some wildflowers he picked earlier on the table. This romance thing isn't his forte. People, in general, aren't his forte. Not that he dislikes them. He just isn't good in social situations. Now, throw romance into the mix, and he is really out of his depth. But she is his wife. This is what she wants. At least, this is what he thinks she wants. He isn't sure, really; it is an educated guess, from a scientist's point of view. He has read about it; he has seen others do it. He believes he has gathered the required amount of data. Besides, knowing her, she will surely let him know if he is doing it wrong. He even procures a bottle of red wine, which cost him a pretty penny. He places the wine on the table with two plastic cups; unfortunately, there are no wine glasses.

Two hours later, Eve returns. Before she can open the door, Adam turns off the lights.

"What is going on? Why—"

"Just hush for a moment," Adam replies, flustered already.

"Hush? What? Who are you telling to—"

"Sorry, I didn't mean to… just one second."

Adam quickly lights the candles. His sideways smile lights up in the dark. Eve can see the table set with the flowers and wine.

"What is this?"

"It's for us. I thought perhaps a romantic dinner? I mean, if you don't like it, we can—"

Eve interrupts him, smiling at his nervousness. "No, no, it's great."

Adam pulls out the chair for Eve to sit in. He uncorks the wine. "Can I pour you a glass?"

"I don't drink."

"Really?"

"I'm your wife. Don't you think you would know that?"

Adam stammers. "I'm sorry, I—"

She slugs him in the arm. "I'm kidding, Adam!"

"Oh, right." Adam pauses for a moment, holding the wine bottle and feeling like a buffoon. "Kidding about not drinking, or kidding about that I should know that you don't drink?"

"Just pour the wine, Adam."

"Right, of course." He pours them both a cup.

"Cheers," she says, taking a sip.

"Cheers," he replies.

"That's not bad. Where did you find this? Do the narcdrops now include fine wine?"

"Boaz knew a black market guy."

"So, Boaz paid off twice in one day."

A knock on the door, and the Compound Chef enters with a food tray.

Adam stands. "Perfect timing."

The chef places two hot plates in front of them. "Leg of lamb with garlic and rosemary. A side of whipped potatoes and lemon asparagus. Enjoy."

"Thanks again, Elliot."

Elliot winks and leaves the room.

Eve is in awe. "How... how did you pull this off?"

"Bribed the chef."

Eve looks over her plate. "This is, this great, but... but I don't eat meat."

Adam is instantly disappointed. "Oh, oh, I am sorry. Um, you can have my veggies."

She slaps him again. "I'm kidding."

"Oh yes, right."

She sips the wine and jokes, "If this is going to work, you'll need a sense of humor."

"Any dead comedians who don't need their LifeCell?"

Eve smiles. "That's not bad."

They eat slowly, savoring the rare meal before them. After a few minutes of silence, Eve speaks. "So, I know we have done this entire thing backward; married first, then dating. It's about time we knew each other's real names."

Adam shrugs it off. "I'm just fine with Adam."

"Oh, c'mon, what's your real name? I'm Naomi."

"We're not supposed to, remember? It's classified."

"I think things have changed in the past hundred and twenty years. Doubt we will get in trouble. C'mon, I told you mine."

Adam shakes his head and returns to his lamb.

"Seriously? C'mon. I think I should know my husband's name."

Adam doesn't reply, but a tiny simper of embarrassment escapes his lips.

Eve catches on. "You don't like your name, do you? Is it embarrassing?"

"Let's just enjoy our dinner, shall we?"

Eve snatches the bottle of wine. "No more for you until you tell me. C'mon, it can't be that bad."

Adam covers his mouth and coughs, "Genesis."

"What was that? Sounded like you said, Genesis."

"I did."

She smirks. "Biblical Genesis? Or were your parents big Phil Collins fans?"

"Funny. Go on and make fun. I have heard them all: 'In the beginning, there was me.' Or, 'After God created me on the seventh day, He realized He needed a rest.'"

Eve takes another sip of wine. "Seems Adam isn't too far off. Shall we keep it at that?"

"Thank you." She stares at him. "What?"

"I have never seen you this chipper. In fact, I don't ever remember seeing you smile."

Adam is still giddy. "Even though I believed what we were doing at Eden, it's hard to feel useful being a Popsicle. What we accomplished today might change the fate of the world."

"If it works, it will."

Eden was all about reacting to a horrible or cataclysmic event. But what Adam and Eve accomplished today was a proactive step in preventing further death. He thought being encapsulated in a frozen tomb at Eden was his calling. Today, he found his true calling. What good was all that scientific knowledge if he could never use it?

They share a smile, truly enjoying the moment. She leans in, expecting a kiss. Adam bites his lip, his mouth suddenly dry. He settles his nerves and leans towards her. But the moment is short-lived.

A Dreck bursts through the door. "It's Boaz. He is dead."

They both jump up in unison. Adam is the first to speak. "What? How?"

"He tried to escape. He murdered one of the guards. A firefight ensued. He was shot dead."

Cephas

Cephas sits in the uncomfortable wooden chair. Like him, it creaks every time he moves. He is on his third cup of stale coffee. Maps and other papers are strewn about on makeshift tables. A sharp breeze sneaks through the slits of his canvas tent—one of many his army has set up in this beautiful valley. One of his Runners bursts through the flaps. "Sir."

"How about knocking first?" Cephas grunts.

"My apologies, sir. I have news about The Canonization."

Earlier, Cephas sent runners to different Internet Cafes that were still operable, but not yet hit with EMPs. He wanted word on Asher's progress.

The Runner, about nineteen, stands there. "Let's hear it."

"Good news. Asher has survived the first two trials."

"And what of Legion and Kenan?" Cephas knows that for Asher to defeat Apex, he will need Legion by his side.

"They, too, are still alive."

Cephas is relieved. "That will be all, soldier."

As he leaves, Neriah strolls in, holding a rolled-up map.

"I guess no one knocks these days."

"Get a door and a real office, and perhaps I will," Neriah replies playfully.

"Coffee?"

"You call that coffee? No thanks. I have news."

"So do I. They have survived the first two trials. And you?"

"Both the nuke and serum are ready," Neriah informs Cephas.

Although he is pleased, Cephas stifles his smile. "Then we are ready for war."

Later, they leave the tent. Cephas ambles the ridge line with Neriah, and examines his army below them. "Question is, how do we get past The Wall?"

"EMP," Neriah says plainly, but Cephas can tell she has a look about her that she knows something he doesn't.

"EMP? The Wall's electrical circuits are hardened. An EMP won't work. We have tried it in the past."

"Not sections 390 through 401. They were damaged in the nuclear blasts. My scouts tell me in Renatus's haste to repair it, the electrical system has not been hardened."

"And you have an EMP?" Cephas inquires.

"Two of them," she smiles. "Just one problem."

"Of course there is."

"Half of Renatus's army is camped out near those sections. Their surveillance drones must have seen our preparations here, and they are preparing for our attack."

"There is no way we could make it through there," Cephas sighs.

Neriah taps her chin. "Unless we use our main army as a decoy, a distraction. Send them through section 390. Then we can take a small contingent, including the nuke and serum, and sneak through 401."

Cephas grunts, "My soldiers aren't expendable; that is a lot of men and women to sacrifice for a distraction."

"We will have them immediately surrender once they are on the other side."

Cephas isn't so sure. "What guarantee do we have that Renatus's army won't just annihilate them right there on the spot?"

"No guarantee, but Renatus will see them as future LifeCells for his army. I should say it's quite the catch for him."

"And we just let him do that?"

Neriah unfurls a map and points to a section. "Here, the crescent mountain range. The only way through is this valley here. A lot of natural rock slides this time of year. If we can beat them there, we can trigger one of our own."

"And kill our army along with theirs?" Cephas says with a healthy dose of skepticism.

"If they follow standard prisoner transfer procedures, our army will be in the middle. We make sure we hit the front and back."

Cephas stares at her. After disliking her for what she did to Sarai and the election, he is beginning to admire her. Her strength, her willingness to do the right thing—Lord knows he has been there. "Have you ever led men in battle before?"

"No."

Cephas raises a bushy eyebrow. "Yet you are well-versed in battle tactics and strategy."

"I am well-read."

"And you are strong and confident, like a seasoned General."

"You forget I have lost a child. My strength has been forged in fire."

Cephas gives her a slight nod. "Yes, yes, it has." He sees her point. No amount of training or classroom lectures can equal the kind of hardening and fortitude that are gained through real-life tribulations.

"So, is it a plan? You are the real General. It's your call."

"It's risky," Cephas ponders. The older he gets, the more risk-averse he has become—not very Dreckish.

"It's war. Besides, the most important thing is getting the Serum to Sarai and the nuke into Zion West."

Cephas begins to wonder if he has the stomach for this anymore. Is it his age? Is it because he has seen so much death and has suffered so much heartbreak? He, too, has been forged in the fire. So much so that his spirit has been permanently burned, but his soul is still intact. He turns to her, a battle raging inside him—between wanting to finally rest and finding the will to fight. "I once thought this way, and I'm unsure if it is right or wrong."

"Which way is that?"

"Win at all costs."

"Do we have any other choice?"

Asher

There are seven of us left on each team. And after almost two days of no sustenance, we are finally adequately hydrated and have a stomach full of food. It's dark, except for our headlamps and the occasional light on the ceiling. We have ventured through our fifth tunnel. Is it the same tunnel? They all look the same.

The third trial in Renatus's new Canonization consists of an underground maze with five levels. Each level, or story, has three levers we must pull that will open a doorway into a stairwell leading up to the next level. We have thirty minutes to find all three. If not, explosives go off in the ceiling and walls, effectively burying us alive with dirt and earth. We have found two already.

But we only have five minutes left.

What makes it particularly difficult is not only the absence of adequate light but also the setup of the doors and tunnels themselves. They seem to spin and rotate every few minutes. The lights flicker on and off. Not to mention the walls are lined with mirrors, further adding to our confusion. Who comes up with this?

"Go down that one," I tell Kenan.

"Haven't we checked there already?" Legion asks.

Flustered, I raise my voice. "I don't know, check again, then. I'll go this way."

We continue to split up, checking the dozens of hallways and rooms for the last lever. I enter another hallway and can't help but wonder what is happening on the outside. It's torture not knowing if Sarai is alright. Has Boaz fooled Adam and Eve into thinking they have a working serum? Is the nuke fully operational? Will Cephas and Neriah be able to even find their way through The Wall? Were they able to recruit any more soldiers? I can't help but think that even if we pull off The Canonization and defeat Apex, we will still lose. Lose the war. Lose my son. When things are going well, faith is easy. Keeping that faith during arduous times is the true test.

I hear a woman's voice over the intercom system. "Sixty seconds." It is casual, like she is announcing the arrival of a train, as opposed to uttering the countdown to our demise.

I search with more urgency. Open more doors. Still nothing. If Renatus's objective was to exhaust us mentally and physically, he has succeeded.

Then I hear Legion yell, "Found it!"

I sprint back towards the center of the floor.

"Thirty seconds," the woman announces. I swear I hear a tinge of amusement in her crisp, feminine voice, like she is rooting for our deaths.

I reach the center of the level. The red door, which is the door to the stairwell, unlocks and swings open. The seven of us file in and trot up the stairs before the level below is bombed and buried.

I don't know if we were lucky or if it was by design, but level two was much easier. In fact we found all three levers and make it out with more than ten minutes to spare. Level three is a different story, though. Eleven minutes left, and two levers still to go.

"Why is this one so difficult?" Kenan pants, practically wheezing from the damp, stale air.

"I think level two was to give us false confidence," I yell back from a different tunnel.

More mind games, compliments of Renatus. The lights flicker. The tunnels that extend from the center of the room rotate like a clock. Doors and rooms are also rotating. I am starting to see double from all the mirrors. I suffer a quick bout of vertigo, and it takes me a minute to regain my balance, to properly figure out where I am. It's enough to drive one mad. I check every door in this hallway. At least I think I have checked every door. The flickering lights and the mirrors are assaulting my senses. I return to the center to try another tunnel. Five minutes left.

Tobias approaches, out of breath. "Got one. One left."

To find them all within the thirty minutes, we must sprint everywhere we go. I suck in deep mouthfuls of musty oxygen as I scamper down another tunnel. It is hot and damp this far underground. I am drenched in sweat. I check door after door and wonder what kind of sadistic and distorted person enjoys watching another human being go through this.

"Sixty seconds," her biting voice returns.

I check another door. Nothing. And another, still nothing.

"Thirty seconds," she taunts me.

I open the final door on the left. There is the lever. I pull it.

"Ten seconds."

I race back towards the center.

"Five seconds."

As I arrive, everyone except for Legion has gone through the door. He is waiting for me. "Let's go, Ash!"

"Zero." Her voice borders on elation.

I dart towards the door as explosions go off above and around us.

"Get in!" Legion growls.

As I approach the door, a massive wooden beam above the door falls towards us. Legion grabs it just before it crushes me.

"Go," he murmurs, using all his strength to hold up the beam, as dirt and debris rain down around us.

I dive in and watch Legion drop the beam and fall backwards through the door. We shut it just as the entire floor is buried.

I take a deep breath, "Thank you."

"Well, if I thought you could have held up that beam, I would have let you," Legion barks back. He has saved me again, an angel on my shoulder. We make our way up to level four.

"This is maddening!" Tobias yells. "How are you all so calm?"

"Not our first Canonization," I reply, referring to Legion and me.

"Speak for yourself. I hate being underground. I'm claustrophobic," Legion banters back, wiping dirt from his shoulders. He turns to me. "I blame you."

"Me?" I feign innocence.

"It seems like yesterday when I was happy in my cabin, sipping tea with Buttons curling up on my lap."

"You telling me you don't enjoy almost falling off mountains or being buried alive? What about the motorcycle ride? That was fun, wasn't it?"

Tobias whispers to me, "Buttons?"

"It's the Legion only I know."

"Shut it," Legion snarls.

We open the door to the fourth floor. We don't need to speak or game plan after surviving the first three. We split up and search different tunnels. I don't know if it is luck or by design, but once again, we finish the level with ten minutes to spare—something Renatus surely wouldn't be happy with. I doubt that is entertainment enough for him and his crowd of blood-craving Lazurites. Where was the tension and anticipation? The last thing Renatus's New Canonization will be is boring; if they're bored, they are harder to distract, harder to control. Surely on the fifth and final level, he won't make the same mistake.

We open the door to the fifth floor.

"Last one," Kenan calls out, wiping sweat from his face. I have never been so hot. I wonder how far Apex and his team have gotten. I really don't want to have to draw straws again. But at this rate, I'll be happy if we make it out of this challenge alive. If we aren't buried alive, the heat alone might kill us. Legion is practically leaving puddles as he rains sweat.

Ten minutes in, Tobias yells, "That's one!"

Two more to go. I hear the grinding of the gears as the middle of the room spins. The tunnels fan out from the middle room like spokes on a bicycle tire. I try to make a mental note of what tunnels I have already been down. The array of mirrors doesn't help matters. Legion is about to sprint down a tunnel to my left.

"Wait, I have been down that one already."

"Are you sure?" Legion asks.

Yet, I am not. "I think so. Pretty sure."

Legion chooses another one. I take the one to the left of his. Five doors later, I find the second lever. We're twenty minutes in. At this pace, we will just make it. I race through another tunnel and check so many doors that I have lost count. I am completely gassed. The salty sweat streams from my forehead, dripping past my lips. I can taste the murky brine.

Five minutes left.

Two minutes left.

"Thirty seconds," our female friend announces over the intercom.

The seven of us converge at the center of the room. Hands on our knees, panting. The room spins again.

"We have checked them all," I state.

Kenan peers around, doing a circle. He studies the tunnels, the entrances. On the surface, they all look the same. This is by design. But on closer inspection, you can see the differences in the grain of the rock, in the chipped surfaces from the massive drills that burrowed them. There's a slight variation in the color.

"Fifteen seconds," she announces coldly.

"It's this one." Kenan points to his right.

"You won't make it back in time," I tell him.

But he doesn't hesitate. As he sprints into the dimly lit abyss, he yells back at me, "Tell my father that I am no coward!"

And then he disappears.

"Ten seconds."

"Five seconds."

The red door leading to the exit swings open. He has found it.

"One second."

I stare down the dark tunnel, expecting him to come running back.

He doesn't.

I freeze for a moment as the explosions start. The walls shake. Dirt and debris drizzle to the ground. I don't hear Legion yell my name. Before the entire floor is buried, Legion yanks me to safety inside the door.

Kenan has saved us.

As we exit the underground tunnels and into the blinding daylight, we see that Apex and his team have not made it out in time. We sprint to our button and press it.

We have won, yet we have lost.

I am flooded with memories of when I first met Kenan. He was so young, just barely an adult. I remember his timid stutter. His humility was the antithesis of being a Lazurite. He was a fish out of water. Watching him grow into the confident, bold man he had become was a great pleasure for me. And his final act of sacrifice has proved to the world who he really was. I hope his father sees it for what it was. Perhaps one day, when this war is over and people recognize the wrongs committed here, Kenan will be celebrated as a hero. He was always loyal. Always a friend. But it is my fault. The final lever was down the tunnel I told Legion not to go down. Kenan's death is on me.

How many more need to die so I can live?

And with so many different lives and personalities inside of me, who are they trying to save?

Cephas

Cephas, Neriah, and Darius lead a contingent of five hundred soldiers to sector 401 of The Wall. The rest of their army, comprising almost 5,000 soldiers, is staged at sector 390.

"Once they set up their EMP and their section goes down, they will contact us," Neriah reminds them.

"What if theirs works and ours doesn't?" Cephas grumbles, referring to the EMP.

"You always this negative?"

"Just being real, when you've been a Dreck as long as I have, these things happen."

Neriah pats him on the shoulder. "It will work. It's time for our luck to turn."

"You a Dreck now?" Cephas bites his bottom lip.

"You tell me."

"Jury is still out."

Darius approaches. "EMP is ready."

Cephas gripes, "I still don't like it. What if they don't honor the surrender? We are sending them to their doom."

"If we don't do this, then we are all dead, including Asher and his friends." Neriah feigns a large smile. "C'mon, Cephas, have faith."

"I do have faith." Cephas's faith has been in short supply lately. And if he's being honest with himself, he realizes he has been negative lately, grumpier than usual. Maybe it's the stress or that he is getting older, and the constant aches and pains are getting to him. A cold gust of wind forces him to turn his bristled cheeks. He never used to get this cold—another item he chalks up to age.

Like an eagle on fire, a large red flare streaks through the air above them.

"That's the signal. Darius, you're up."

Darius activates the EMP. "Here goes nothing."

A loud pinging noise. Then, the blue electrical current that comprises The Wall flickers momentarily before returning to life.

Cephas frowns at Neriah. "Now you're a Dreck."

Another sizzle and a loud cracking noise. Sector 401 of The Wall powers down.

Neriah clears her throat. "Faith."

"No time to waste," Cephas barks.

They lead their troops through the open portion of The Wall. Just to the south of them, on the other side of a ridge, their main army should be in the middle of a surrender right now. Cephas prays that this is what is happening and that they are not being annihilated. They march at a quick pace. They have to beat the Lazurite army to the crescent mountain range, or their plan is for naught.

"Drones!" Darius warns.

In the far distance, two HeliDrones hover towards them.

"If we're spotted, it's finished." Cephas's tone is dire.

Neriah motions to their right. "That way, to the trees."

Their brisk march turns into a sprint.

"Hurry now!" Cephas barks, even though he is falling behind. *Maybe I shouldn't have come. I am only slowing them down.* But his moment of self-doubt inspires him to run even faster, harder.

The drones draw closer. They are now a hundred yards from the forest's cover. If they are spotted, not only will their ruse be up, but there is a chance their surrendered army will be terminated because of it.

"It's gonna be close," Neriah spits.

Just before the drones arrive, they have reached the safety of the trees. Cephas is one of the last. His knees hurt, his ankles ache, and his back is sore. He heaves for oxygen.

"You okay?" Neriah whispers.

Cephas has yet to find the requisite amount of air to answer.

Hiding under the large canopy of the forest, they sit and wait, careful not to move or speak as the drones hover above them. A tense moment as they linger.

"You think they saw us?" Cephas whispers back.

"They're still searching."

"If we're here much longer, we're not gonna make it to the Crescent mountains in time."

Neriah places her hand on Cephas's back. "You look like you could use a few minutes."

"Just wait until you're old."

Darius places his finger to his lips, signaling them to keep it down. A waterfall of sweat streams from Cephas's forehead. He finally catches his breath, but doesn't realize he is holding it as the drones fly just above them.

"Can we shoot them down?" Cephas asks Darius.

"Maybe. We would have to hit both at the same time. Otherwise, the other one will transmit our location."

"We might not have a choice."

But it's a moot point. The drones hurry off like unsuccessful hunters at the end of the day.

"Time to move," Neriah tells them.

Muscles click and bones creak as Cephas pulls himself to his feet. Even though it's cold, his shirt is drenched with sweat.

"You sure you're okay?" Neriah asks, this time with more concern.

"I'm not staying behind if that's what you mean. Let's move."

Four hours later, they arrived at the Crescent Mountain range. The wind still batters them, but at least it keeps them cool during their march. Cephas plops on a rock and gulps down a jug of crisp water. He peers down at the valley below them, where they expect the Lazurite army to march through, holding his army hostage. "We have beaten them here."

Neriah sits next to him. "Darius has placed bombs on top of the ridges on both sides."

"Then we wait."

"Perhaps you should say something to the troops?" Neriah suggests.

With Jude gone, Cephas thought he wouldn't have to anymore; it was always Jude's idea. This wasn't his strong suit. "I don't think they want to hear from me."

"That is where you're wrong, Cephas." Her tone turns cheeky. "And seeing someone your age still portray strength and vigor just might encourage them to do the same."

"Funny. If I must, I suppose."

After a quick bite of OatBars and dried venison, his army has gathered around. Cephas finds a stump to stand on.

He clears his throat. He doesn't have the fervor of his last speech; his tone is almost melancholy but not defeatist. "Look, many of you have been with me since the beginning. Many of you have not. Some here are Drecks. Some are converted Lazurites. Some of you neither, but have realized what we are fighting for. But that doesn't matter anymore. We are all Americans. We are all fighting for the same cause. We have been dubbed The Defiance. I did not come up with that name. It is how our enemy branded us. Personally, I have never liked it. It is they who defied our freedoms. Defied our lives.

Defied a country that was once free." Cephas takes a breath, cracks his neck, grits his teeth, and zeal begins to sneak into his voice. "But it will be us who takes it all back. Not everyone here will come home from this. But if we don't fight, there will be no home to return to! Soon, there will be no more Defiance. No more Dreck or Lazurite. No more Zion or MiddleLand. No more protocol. No more death games. No more Wall. That is what they wanted. That is how the corrupt come to power, by division." He spits. "Let me tell you something; what was once divided will be united again."

A soldier from the crowd yells out, "You guaranteeing victory?"

"Look, I'm too old to guarantee anything. I can't guarantee my knees will hold out for this battle." A few chuckles. "I have lived a long time. I have seen a lot of things. At sixty-seven, I am old enough to know there are no guarantees. Not on this side of heaven, anyway. I can see how many of you look at me. You see an old man, too old to fight, too old to lead. Perhaps you are right. But neither age nor anything else will stop me from doing what is right. Sometimes, I feel like retiring to the rocking chair. Perhaps tending a garden like my wife used to. War is a young man's game. But I refuse to be quiet as I enter the twilight of my life. I will finish strong. When I leave this world, people will know that I was here. You want guarantees? What I can guarantee is that down in that valley, we will give 'em hell. We will fight like our children's lives depend on it. Why? BECAUSE THEY DO!"

Raucous cheers erupt from the five hundred. Cephas waves at the air, trying to settle them down. "We are outnumbered, but that is nothing new. It's going to come down to who wants it more. You may not realize this, but you're more powerful than they are. They have underestimated us. To them, this battle is a mere formality. They expect to win. We expect not to lose. There is a difference. They fight to retain power and wealth. We fight for freedom, for our very lives. But make no mistake, we will bleed for every inch. We will be dying for each one of those inches. But when it is all said and done, we will be the ones standing!"

Another round of cheers erupts as Cephas steps down from his stump and marches through the troops, shaking hands and patting shoulders. A scout approaches him, out of breath.

"Sir, they are here."

Asher

Our winged flying suits are red and black. The jetpacks strapped to our backs are lighter than I would have imagined. We stand atop a mountain as the sun is on its way down. What I can only describe as joysticks are strapped to each of our hands. With them, we can control our flight and the plasma guns attached to our wings. Renatus also let us wear parachutes in case we are shot down. Perhaps he is afraid to lose any more men before the final showdown.

To my left, Legion is struggling with his jetpack.

"Here, let me," I tell him while trying to connect the straps that keep his jetpack attached. It's a bit too tight. "Suck it in a little." He pulls in his stomach, and I am able to successfully attach the straps around his chest and waist. "Need to lay off the pancakes," I joke. But he is in no mood. There are six of us left on each team, and this is the second to the last trial.

Then, from behind us, like a giant eagle, Renatus lands, wearing the same winged suit. Not surprisingly, he doesn't have a parachute. Why would he need one?

"Good evening, aviators," Renatus states with a smile as he strolls by both teams. "Anyone afraid of flying?" No one takes the bait. He clears his throat and points to a mountain range about twenty miles away. "There. Directly north. That is the endpoint. That is where you will find your button. Just as before, get your team there first."

"And if we are shot down or crash?" I ask.

"That is the same as a kill, but this time, you have your parachute."

"So kind of you," Legion spits sardonically.

Renatus waves his hands in the air as he often does. "Well, I figured you made it this far; might as well let you make it to the end. This trial is more fun than anything else. A little bit of a breather before the final trial."

Fun. Right. The loser is still harvested, and a parachute doesn't mean we won't get shot or killed.

"Oh, and watch out for the drones," Renatus adds.

Wonderful.

Apex and his crew are to our left. He smiles at Legion. "Don't crash, brother."

Legion doesn't look at him. I notice tremors in his left hand. "You all right?"

"You know how I said I was claustrophobic? I hate flying even worse."

I pat him on his shoulder. "Just don't look down."

"What's the plan?" Tobias asks.

"If we fly ahead of them, they have a better chance at shooting us down. If we get too far behind, we will lose."

He holds up his hands and looks at me as if to say: *What kind of answer is that?*

I am tired and frustrated. We all are. "What do you want me to say? I have never flown in a death race before wearing a jetpack and a winged suit. Best I can say is split up and try not to get shot." Not the most inspirational thing I ever said, but what can I say? I'm drained.

To my left, I spot one of those annoying reporters covering The Canonization. His tall hat is purple, and his suit is bright yellow. I have avoided him thus far.

He approaches and shoves a microphone in my face. "Asher, is there anything you want to say to your fans out there?"

I want to look into the camera and tell everyone to go home. "*Turn off your HoloTube. Go to a park, play with your kids.*" But instead, I play along. "I have fans?"

"Well, you are the defending champ."

I wonder how I can secretly warn Sarai about Boaz and the serum. But I have nothing. Besides, Renatus would catch on and edit it out. "What are my odds of winning?"

"Ten to one."

I smile. "Ten to one? No respect for the reigning champion?"

"You think you're going to win? Defeat Apex?"

I stare deep into the camera. Serious. "Freedom will win."

Renatus makes a slicing motion at his throat, telling the reporter to end it. The reporter turns back to the camera. "And there you have it, folks. Asher, The Traitor of Zion, is confident he can repeat."

After the reporter finishes a bit with Apex, Renatus stands before us. "Ready?" We slide on our goggles and fire up our packs. We were able to practice with the packs and suits this morning for a couple of hours, but it wasn't enough. It's like asking a pilot to fly a 747 after only training in a flight simulator.

"Go!" Renatus yells.

I press a button on the controls in my left hand and am rocketed into the air. Tobias whizzes by me, and Legion almost slams into me. Touchy and finicky, these suits are. I am finally able to straighten out, and head north towards our destination. Renatus flies above us, watching the action just the way he likes to, from a God's eye view. A plasma blast flies right by me, coming from a Lazurite flying behind me. I spread my wings and slow down; he flies right past me. I press the buttons on the controller in my right hand, and plasma shoots from my wings, missing him by a mile. Again, this isn't easy. I try to reposition to get right behind him and try again. Before I do, a hole is burned into his left wing. He spirals to the ground before deploying his parachute. Behind me is Legion.

"Good shot."

"I can't breathe in this thing," he mutters.

Then one of ours is hit, Apex behind him. He floats to the ground. There's a blast from above. "Legion, look out!"

A drone fires from above us. Legion dodges. I am surprised how nimble he is for his size; he has obviously acclimated to the controls quicker than I have. Apex takes out another. Legion pulls in front of him, slows his speed, and slams his foot into Apex's chest. He loses control momentarily, falling towards the hills below, but then regains control—speeding toward us.

We are about halfway there now. I fly back and forth, dodging the shots from two Lazurites behind me. One of my wings is grazed, but my flight is still steady. I dive. They dive. I can't shake them. Legion and Tobias are dealing with their own problems at the moment. I peer up. Another HeliDrone emerges, taking shots at Tobias, but it is right above me. I fire two plasma shots directly into its belly. The hit is good, and it loses control. By the time the Lazurites behind me see it, it is too late. It crashes into both of them. I peer to my left just in time to see Apex take out Tobias. Legion is flying hard and fast towards our destination. Apex is catching up.

Getting comfortable being a bird, I jet high above both of them. There, I almost run into Renatus, who is enjoying the show. He flies gracefully beside me. I am tempted to shoot him down, but what good would that do? The exhilaration of soaring through the sky has cleared my head. The adrenaline has snuffed out my headache. It is a rare moment when I can block out the chaos in my head, and an uncommon occasion when I do not worry about Sarai and Silas. At this speed, so high in the air, close to the sun with crisp wind on my face, I am forced to concentrate on what is directly in front of me, to be in the moment.

But as always, my thoughts drift towards Sarai. As I close my eyes, I can see her. Wind in her hair. She is shotgun in my five-hundred-horsepower convertible pony as I navigate the mountain roads high above the ocean. I see her. Smiling. Laughing. I see her. Faded Van Halen Tee. Her singing voice is terrible, but that doesn't stop her from howling along as we blast Bon Jovi on the radio. We wind our way down and finally park near the beach. I see her. Small toes nestled in the sand. No longer afraid, she dives into the ocean, the waves pushing her back to the shore. I see her. No scourge. Just a smile and a heart full of love. This is what could have been. What might be.

I open my eyes. I am so high in the sky that everything below me seems like far-removed, earthbound problems. Small. Even Renatus seems benign as he lithely glides above me.

But this is not the world I live in. It is not reality. I am in chaos. We are at war. Renatus is anything but benign. Sarai is not free.

It's time to re-engage. I fire up my thrusters and begin to dive at Apex. But he knows I'm coming. He flips onto his back, facing up at me, and fires three shots. Two of them hit my right wing. I flutter for a moment before going into a tailspin. Halfway to the ground, my parachute deploys. I am helpless as I sail to the ground, watching Apex and Legion bump one another on their way to the finish. Renatus races after them.

I hit the ground and roll in an attempt to save my knees. I remove my parachute and wings. I can barely see Legion and Apex land on the mountain, where the finish line is. Who will press the button first?

CHAPTER NINE

Eve

"I DON'T LIKE STAYING behind," Eve grumbles, reading a new book.

"We're following orders," Adam responds. "You think being military, you would be a bit better at it."

Against their wishes, Cephas had ordered them and the hundred from Eden to stay behind. If they lost the war, they would be the last surviving remnant of The Defiance. And much like their original commission at Eden, they were to be the ones to start over, build another Defiance, and live on to fight again. Besides, many were scientists, engineers, teachers, and artists without military training.

"I just feel so useless." Eve sets the book down and paces the cold floor of the sterile research room in Cephas's underground compound.

"Useless? We just created a reverse-protocol serum and managed to make a century-old nuclear weapon operable."

"Which will be useless if they can't defeat Renatus's army."

"Orders are orders."

"So we just sit here?"

"For someone who had no problem signing up to be a catatonic Popsicle, you're sure restless."

"That's different."

"Cephas did say we might have to rebuild The Defiance. I thought we could get a head start, perhaps make some of our own," Adam winks.

"Having kids? That's not a bad idea, Genesis."

"Here we go."

"What? You can call me Naomi."

Adam grabs Eve's hand. "No matter what I say, you're going to keep calling me Genesis, aren't you?"

Eve smiles. "Probably."

He pulls her closer. "Can I convince you otherwise?" His confident-sounding tone camouflages his nervousness.

"Probably."

He brings her in even closer for a kiss. Eve can feel his anxiety. He stops, a few inches away from her lips. She can sense how uncomfortable he is with intimacy, so she pulls him in the rest of the way. Their eyes close.

But they flash open to the sound of a massive explosion above them. The room shakes, and the lights go out.

"What was that?" Eve looks up at the still-shaking ceiling.

Then, the sound of plasma blasts, and two more explosions.

"We're under attack," Adam declares. He sprints to the closet, grabs two Gen2 plasma rifles, and hands one to Eve.

Adam slowly opens the doors and peeks into the hallway. "Clear."

They both exit and scamper towards the stairwell. Their military training kicks in. Adam opens the door to the stairwell just as Eve enters, gun pointed upwards. Adam covers her flanks. "Clear." As they hustle up the stairs, Eve spots it. A Lazurite on the top floor has just dropped a plasma grenade. It is falling right above them.

"Keep moving!" Eve yells.

It's too late to go back down. They have ten stairs before reaching the next level. Their thighs burn as they take four stairs at a time, using the railing to help propel them upwards.

"We're not gonna make it!" Adam murmurs.

They arrive at the platform for the next level just as the plasma grenade lands at their feet. It detonates as Adam shoves Eve through the door onto the next floor. The detonation reverberates at their feet. Adam's heart rate is elevated, to say the least, and not just because of the attack. This is the closest he has ever been to Eve. They share a quick moment in recognition of this. Then, quickly, they are both back on their feet.

"There's another stairwell in the back!" Eve hollers. They race to it, open the door, and sprint up the dark stairwell. Adam misses a step and falls. Eve helps him up. "Too much time in a lab these days."

Moments later, they exit the back side of the bunker into the blinding sun.

They peek around the other side of the bunker. Lazurite soldiers march through and around Adam and Eve's dead counterparts—all hundred of them from Eden.

"We have to go," Adam whispers.

"What about the kids?" Eve suddenly remembers.

"I haven't seen them."

"We have to go back down. They're always playing hide and seek in the bunker on the lowest level."

After racing down the stairs at full speed, they reach the bottom level. Eve is surprised at how naturally her motherly instincts have kicked in. Perhaps she would make a good mother. In the hallway, she spots Timothy. "Timmy! You okay?"

"Yes, ma'am."

"Where are the others?" Adam asks.

"This way." Timothy leads them into a storage bunker at the end of the hall. Inside are the other children, scared and shaken. The room is more like a fallout shelter. It has food, water, and giant steel doors.

"You're going to be okay. Everything is going to be okay," Eve assures them.

"Now what?" Adam whispers. "It's too dangerous to take them up top."

"They could stay here. They have food and water, and no one is getting through that door." Eve raises her voice. "Listen up, everyone. You are going to stay here, but just for a little while. There is food and water. And don't open that door for anyone but us. We will be back."

"When?" one of the kids asks.

"Soon. Very soon."

Adam turns to Eve. "We should go now."

Eve does a mental count; she doesn't see any red hair. She grabs Timothy. "Timmy, where is your brother? Where is Lucas?"

He shakes his head and stares at the ground.

"Tell me, Timothy."

"I'm not supposed to tell anyone."

Eve bends down to his level and turns his body to face straight with hers. "It is very important that you tell me where he is. He could be in trouble."

"Will I be in trouble?"

Eve is stern. "You'll be in trouble if you don't tell me."

Timothy still stares at the ground. "He wanted to help, is all."

"Help do what? Look at me, Timothy. This is important."

"He went with Cephas and the rest of the army."

"What?" Adam says.

"He... he wanted to fight. Fight the Lazurites. He stole some exoarmor and a helmet so he could pretend to be a soldier. Is he gonna be okay?"

Eve feigns a smile. "Yeah, Timmy, he'll be fine. In fact, Adam and I are going to go find him."

After locking the bunker door and racing back to the top, they once again find themselves outside. Smoke and bodies everywhere. They perform a running crouch to the safety of the woods behind them. They don't slow down for another thirty minutes.

"How did they find us?" Eve asks.

"Maybe Boaz? Maybe he had a tracker?" Adam suggests.

"I knew we couldn't trust him."

"Yes, he made that quite evident."

Eve stops for a moment. "They're all dead. We are the last ones from Eden."

"Ironic to think we have been with them for over a hundred years, yet we didn't even know them."

"To live all this time and then to die suddenly like this."

"So much for starting over and rebuilding The Defiance."

"Now what?"

Eve grits her teeth. "Now we join the fight. And we get Lucas out of harm's way."

They hear a twig snap.

"Get down," Adam whispers.

They ready their plasma rifles, waiting for Lazurite soldiers.

"Weapon's down!" a man's voice from behind them. They freeze. "You are surrounded."

"We're not surrendering," Eve whispers to Adam.

The voice yells out, "We're not going to hurt you, Adam and Eve from Eden."

Adam recognizes the voice. He stands with his hands up, and so does Eve. The man speaking is Jethro. Next to him is Red Beard.

The Sitkans.

"What—what are you doing here?" Adam stutters in shock.

"Looking for Cephas and the rest of you crazy Drecks. Heard his compound is south of here."

"It was," Eve breaks the bad news. "Lazurites."

"What happened? We late? War over?"

"No, Cephas and his men are battling right now. We were on our way to find them."

Jethro strokes his long black beard. "Then we shall join you."

"How did you get through The Wall?" Adam asks.

"A section was open near 390." He spits. "This country has changed a lot since the last time I was inland."

Adam says, "You're telling us."

"How many men do you have?" Eve asks.

"A hundred and three. All warriors. Every one of them."

As the Sitkans can live off the land in Alaska in the winter, Adam and Eve don't doubt their resolve or courage.

"What made you change your mind?" Eve is curious.

Jethro spits. "It was that damn Thomas Paine quote."

Adam recites it, "*'Those who expect to reap the blessings of freedom, must, like men, undergo the fatigues of supporting it.'*"

Jethro raises an ancient Smith and Wesson shotgun. "Show us to the war."

Asher

It was a tie. Apex and Legion pressed their buttons at the same time. Neither team had to sacrifice someone. We are now down to six on each side.

This final trial is similar to the last time I was here. It isn't a physical test but a test of our mental acuity, but that doesn't prevent me from sweating. The room we are in is a fifteen-by-fifteen-foot square. There is one locked exit door. On the floor are ten tiles mixed in random order. Each tile has a number on it, from zero to nine. On the wall to our right are ten indentations into which the tiles will fit perfectly.

"What is this?" Legion asks.

"Another mental test," I reply.

The door slides open, and a Lazurite guard enters. He hands me a sheet of paper. "Good luck." His tone is indifferent. As he exits, the door slides shut with a thud.

A digital countdown is displayed on the ceiling. Its red numbers begin to count down, starting at fifty-nine minutes and fifty-nine seconds.

"That can't be good," Legion says to no one in particular.

"What does the note say?" Tobias asks.

I read it to them. "Place the numbers into their proper slots before the countdown hits zero. If unsuccessful, the room will no longer be supplied with oxygen."

Like the guard, even the note is apathetic. *No longer be supplied with oxygen.* What a sterile way of saying that we will suffocate to death. Nothing like working under pressure.

"Correct order? What does that even mean?" Tobias asks, as confused as we are.

"It won't be the obvious," I state.

"Yet, we have to try. Low-hanging fruit first," Legion suggests. "Zero through nine."

We place the tiles into the wall, starting at zero and ending at nine. Nothing. The red light above the exit door stays on, and the door doesn't budge. We try the next obvious and move them in descending order, from nine to zero. No luck.

"I wish Jude were here; he would figure it out," I say quietly, almost to myself. Jude was the puzzle man. I miss him more than I let on. I can't imagine how hard it must be for Cephas. Jude's humor always had a way of cutting the tension, bringing the temperature down a notch in stressful situations. Cephas hasn't been the same since he died.

"Maybe it is smallest to largest, but not in the way that we think?" Tobias proposes.

"What do you mean?"

"Start with one and finish with zero. Each number is larger than the last one, with the last number being nine-zero, or ninety."

It's worth a shot. We try Tobias's suggestion, but with no luck. We inverse it, and still nothing.

"What is the correct order? This doesn't make sense," Tobias sighs.

Nothing makes sense anymore.

Thirty minutes left. It is sweltering inside our little heat box.

I am exhausted. Not only have my headaches returned, but my brain is feeling like mush. We start throwing out random ideas, willing to try anything at this point.

"Is it a date?"

"That would be eight numbers, not ten."

"Is it a specific time? Using milliseconds?"

"That will still only be eight digits."

Time. Maybe they are onto something. Epoch time can be ten digits. In computer science terms, Epoch time is the number of seconds since January 1st, 1970.

Epoch time? How do I know that? Maybe one of the many LifeCells that have invaded my system belonged to a mathematician? Only I have no memories of any such person. But somehow, I know what Epoch time is, and I don't recall hearing it before. I start running the numbers in my head. It takes me a few minutes to reach today's Epoch time. It begins with two fours. That rules that out. I shake my head. I was never good with math. I *must* have inherited it through a LifeCell—my head throbs. The heat is overbearing. I have to sit. Not knowing what is happening with Cephas and Sarai is driving me crazy. But I have to focus. I have to do my part.

Fifteen minutes until we run out of oxygen.

"Perhaps the numbers represent letters, and it spells something?" Legion suggests.

"Like what? It could be anything," I respond, frustrated.

Tobias starts spewing out words. "Renatus, Zion, Canonization, protocol."

Legion huffs, "None of them are ten letters."

Is it unsolvable like last time? Is Renatus just toying with us again? Surely he wouldn't use that logic again, would he? Then again, he can't let us all suffocate; who would fight Apex in the final showdown? Legion and Tobias begin randomly placing the numbers into the wall.

"What are you doing?" I ask.

"Trying anything, not giving up," Legion grunts back. Underneath him, the ground is soaked with sweat. He smells like a rancid onion—we all do. Renatus has a talent for physically and mentally exhausting you before stepping into that arena. I wonder if Apex has made it out. He was probably given the riddle beforehand.

Legion punches the wall. "I don't get it."

Five minutes.

I close my eyes and try to concentrate, try to will to the surface the mathematician inside of me. My mouth is dry, and my head feels like it will explode.

Then I have a memory: I can see him in the mirror. He has wild white shoulder-length hair, a nicely trimmed beard, and bantam-round spectacles. He asks his students questions while drawing equations on a chalkboard. He had children. Two sons. They both died fighting against Zion. I shed a tear for a memory that isn't mine. I know it's not real, but the emotions are.

"Don't give up! Get up here and help us!" Legion barks at me, still trying random numbers. But I remain where I am. I can see the numbers dance around in my head. It's a riddle he used to tell his sons. He also handed out chocolate bars to any of his students who figured it out.

One minute left.

"Get up, Asher!"

I remain seated, eyes still closed. The numbers are starting to come together in my head. I am not sure why or even know what they mean. I think my subconscious has figured it out before my brain.

Thirty seconds.

I see the numbers clearly now: "**8-5-4-9-1-7-6-3-2-0**".

I stand. "I got it." My brain has caught up with my subconscious. I place the tiles into the wall in the exact order I see in my head.

"What is it? I don't get it?" Tobias asks.

"It's alphabetical," I smile, thankful that the mathematician who was sacrificed didn't die in vain. I place the last tile into the wall. The light above the door turns green, and the door slides open. We gulp mouthfuls of fresh oxygen.

As we file out, Legion examines the numbers and figures it out. "I see."

Again, we exit into the overbearing sun. I have to shield my eyes. It takes me a moment to see that Apex and his team have already made it. Apex smiles at Legion. "You were never good with numbers, were you, brother?"

Legion ignores him. Tobias pulls out the straws.

Looks like we will be short one for the final battle.

Even when we win, we lose.

Sarai

I exhale in relief. Asher has done it. But now he must face Apex. I am slightly comforted by the fact that he will have Legion by his side.

From the Sultan Suite, my father shuts off the HoloTube. I don't want to antagonize Renatus, but I can't help myself. "He did it again. What will you do when he defeats Apex?"

He stares at me with his icy smile. "That won't happen, Sultana. Asher and Legion have survived only because I wanted them to. Everything that has transpired thus far is according to my design."

"You underestimate him; you always have. No one thought he would beat Legion either."

"Not this time." He says it confidently, which worries me. Is it a foregone conclusion? Is it rigged? I feel so trapped and helpless up here. I wish I could be down there with him. Fighting beside him. I wasn't built for all this sneaking around and pretending to like it here. Pretending to like my father as if we are a normal family. I want to know that I'm good and that my enemy is evil. I want to fight them—directly, look them in the eye. Fair and square. I want to know where they stand, and they know the same about me. This is too much like politics, where the truth and lies are intertwined; that is where sincerity goes to die.

But he has my son. I have to play his game. Hopefully, it won't be much longer. I just want it to end one way or another.

"Will Mother be joining us for dinner?" I ask in the most placid and submissive voice I can muster.

"I'm afraid not."

"What happened? She not feeling well? Did she not want to watch today?"

He stares straight ahead, his voice calm, frigid. "Your mother has been busy lately, hasn't she? Putting her nose where it doesn't belong?"

I tense up. He knows. I am suddenly cold. A cutting chill descends upon the suite—an invisible breeze batters my face. I swallow and wince as bile escapes my stomach and traverses up into my throat.

"Where is she, Father?"

He yawns as if he's bored. "Snooping around. Always snooping."

My hands shake, "Where is she, Father? Where is my mother?"

"Surely your tutors taught you about King Edward II?" He stares at me, unblinking. "He was betrayed and overthrown by his wife, Isabella of France. They called her the She-Wolf."

"That was because he was inept."

"Ah, yes, your tutors did do their job. Do you think I'm inept, daughter?"

I don't dare answer.

He holds out his thumb and finger, a small space between them. "Perhaps just a little? Perhaps I was. That was my bad. Using your brother as my password. Too predictable. Did you think I would not find out? Do you think there is anything that happens in Zion that I don't know about?"

He knows I am helping The Defiance. I'm only still here, and not in jail or dead, because he wants me to watch The Canonization. He wants me to watch everyone I love dearly suffer and die.

"Tell me, daughter, why do you think your mother returned?"

A single tear glides down my cheek. My posture turns rigid. "I don't know."

He fiddles with his sash. His lips move rapidly. "Sure you do. You know, I always thought you were the family's stubborn one. You always went your own way, had your own ideas. I wasn't surprised when you betrayed me. Hurt? Yes. But your mother, I never expected you two would be so alike. So clever. I didn't think she had it in her. I am impressed, actually. She could have been a great queen if she had played for the right side."

He is no longer serene. He stands, picks up a chair in front of him, and throws it from the suite. It tumbles onto the seats below us, almost hitting a janitor sweeping up the discarded trash. "Like you, she has been seduced by Asher. Charmed by the way of the Drecks. I can handle such treachery from my enemies, even my friends. But from my family? The same family

I have given the world to! A palace. Eternal life. And this is how I'm repaid. My heart aches, Sarai. The stab in the back hurts more than the one in the chest."

"What have you done with her?"

"When I first met your mother, she was a maid, and I was a mechanic. We were both poor. But I was ambitious, and she had a natural regality about her. Someday, I knew I would be king, and she would be queen. She transitioned nicely into what became our royal existence. She loved me when I was poor, when I was a nobody. Ironic how it took me giving her everything for her to hate me."

"Where is my mother?"

He slides back into his seat. His tone hollow, tranquil, even. "She's a She-Wolf now. She's where all traitors go."

SeaPen.

Cephas

"Are the explosives in place?"

"Yes, Neriah," Darius replies.

Through his binoculars, Cephas watches the Lazurite army march through the canyon. His army, now hostages, have been corralled in the middle, just like Neriah said they would be. Half of his 500 soldiers are perched on the other side of the ridge, waiting for the bombs to go off.

Cephas is still a bit skeptical. Afraid he might take out too many of his own soldiers in the process, he turns to Neriah. "You sure this is a good idea?"

"Define good."

Cephas concedes that it is a fair point. This is probably the best they have at the moment. And for a Dreck, it's not bad.

"I'll rephrase the question: Is it a bad idea?"

Neriah says, "Define bad."

"No wonder you went into politics."

Cephas grimaces and peers down at his boots, which are a size too small. He wiggles his toes, trying to coerce blood to them and his aching feet. His back, his knees, now his feet. At least the pain had nowhere else to go. When they beat Renatus ten years ago, he didn't picture this was how he would be spending his golden years. Soldiering was a young man's game. His body begged for the rocking chair. But he was a finisher. He always was. He didn't plan on sitting on that proverbial chair until this was over. Besides, Cephas knew all too well that without a cause, without a purpose, he would grow bored. And he knew that nothing good ever came when he was bored. That was how the Tonic first crept into his life.

Tonic.

Through his overwhelming pain and stress, the Tonic is calling for him again. He battles off the temptation with a quick prayer.

Darius holds the detonator. "Say when."

Cephas is still lost in thought. "What?"

"Tell me when."

Cephas peers through the binoculars. He has to time it just right. Set off the explosives too early, and the landslides miss the Lazurites in the front and hit his surrendered army in the middle. It's the same outcome if it's too late.

"Not yet," Cephas whispers. His hand starts to shake. Again, he wonders if he has the stomach for this sort of thing anymore.

Why do they face nothing clear-cut and simple? Why does every choice have a sacrifice, no matter what he chooses? Just like his decision to ambush Renatus so many years ago, which cost him his brother Silas—at least for a while, while Silas was entombed at The Mountain. Or his decision to send Asher into Zion, cloaked as a Lazurite. Or his decision to go to Eden, which cost him Jude. Or how joining The Defiance cost him his wife. He used to be decisive, but now he is beginning to question everything. *It's a lack of faith*, he tells himself. He closes his eyes for a moment and steals a quick prayer. He realizes that if his faith has taught him anything, it's that nothing good can come without sacrifice.

He opens his eyes and takes another look into the canyon. "About a hundred more feet." And then, suddenly, they stop marching.

"What is going on?" Neriah asks.

"I don't know, they have stopped."

Cephas spots the Lazurites pulling food and water from their packs. "It looks like they are eating." As Cephas scans the ravine with his binoculars, he stops at a Lazurite guard who seems to be looking straight at him with his own binoculars.

"Down!" Cephas growls.

They duck behind the rocks.

"What?" Neriah asks.

"A guard is looking up this way."

"Did he see you?"

"I don't know."

Darius rolls on the ground around the rock and, from his belly, peers through his binoculars. "He's coming up here. What do we do?"

Cephas shakes his head again. It's never easy. "Get ready to blow just the front. It will only hit a portion of their men, but maybe it will cause enough chaos to help us attack."

Darius readies the detonator and takes another peek below him. The Lazurite soldier surveys the area momentarily, then turns and marches back down the hill. "He's heading back down the mountain. I don't think he spotted us."

A collective exhale. The next thirty minutes seem like thirty hours as they wait for the Lazurites to finish their lunch. Cephas watches in disgust as the Lazurites eat and drink in front of his surrendered army, teasing them with water and food, sometimes kicking them as they march by.

"They're moving again," Darius informs them.

"Get ready," Cephas whispers.

The army marches forward, with his brethren wedged in between. He must get this right or risk killing many of his own. He takes a deep breath and ignores the sweat sliding down the crags in his weathered cheeks. "Now!"

Darius activates the detonator. Within seconds, the ridge shakes from the four massive explosions. The landslide is bigger than they expected. A tsunami of rock, dirt, and trees barrels towards the ravine. Through his binoculars, Cephas can see the shock and awe in the faces of the men below—Lazurites and Drecks. It only takes seconds to find out if their gambit worked.

It did. Sort of.

The rear landslide was too late and completely missed the tail of the Lazurite army. The front, however, has engulfed the front portion of Renatus's battalion. In fact, it was too effective. Cephas and company watch in horror as some of their men are also buried under the avalanche of mountain debris.

Cephas glances at Neriah, not quite an "*I told you so look*", but it's close. He can't blame her, though. The final decision was his. Besides, what other choice did he have?

Cephas waves a red flag in the air, signaling the other half of his 500 on the ridge across from them. "Go!"

They storm down the mountain and into the ravine. With them is a volley of plasma blasts mixed with actual bullets and gunpowder. The brilliant and blazing sun casts an orange aura around the smoke, dirt, and debris still wafting into the air.

Just coming out of shock, the remaining Lazurites finally aim at Cephas and his horde surging into the ravine. The surviving Drecks, those who weren't buried under the landslide, join the fight in close-quarters hand-to-hand combat, trying to steal the Lazurite's weapons. Cephas fires his plasma gun in his right hand and the COLT 45 in his left.

The next twenty minutes are pure carnage and chaos. With over half the Lazurite army buried under the landslides, their own troops finally aren't outnumbered. The portion of his army that was held hostage is now armed, but many still aren't.

"This way!" Cephas orders them as he leads them behind one of the mountainous landslides for additional cover. It is costly, but they are gaining ground. "It's just a matter of time," Cephas states confidently. They have the upper hand, as more and more of his men take arms from the downed Lazurites.

Cephas barks to his men behind him, "Get ready to fan out and surround them." *Victory is finally ours*, he thinks.

But then.

"Wait! Up there!" Neriah yells.

A thousand soldiers march down the ravine, dressed in exoarmor with white and blue helmets. Cephas takes a closer look with binoculars. The man leading the army is short and skinny. Streaks of blond invade his black hair. Cephas recognizes that self-indulgent smile.

Czar Percival.

"Who is it?" Neriah asks. "They with us?"

"It's the French," Cephas spits. "And no, they are not on our side."

"What are the French doing here?"

"I heard they want the Statue of Liberty back."

Percival yells a command, and his army charges into the ravine. Percival is now at the back, of course.

"Take cover! And don't stop shooting."

"This isn't working. We need more weapons." Neriah spits while taking out a Lazurite to her left.

"For every one of them we take out, we need to arm one of ours," Cephas replies while firing double-fisted. Easier said than done. Every time one of them leaves the cover of the landslide to retrieve the weapons from a downed Lazurite or French soldier, they are shot at, and often hit.

One of his men returns with a Lazurite plasma rifle, but has paid dearly for it. He bleeds from a massive wound in his chest. Knowing he won't make it, he hands the gun to Cephas, then slowly lies down and closes his eyes.

Cephas fires a couple more shots at the enemy and turns to see more and more of his men arrive at their location, still unarmed. He points at them. "Follow me."

Cephas jumps up from the safety of the landslide and scampers towards a platoon of dead Lazurites. His men follow. While ducking and weaving among plasma blasts, they pilfer their weapons and high-tail back toward the landslide. Cephas scoots over rocks, debris, and bodies.

Then it hits him. He falls to the ground. It feels like a moose has stomped on his back. He grits his teeth as smoke and blood emanate from the hole that the plasma has created in his exoarmor. *At least my feet don't hurt anymore.*

One of his men stops. "Sir, you okay?"

Cephas waves him off. "Just go!"

But he doesn't. He helps Cephas up and to the cover of the landslide. "You okay, sir?"

He lies, "I'm fine."

A concerned Neriah checks his wound, then frowns.

"That bad?" Cephas whispers to her.

"It's not good."

Cephas grabs a Dreck and pulls him close. "Bring me Darius, and hurry."

Rock and dirt erupt into the air as a brigade shoots at them from their left flank. On their right is Czar Percival and his army.

"We'll be surrounded soon." Neriah fires at the new threat to their left.

Cephas joins her just as Darius arrives. "Sir?"

Cephas grunts in pain. "Darius. Grab three men, take the serum, and get to Zion West while you still can. We will stay and cover your exit."

"But Cephas, we can still win this, we can't give up—"

Cephas shakes him with his meaty paws. "Listen to me. If we don't get that serum to Sarai, all is lost; all this will be for nothing. Now go! She is expecting you."

"And what about the nuke?"

"We'll keep it with us in case you don't make it. That way, at least either the nuke or serum makes it."

"You sure?"

"I'll get it there, son. Go."

Darius peers at Cephas's wound and does his best to conceal his concern.

"Don't worry about me, just go. Don't stop until you get there."

Darius looks to Neriah, who nods in confirmation. Darius takes off.

A hail of plasma engulfs them as they try to fight on two fronts. Neriah examines Cephas's wound. "You're going to need a medic."

Another plume of dirt and rock emerges next to Cephas. "At this rate, I won't."

Neriah says, "I'm starting to think my idea was a bad one."

Cephas smiles, revealing his blood-stained teeth. "Define bad."

Neriah fires to her left. Cephas shoots in front of them. They are quickly losing men. Cephas turns his attention back to his left when he hears a suppressed shriek. It is Neriah. Smoke fizzles from her chest as she stumbles backward, practically into Cephas's arms. From the corner of his eye, he can see that it was Percival who shot her.

"Neriah!" Cephas holds her tight and away from harm as he scans her wound. The plasma got her heart and lungs. Her breathing labored, her fists involuntarily clench.

"C'mon, Neriah, stay with me. Stay with me."

Her entire body convulses. After Jude, Cephas isn't sure he can handle someone else dying in his arms.

Her voice is cracked. "I'm sorry, Cephas."

"Don't do that, don't say that. You have nothing to be sorry for."

"Yes. This plan of mine was... it was foolish. I thought I could lead. I thought I was qualified. I thought I was a Dreck."

"This isn't your fault, Neriah. Stay with me."

"Tell Asher and Sarai that I'm sorry. I am sorry about Silas." Her eyes flutter closed. Her chest is no longer moving.

It may have been foolish, but now you have died a Dreck.

Cephas picks up her lifeless body. She is folded at the waist atop his broad shoulder. As he weaves in and out of plasma blasts and shrapnel, he hollers to his men what, unfortunately, has become another Dreck axiom.

"Retreat!"

Asher

A Lazurite with copper skin and small hands securely places the Guillotine Ring around my neck. He is close enough for me to smell his pungent, musky cologne, now in vogue with most Lazurite men. His hair is cut short, which is the latest fashion. I leave my four remaining companions, and I'm whisked through the hallway bejeweled with marble and ornate wainscoting. He escorts me into Renatus's study. The last time I was here, I had just defeated Legion and won The Canonization. That was ten years ago. I remember stepping into this room, thinking I would be put to death for not killing Legion. Now, I am having those same feelings. I shake off those thoughts. Why would he kill me now? He needs me to fight in this final battle.

The lights are low, and the room feels tinted and dark. Renatus sips on bourbon while reading what looks to be a report. He wears all black with a red sash, and his face and head are freshly shaved. His eyes, as always, are spirited and spry—especially when he is excited about something.

"Ah, Asher, have a seat."

I do. He pours me a bourbon. I take it. Normally, it's a bad idea the night before battling a giant, but I figure it will help me sleep.

He holds up his glass. "Congratulations on surviving the trials."

Not wanting to be rude and set him off in any way, I reciprocate and hold up my glass before taking a sip of the expensive dark spirit.

He shakes his head. "It's a shame about Kenan and Amos. I really thought they would make it through." All I do is nod, trying not to get emotional about Kenan.

"But, they sacrificed themselves for the greater good," he says.

Internally, I scoff. Sure, that was the case for Kenan, but Apex intentionally killing Amos so he could win a trial is not something I would call a sacrifice. He takes another slurp of bourbon. "What you and your people fail to understand is that is what Zion is all about: sacrifice for the greater good."

I should probably keep my mouth shut, but I can't help myself. "You mean the killing of innocents so you and your ilk can live on perpetually?"

"I am a born leader, destined to bring great prosperity to Zion. It behooves Zion for me to live on." He sets his drink down with a clank and leans in close, his countenance sober. "If I thought there was someone else who could do it better, I would gladly give up my life for them."

What makes it worse is that he is not lying. He truly believes what he is doing is righteous and that he was intended to lead and live forever, that no one else could do it better.

"I know of someone," I say wryly.

He chortles, "I always liked you, Asher. We are not that different, you and me. For I, too, know what it is to feel the swoon of despair. It's too bad we couldn't make this work. Such it is with in-laws sometimes."

His jokey response lands flat. He then stares quietly at me for a moment, enjoying my tension and anticipation as to why I'm here. I don't give him the pleasure of asking; instead, I act bored. I see a hint of irritation on his face. He stands and finally speaks.

"So, this is how tomorrow is going to go. You and your team will put up a good fight. A bloody fight. I don't want it to end too early. You are free to kill anyone you like, except Apex. But in the end, you will lose. You and Legion will die at the hands of his brother."

My mouth slowly drifts open as I can't hide my shock. "You want us to lose on purpose? Have you no faith in Apex?"

"Not at all. In fact, I think he will decimate you." He clears his throat, "I just can't have you getting lucky again, is all."

I am still jarred by his request. Pride has always been his weak point until now. I thought it would cause his fall. But to admit that Apex could possibly lose is something I would have never expected.

"Hmm... I didn't think Lazurites would need Drecks to take a fall in order to win. So much for Zion superiority."

I have annoyed him. "You are in this position because we are superior."

"And if I refuse?"

"If serendipity decides to smile upon you again and you win, you will still lose. Your wife and son shall perish. And you will die anyway. Then, I will store you and Legion inside my mountain, bringing you back once a year to die all over again in what I will call the *Legacy Battles* for future Canonizations. That will be your new life. Your purpose. To battle once a year. That will be your one day to live. You will be dead the other 364."

"What will you do a hundred Canonizations from now when you have exhausted every twisted and perverse possibility? Surely, you will get bored with us killing each other."

"I will never tire of watching your blood spill, Asher. And you have no idea the depths of my imagination. I am just scratching the surface."

"If not you, then your audience will get fatigued by watching the same people die in the same manner. How many times can they see one burned in hot oil? Attacked by tigers? Cars dropped on them?"

"Oh, Asher. Human nature isn't inherently good. Immorality is our default behavior. Not only do they lust for violence, they expect it. Don't take my word for it. Just look at history—war after war after war. You have misjudged the populace. That is why you are in the arena, and I sit in the Suite of Sultans."

"Maybe. But you misjudge what those who fight against evil are willing to sacrifice."

"That is where you are wrong, Son of Silas. I know exactly what you and my daughter are willing to sacrifice. And why. That is why you will die tomorrow."

I try to muzzle my anger. He sees it welling in me. My face reddens. My body flushed with heat. He smiles and continues.

"If you don't do as I ask, your wife and son will have no grave. After I reap their LifeCells, I will bury them in the cold reaches of the Pacific. They will not be remembered. They will not be martyred. Neither will you, as you will live on eternally to fight and die. To fight and die. Over and over. You will exist for entertainment, nothing more. Your pain and suffering will never end. Your yearning and desire for your family will not fade with time. For a hundred years, it will only be a hundred days for you. Every time you are brought back, it will be like you just saw them yesterday. Zion will own your body, and I will own your soul."

The room suddenly shrinks. My vision is bombarded with crimson hues. I have trouble finding oxygen. For the first time in my life, I think I'm going to faint.

Sarai

Since being banished from the protocol facility, my father has had me under lock and key. Except for being let out to watch the trials, I have been locked in my room with nothing to do but mourn for Hagar and wonder about our plan. Is the nuke operable? Have they created the reverse protocol serum? And if so, will Darius make it here with it?

I check the time. I am supposed to meet with him in less than three hours. I need to get out of here somehow.

I take a gander at the mirror. I pull my frizzy, oily hair into a ponytail. I think about putting on some makeup, but what's the point? My eyes are bloodshot, and puffy blue bags droop below them. Wrinkles fan out from my eyes like wings. The lines on my forehead look like cracks in concrete. How have I aged so quickly? The question is rhetorical. I know the answer. My father's war has done the same to Asher. At least we'll be old together. Assuming we survive this.

I rifle through my closet and find my black workout fatigues and Def Leppard sweatshirt. I grab my scourge from underneath my mattress and coil it up, then tie it to my chest. I zip up the sweatshirt to cover it. I take a deep breath and steel myself. I knock on my locked bedroom door. A tall, sinewy guard answers. His hair has been cut short. His eyes are vacant. His aura is frigid, and he gives off a melancholic ambiance. It's the look of someone who doesn't want to be here but knows they have no choice. I could try to use that to my advantage, but if it doesn't work, I'm stuck here.

"What is it, Sultana?"

"I need to use the restroom."

"What's wrong with the one in your quarters?"

I feign embarrassment, then lie. "It's clogged. Now, unless you want to unclog it for me, I suggest you escort me to one of the guest bathrooms. And quick."

He ponders for a moment. He could call a maid or the floor janitor, but I do the pee-pee dance, telling him there is no time. Besides, he may not want to be here, but he is still a prideful Lazurite guard who wouldn't be caught dead with a plunger.

He opens the door, one hand on his plasma gun. "This way, Sultana."

As I walk in front of him, my shoes squeak on the freshly polished marble floors. The longer I'm here, the larger this place feels. The wide hallways and tall ceilings are unnecessary. "I don't recognize you. You must be new. What's your name?"

"I'm not supposed to speak with you."

"What? My father afraid you might succumb to my charms?" I wink at him.

He stops, rigid, and doesn't look me in the eyes, but stares above me. "What's the danger in giving me your name?"

"It's this door. And make it fast." He points to the restroom.

"Thank you." I enter the bathroom and close the door. I gaze at myself in the gold-trimmed mirror once more. I guess if I were going to charm him, I should have put on some makeup. Or at least showered. I take a whiff and cringe. I grab my scourge from underneath my sweatshirt and uncoil it. I almost feel sorry for the guard, but he has made his choice, and I don't have one. I flush the toilet and mock washing my hands. With the water still running, I swing open the bathroom door and whip my scourge. Like a snake, it wraps around his neck. The electrical surge knocks him to the ground. He seizes for a moment, then is knocked unconscious. I drag him into the bathroom and roll him into the bathtub.

I check his pulse; he is alive but will probably be out for the next hour. I crack the bathroom door and peek out. All clear. Before leaving, I lock the bathroom door. I quickly scamper down the hallway, shoes mildly squeaking. I should have worn something else. Just before I reach the corner, two more guards come my way. I duck into one of the guest bedrooms and softly shut the door. I hear their boots stomp on the floor as they pass me, chattering about an attack on The Defiance. I hope Cephas and his army can make it here. I hope they weren't ambushed.

After they leave, I slither into the hallway and sprint towards the back door. I make my way outside and into my father's garden. A moment later, I run into another guard. He has no deference for me; he doesn't refer to me as Sultana.

Instead, he says, "What are you doing out of your quarters, traitor?" Unlike the one I left in the tub, he is generously built and has the look of someone who can't wait to dole out violence. I don't give him a chance. I whip my scourge towards his neck. He sidesteps, but it still wraps around his arm, his armor dulling the electric current. He yanks his arm towards his chest, pulling me towards him, then smashes his elbow into my chest. I go flying backward.

"I don't care whose daughter you are. It's time you were taught some Lazurite manners, you Dreck-loving traitor." He tosses my scourge behind him. He arrives just above me and tries to pick me up, but I slide underneath him, just between his legs, lifting my foot as I exit behind him, hard into his groin. He drops to his knees for a moment, giving me just enough time to gather my scourge. Before he can grab his plasma rifle, I rear back and hit him in the back of the head with my electric whip. He convulses a moment before dropping to the ground. It takes all my might to drag him into the row of passionflowers, where he will be out of sight.

I spit. "How's that for manners?"

It takes me another thirty minutes of hiding and dodging before I make my way outside the perimeter of the compound. I avoided the guards, but probably not all the cameras. I am hoping my hood is enough to disguise me.

An hour later, I traverse a rocky cliff overlooking the blustering ocean. My hands shake every time I look upon the deep blue that snatched my brother and son. It's everlasting and vast. Beautiful yet terrible. Its waves are unsympathetic to the eroding shoreline. Aloof to the way it has bruised my soul. But it is only doing what it is meant to do. I have to one day accept that.

Darius isn't here yet—if he's coming at all. Soon, my father will be alerted to my absence, and men will come looking for me. This complicates things, but I didn't have any other choice.

The sun breaks through the clouds, its fingered rays descending upon the blue Pacific. I have tried to block him from my mind so I can focus on the tasks ahead, but seeing God's handiwork, I can't help but think of Asher. That he will be in the arena tomorrow with Apex. Even if he wins, my father will probably kill him anyway. And if Darius doesn't show up with the serum, my son will soon be dead.

Then, a whisper. "Sarai."

I turn; it's Darius with three others. "You made it. Tell me you have good news."

He hands me a small metal case and smiles. "It works, Sarai." I exhale in relief. Finally, positive news. "Inside are two vials and a needle. Each vial should be enough for one person."

"And the nuke?" I inquire.

"That, too, is operable. But Cephas and his army have it."

"That makes our plan harder but not impossible."

"He said he would get it here."

"And what of Cephas?"

He solemnly watches the ocean with heavy eyes. "He was... they were under heavy fire, surrounded when I left." He notices my eyes squint in sorrow. "Hey, this is Cephas we are talking about. He'll come through. He always does. He's too stubborn to die."

I'm not so sure this time, but I nod in agreement. He turns away from the ocean and stands closer to me. "What will you have us do next?"

"You have done enough, Darius."

"With all due respect, we are not bowing out until this is finished. We are Drecks, remember?"

"Then return to Cephas. Help them in any way you can."

"And how will you get into The Mountain to administer it?" He is referring to the serum.

"I don't know."

CHAPTER TEN

Cephas

Cephas's breathing is still labored as blood once again seeps from the bandages covering the plasma wound on his back. They have been in full retreat for almost twenty-four hours straight now, stopping here and there to skirmish with the enemy in the thick woods.

After thirty minutes of nearly sprinting, Cephas's legs give out. He falls to his old knees. His muscles burn and ache. His lungs can't keep up. He is physically exhausted. His mourning for Neriah and his anger at Czar Percival have left him mentally drained.

More death. More pain. More suffering. When will it end? He knows it might never end, not until he leaves this earth.

"Sir!" a Dreck yells for him. "Let me help you, sir."

Cephas is so winded he can barely speak. A scattering of plasma blasts almost hit him. He spots two Lazurites to his left. Cephas fires his COLT 45 and takes out one.

The soldier next to him takes out the other. "Cephas, sir, we must go. Now!"

Cephas stands and immediately falls again. He looks up at the Dreck with weary, bloodshot eyes. "Go, soldier, go, and tell the army not to stop until you get to Zion."

"I won't leave you, sir."

"Yes, soldier, you will. I am wounded, probably fatally. My legs have no more strength. Now go and leave an old man be. That is an order, soldier."

More explosions as trees splinter and dirt rockets up from the ground—plasma grenades. More Drecks show up and circle Cephas. "We will carry you, sir."

But immediately, three are hit by plasma and go down. Cephas peers up and sees that the Lazurites and French have them flanked on both sides.

"We have nowhere to go," Cephas tells them, blood trickling from his nose.

"Then we will stay and fight with you." The soldier places his hand on Cephas's shoulder. "Drecks to the very end."

Cephas spits blood, "For once, don't be a Dreck and leave me here."

"And what? Act like a Lazurite? Never."

Cephas cracks a smile and wheezes. "Don't make me write you up for insubordination. You know, as a soldier, you don't get to choose what commands to obey."

"If the orders are folly, we do. Leaving you is not an option."

Another Dreck with a thick, dirty mustache also grabs Cephas's shoulder. "We have fought with you. We have laughed with you. We have battled demons with you. It will be an honor to die with you."

Through the pain, Cephas manages to smile. Even if they lose today, he has solace in the fact that he has taught his men well. He is astounded by their courage and bravery. Their sacrifice. Like him, they are salt-of-the-earth people who want nothing more than to work, raise their families, and be free. If he dies today, he is okay with it. They have done their job and held them off long enough for Darius to deliver the serum. He has peace. He knows where he is going when he leaves Earth. His bloody fingers grab the soldier, his teeth gritted. "Drecks to the very end!"

"Those are orders we can obey, sir."

With that, they make a last stand. A final volley of bullets, plasma, and bombs. Men from both sides drop. There is no Legion or Sons of Levi to save them this time. Cephas begins to pray. Not to be saved necessarily; in fact, he doesn't make any requests. It's more of a conversation, really, with God. He tells him that if today is the day that he meets Him, he is okay with it. He is ready. He can suffer misery no longer. He wants to see his wife again. He wants to return to the garden, watching her plant sunflowers, sweet peas, and marigolds. Admiring her curly copper hair frolic on her shoulders as she dances to her favorite Irish ballads. Sometimes, when she thought she was alone, she would even try to sing them. And the scent of her perfume: herbal, floral, with notes of citrus. He closes his eyes and can smell her as if she were standing before him. And her cooking. He hasn't had a decent meal since she passed, at least that is what he liked to tell people. It's not entirely true, but it was his way of complimenting her to people after her death. How he longed for her Shepherd's Pie and Irish Soda Bread. And her Colcannon. He can taste the scallions, leek, and garlic lathered over potatoes swimming in brown butter.

He is suddenly overwhelmed with joy. Contentment even. To die next to his brothers and friends is a great honor. His only regret is not being able to say goodbye to Asher and Sarai. But he has made his peace with his nephew, and imparted all the wisdom that he had. He has no more to give.

Yes. He is ready.

Ready for no more struggle.

No more addiction.

No more pain.

But.

God has other plans, it seems.

Suddenly, dozens of Lazurites on their left flank fall, shot in the back. After that, dozens more.

Cephas grunts in confusion, looks to his men. "What is going on? Who is that?"

"No idea, sir."

Then they see it.

Adam and Eve with Jethro, Red Beard, and the rest of the Sitkans.

Cephas smiles, and with renewed energy, he barks, "Don't let them regroup!"

They charge the Lazurites. Between Cephas and the Sitkans, they easily take out the Lazurites on their flank. Once joined together, they charge the remaining Lazurites and French, who quickly become overwhelmed. Most of them retreat to the woods. Including Czar Percival.

A Dreck approaches Cephas. "Sir, should we take chase?"

Cephas wants to. It brings him no joy that Percival has escaped. But avenging Neriah at this moment is an emotional decision. A selfish one. He knows they must stay on task and deliver the nuke to Zion West.

Cephas shakes his head. "Let them go. There has been enough killing for one day." He then approaches Adam and Eve. "Seems you are more than just scientists."

"We are Marines first," Eve answers.

"I thank God for that. Thank you."

Jethro stands next to Red Beard with his arms folded. Cephas trudges over and shakes his hand, exchanging blood and dirt in the process.

Cephas winks. "It was the Thomas Paine quote, wasn't it?"

Jethro reveals his chipped, crooked teeth. "Shut it."

"You coming with us all the way to Zion West?"

"I didn't take a long boat ride to quit halfway."

There is an instant and unspoken camaraderie between Cephas and Jethro—two old warriors, underdogs, ragged and weatherbeaten.

Jethro surveys Cephas's army. "Quite the motley crew you have gathered. Is this all of you?"

"Yes. Is there a problem?"

Jethro's grimy fingers push down on his oily, sooty eyebrows. "Nope. If I'm being honest, the only way I know how to operate is when the odds are against me."

"Then you'll feel right at home."

Eve approaches Cephas. "You haven't seen Lucas, have you?"

Cephas narrows his eyes in confusion. "Lucas? The boy?"

"Yeah, his brother said he stole some armor and a helmet. Sneaked in with your army."

But they have their answer. And it's not good. A Dreck trudges past them, carrying Lucas's lifeless body.

Cephas sighs and closes his weary eyes. "He was just a kid. Just a kid." But the truth was, Lucas wasn't the first teenager to lose his life in this ugly war.

Eve turns away, trying to sniff away tears. Adam holds her. "I should have kept my eye on him more. I should have watched over him."

Adam holds her tighter. "Don't do that, Eve. This isn't your fault."

As the adrenaline wears off, Cephas grimaces from the deep wound in his back and begins to wonder if he can make the journey. He scans the dead littered around him. He thinks of Neriah. Of Lucas. He can't take much more.

He then addresses his men. "We have paid a massive price, but we have won this battle. I don't know about you, but I'm tired of fighting. Tired of death. One way or another, this ends soon. Now it's time to move on to Zion and win this war."

Amidst cheers, Cephas takes three steps and collapses to the ground.

Asher

It's 3:21 AM, and my head is throbbing. I'm not sure if it's from the bourbon or protocol. Every time I close my eyes, I see the memories of the people whose LifeCells I have reaped. Not just see, but feel. They are getting stronger and more intrusive. They only partially disappear when I take my thoughts captive, when I willfully and purposely think of Sarai and Silas. Our tin boat. Our lake. When I leave those memories, they morph into my parents, specifically my father. I can vividly see him floating in the pink substance, having just given me his LifeCell. I reminisce about that moment and see his face. It's full of peace. Not a hint of regret. Although barely perceptible, I think I see the slightest upturn of his lips. Thinking back, his entire life has been a sacrifice. For me, for my mother. For Cephas. For The Defiance. It awes me, but at the same time, does not surprise me. I would do the same for Silas. Perhaps I'll get lucky and fall asleep on that thought?

No.

I close my eyes and see the bombing at the bazaar. I can smell the charcoal soot. The raw, smoggy vapors of the freshly deceased. The dead children. Neriah carrying her lifeless son. The vacant eyes of the mothers in shock. I can hear the lament and heartbreak—the shrieks of despair. I have asked for forgiveness and have forgiven myself, I think. Will I forever be haunted by these images? The sounds of that day make me nauseous. Who wouldn't be?

It's no use. I open my eyes. I'll be awoken in two hours anyway. I guess I'll be facing Apex on no sleep. I wonder if Apex is nervous. He's probably sleeping like a baby. I can only hope that his overconfidence will be his one weakness. But considering what Renatus said, does it matter? I'm not sure what to do. How do I even decide? If our plan works, then Sarai and Silas should be okay. But if I don't take a dive and win, and the serum doesn't work, and the nuke isn't delivered, then we will all die.

But I know Renatus. Won't he just kill Sarai and Silas anyway? As for me, I have a feeling he will bring me back for the Canonization every year, no matter if I win or lose. I can't think of anything worse. Will I be fighting in his heinous games for the next millennia? And never see my family again? Will they forever be waiting for me in heaven?

And Legion. I can't ask him to die at the hands of his brother on purpose, can I? And what about Tobias and the other Drecks still remaining? Do I ask them to die for me and my family? Haven't they done enough already? I can't help but think it is on purpose. Renatus has diabolically stuck me with an impossible choice. I think he enjoys our mental anguish just as much as the physical. I just want it to be over. My fortitude is waning. I take an honest appraisal of what I have left in me. Physically and mentally.

It isn't much.

Why me? Why is the burden mine? I didn't ask for this. I never wanted this. But I have to put things in perspective. I am still alive. Sarai and Silas are still alive. Hope is still alive. For many, that is no longer the case. Drecks and Lazurites alike have lost everything in this war. Why am I still here? I have to believe it's for a reason—too many have died for me to still have breath in my lungs. As long as my heart is beating, I must continue. I must fight on.

I close my tired, stinging eyes.

When I open them again, I am being escorted into the arena. I barely recall eating breakfast. Time has sped up and slowed down at the same time. My feet feel like they are in buckets of concrete, and I am walking in slow motion. The crowd's cheer is ear-piercing as the Lazurite guards shove me into the middle of the massive coliseum. I scan the horde of fans, and I see that almost everyone is dressed to the nines—fancy gold and silver robes. Their wrists, fingers, ears, and necks are laminated with emeralds and diamonds. I guess watching us spill one another's blood is now a primping event. I also notice that there are not a lot of old people in the crowd. Is it because they are wiser with age and have finally found the folly in Renatus's blood games? Or is it because Renatus has deemed them no longer useful or productive, and they are therefore waiting to be harvested?

The wind agitates the dirt under my boots, the swirling dust particles like smoke. The sun's rays amplify the effect, adding gravitas to our introduction.

Next to me are Legion, Tobias, and the two remaining Drecks. They look like they slept about as well as I did. I peer up at the Seat of Sultans. Renatus isn't there yet. Then there's a raucous ovation. We turn and see Renatus entering the arena. He marches towards the center. Gold flakes have been added to his red sashes, and glitter in the sun. There is a glint in his eye; this is the day he has long awaited.

"Welcome back, everyone! After ten long years, we have returned!" His voice rumbles from the massive speakers that litter the arena. "Last year, an earthquake robbed you of what you are about to see. For that, I am sorry. But in a way, it was a blessing. For not only do we have Asher and Apex to feast on, but Legion too!"

A full minute of jubilant applause. Again, I look around at the faces in the arena. Some fat. Some dirty. Some poor. Some rich. I wonder how they have once again become brainwashed by Renatus's charms, by Zion's charisma. Have they not anything else to live for other than this manufactured distraction of violence and death? Can they not see what is happening? That they are being fooled? That Renatus would not think twice about putting them down here with me, or storing them in The Mountain if he thought it could benefit him? Do they not realize they are simply a domino in Renatus's train of corruption—and that they will eventually fall to serve his glory? Like pigs, they are fattened now, only to be feasted on later. Almost every time, they take the temporal gratification over anything lasting.

Renatus explains how today will proceed. "Asher and his team have five remaining survivors from The Trials. Apex has six. They will face off to the death until only one team remains." He smiles at us, then returns his attention to the crowd and, as usual, spews nothing but lies and deceit. "We don't do this for entertainment. It's not for our amusement. We do it for bravery; we do it for valor. We do it for Zion!" The masses eat it up. "For Zion is special. For Zion is strong. And it must be proven to those who wish our demise. It must be sanctioned with blood!"

I stop listening to the propaganda for a moment and huddle my team together. "Listen up. Renatus wants us to take a dive."

"What?" Legion frowns. "Never."

Tobias asks the pertinent question. "And what if we don't?"

"He will kill Sarai and my son." I turn to Legion. "He will keep us in The Mountain, bringing us back once a year to fight in this vile contest. Forever."

There is a moment of contemplation.

Legion turns to me. "What do you think we should do?"

I kneel, scoop some coarse sand from the arena floor, and rub my hands together. "We have been oppressed and brutalized for decades. They have ripped our families apart and have made us slaves. Everyone here knows what it is like to experience thirst and hunger. And I'm not just talking about food and water. I'm talking about freedom and justice. We have been second-class citizens long enough. I think we should take those years of bottled-up aggression and fear and unleash them! Hold nothing back. Leave it all in the arena. Show them the way of the Dreck. For today, my brothers, it finally ends."

Sarai

The protocol facility is heavily guarded. My father has banished me, so I can't just waltz in. Besides, surely they are searching for me by now. Inside, my son waits to die while my brother waits to be resurrected. I can't let either happen. There is no way inside The Mountain except through the front door. I shake my head and tell myself this is impossible. I'm running out of time. Maybe I can pay off a Lazurite guard or a protocol scientist to do what needs to be done. I shake my head; it's too risky. If they disagree, Renatus will find out, and the ruse will be up. Can I force them somehow? Threaten their families? No. Now I'm sounding like a Lazurite.

Then I hear that familiar swoosh of rotors above me. I duck down and hide behind a thicket as the HarvestDrone hovers above The Mountain. I again watch in revulsion as the tube extends from the HarvestDrone and into the roof of the protocol facility. Two Drecks, incapacitated by DemonDust, slide down the tubes and into the belly of The Mountain. Soon, their LifeCells will be harvested—a well-oiled machine of extermination and rebirth. You wonder what mindset it takes to come up with this, much less follow through with it. As the HarvestDrone takes off, I suddenly have a realization.

HarvestDrone.

That's it. That's how I get in. I just have to find some DemonDust. I shake my head, thinking this sounds like a plan my husband would come up with. My father doesn't do narcdrops in Zion; he saves that for The Middle. I'm going to have to find a black-market dealer.

An hour later, I am on the outskirts of town. It's seedy for Zion but still nicer than anything in The Middle. I don a hood, a Def Leppard hat, and sunglasses. The serum is tucked away in my black *Back To The Future* backpack. There is a bar two blocks over that Hagar had warned me about. He said that would be the place if you were looking for anything illegal. I make my way over to the next block. A three-man Lazurite patrol turns the corner. I peer at my feet and keep walking as they pass me. I exhale as I reach "Jack's Bar."

I enter and peer around. It's dark but clean. I stroll in like I belong and approach the bartender. Soft rock plays in the background.

"What can I get ya?" he asks.

I lean in. "Something that isn't on the menu." He nods his head to my left. A pudgy man with slick black hair and a red leather jacket sits in a booth in the back. He wears brown gloves with the fingers cut out. I nod and swagger over. The man's armed bodyguard stands to his left. He has a Ruger 9MM attached to his hip. Before either can move, I swing into the booth seat across from him. His guard steps towards us, but Leather Jacket waves him off.

"I'm looking for some Dust," I say plainly.

He eyes me, all of me. "What's a pretty lady like you want Dust for?"

"You a dealer or a psychiatrist?"

He smirks and sips his Scotch. "Wouldn't you rather have a gun? Protect yourself from the invading Drecks? And not the stuff Harry sells down the street. I'm talking about Gen2 plasma. Or better yet, gunpowder weapons."

"I can handle myself, just the Dust."

He surveys me again. "You don't look like a duster."

"It's a wonder you stay in business. You always make your transactions this hard? You want my full medical history? Wanna hear about all my childhood trauma?"

He smiles. "I have what you need. How much?"

"One dose. It has to be the new stuff."

He raises an eyebrow. "Man, you must really want to escape. You sure you don't want the traditional?"

"I'm sure." The newer incapacitating formula is what the Harvest-Drones scan for.

He pulls a metal briefcase from underneath the table and flips it open. He hands me a bag of the blue-green powder. "Careful. This is enough for a two-hundred-pound man, so take it accordingly."

I pull my BitTender card from my pocket, which I had stolen from one of the Lazurite guards in my father's palace. I only hope they haven't deactivated it yet. I hand it to him. He scans it with a reader connected to his watch. The beeping noise it makes doesn't sound good. "Sorry, missy. Declined."

This isn't good. What I'm about to do next isn't the smartest thing I have ever done, but neither is this entire plan. Besides, I am out of options. I pull down my hood, take off my glasses, and hat. "How about I pay you back later?"

It takes him a minute, but he recognizes me. "Sultana?"

I nod.

"I don't understand, why would you—"

"Does it matter?"

He briefly studies me, then finally, "I can't give that to you."

"Why?"

"Because you're Renatus's daughter."

"I'm actually a traitor to Zion, remember? Since we are both breaking Zion's laws right now, how about you cooperate, and I won't tip off a Lazurite patrol about your little operation here."

He laughs. "You don't think they know? They're on the payroll."

"Then maybe a few of my Dreck friends might pay you a visit. When this is all over, I think Legion and I might come here for a drink."

He bristles at the mere mention of Legion. Then I catch him making the smallest glance towards his bodyguard. I immediately pull out my scourge. "I'll have this wrapped around your neck before your man can pull the trigger."

Leather Jacket freezes. His guard still has his gun trained on me.

"Do you really wanna be responsible for killing Renatus's daughter? He may think me a traitor, but make no mistake; no one hurts his family but him."

He waves his guard off once again. "Put the gun down."

"Wise move."

"Keep it," he tells me. "I don't sell a lot of that stuff anyway."

I get up. "Much obliged." As I head towards the door, I hear him clearing his throat. "Sultana, should I bet on your husband?"

"What are his odds?"

"Ten to one. You think he'll pull off another upset?"

"Let me put it this way: after tomorrow, you should look for a new profession."

Asher

The faint sound of drums.

Thump.

As they get louder, the tension increases.

THUMP.

I peer to my right—beads of sweat percolate on Tobias's red cheeks. To my left, Legion is stoic. Even though he no longer wants this, I must remind myself that he is bred for this. My knuckles are white. My fists unconsciously clenched.

THUMP. THUMP.

A metal gate on the east side ominously slides open.

THUMP. THUMP. THUMP.

The same goes for my heart. I fiddle with my exoarmor and clear my throat. My foot taps the dirt. Legion bounces side to side, wringing out his hands. Tobias chews on his fingernails before licking his lips. I unclench my fists and stretch out my fingers.

THUMP. THUMP. THUMP. THUMP.

Smoke oozes from the tunnel behind the open gate, like a demon ghost announcing its arrival. Then, as if planned, a lone dark cloud parks in front of the sun, casting a dark shadow over us, mirroring our somber mood. Our breathing is almost in unison—deep, slow breaths—fortifying our lungs for battle. The crowd stomps its feet in unison with the drums.

THUMP. THUMP. THUMP. THUMP. THUMP.

The drums suddenly stop. The crowd goes quiet. Deathly quiet. The smoke clears. The sun shoos away the murky cloud. From Renatus's half-smirk, this is the effect he was going for. Tension thrives in silence. The crowd peers in anticipation towards the open gate. Still nothing. Legion nudges me. "Perhaps they changed their mind." I forcibly exhale, needing that bit of comic relief.

Tobias's left hand shakes uncontrollably; he tries to calm it with his right. I can feel his surge of anxiety. "Easy, Tobias. We got this. Apex is just a man like you and me." His voice cracks. "What's taking so long?"

"Renatus is enjoying the anticipation of what he thinks will be our death." He knows the longer we wait, the more nervous we become.

There are murmurs from the mob. They are getting impatient. They want their pound of flesh.

Renatus finally stands, his hands raised, silencing the crowd. "People of Zion. The wait is over. I give you Apex!"

Raucous cheers as Apex and his five remaining Lazurites strut through the gate and into the arena. Apex peers at us like someone about to shoot fish in a barrel. He thinks it's already in the bag. He makes a show of counting the five of us. He then turns to his men and pretends to count them as well, playing to the audience.

"Well, this isn't fair, is it? Six to five?"

The crowd boos, and many of them give a thumbs down. "How about we make this fair?"

A loud applause.

I watch in shock as Apex turns, rears back his mighty fist, and punches one of his teammates square in the chest. The man is lifted off the ground and lands on the sandy arena floor. Lifeless. A massive dent in his exoarmor.

"Now it's fair!" Apex bellows as he lifts his hands to the crowd. Renatus can't hide his chagrin as four arena guards drag the dead Lazurite from the coliseum. It's obvious Renatus can't completely control Apex. Maybe no one can. But it's too late to play that card and try to convince Apex to join our side.

I gather my men. "Okay. One down. Keep your eyes open. Look to the ground and the sky. I have a feeling whatever hell is about to be unleashed won't just come from Apex. Let's spread out; take out the weakest Lazurites first, save Apex for last."

Tobias whispers. "Shouldn't we do the opposite? Take out Apex first, then the rest is easy?"

"Normally, I would say yes, but Apex will want to draw this out. Make it last. Prolong our suffering. It is obvious he doesn't care about the other Lazurites. And because of that, they won't be as deadly. Apex thinks he can take us all on by himself. That will be his downfall."

"Agreed," says Legion.

I peer at them with a certain gravitas. "Today is for your families. For your children and their children. For the Drecks that died before us. For The Defiance. For freedom. Am I the only one tired of living behind a wall, only to be seen as a commodity? Renatus rules by fear and fear alone. What do *we* fear, gentleman?"

In unison, "Nothing."

My little speech started with a tinge of false bravado, but now I have even amped myself up. I raise my voice. "What is it that we fear?!"

"NOTHING!"

"What can man take from us that God can't give back?"

"NOTHING!"

"It has been one of the great honors of my life to share your company. There is no other I would rather bleed with." I sniff away my emotions, and we stand together. I try not to think about the outlandish and barbaric things that await us. I scan the arena and don't see anything unusual yet. Perhaps Renatus has gone back to an old-fashioned gladiator-style duel. He probably did a poll to determine what the people wanted.

I couldn't be more wrong.

It begins with drones swooping in, flying over the arena, and randomly dropping weapons. Scourges. Ricochets. StunClubs. Voltaic maces and swords. Energy-propelled spears. Our exoarmor can blunt some of the effects of these weapons, but not by much.

Apex pounds his chest and motions for his men to charge. On their way towards us, they scoop up weapons. We do the same. I grab a ricochet, of course, and toss it towards a Lazurite to my left. I miss. He ducks, then rolls. I watch Legion swing his StunClub, knocking a Lazurite into the arena's wall. To my right, Tobias dodges an energy-propelled spear, only to be hit in the back by a scourge. I fling my weapon and hit the soldier standing behind him. He goes down, but is not out.

All the while, Apex watches with folded arms, looking bored even. What is he waiting for? I can see Renatus from the corner of my eye, showing signs of irritation. Yes, he wants Apex to put on a show, but he doesn't want to take any chances. Suddenly, four gates open, and four Rollers shoot out.

"Rollers!" I warn my men.

One of them rolls straight towards Apex, who casually jumps over it, letting it slam into one of his men. Four to go. The Rollers bounce off the walls and slide around like a game of pinball. After a few nifty moves, we are able to avoid the Rollers, until they finally come to a stop and deactivate.

"Drones!" Legion bellows.

I peer to the sky and watch as four HeliDrones indiscriminately drop plasma bombs. Now, we are dodging things from the sky. If Renatus's plan is to wear us out, it's working.

"Look out!" Tobias yells.

In my peripheral, I spot the glowing end of a voltaic mace being swung towards my head. I duck the sizzling, spiky ball of metal and kick his legs out from underneath him. I step back and detach my ricochet from my belt. Before I can throw, a sudden, sharp, sizzling pain pierces my left shoulder. An energy-propelled spear has pierced my exoarmor and punctured my shoulder. Momentarily distracted, I don't see the Lazurite take another swing with his mace. Before it finishes me off, Legion throws me to the ground, and at the same time, he boots his mighty foot into the Lazurite's chest, knocking him to the ground.

"Thanks," I manage.

"You're about to retract that, thanks," he replies, grabbing the spear and ripping it from my shoulder. I grimace in pain and drop to my knees. Before I can take stock of my new injury, Legion hurls the spear like a professional javelin thrower, and it sticks into the back of another Lazurite. Three more to go.

Legion pulls me up. "You okay?"

"Oh yeah, never better," I reply facetiously.

I look up at Renatus, who is staring daggers at me. It's evident to him now that we don't plan on taking a dive. He rubs his chin and shakes his head, giving me a final warning.

I stand and defiantly hold up my ricochet—the symbol of hope—the symbol of defiance. The crowd cheers, further vexing Renatus. Legion and I rejoin the fight while wondering what Apex is waiting for.

Sarai

I warily eye the packet of DemonDust. Is it the correct variety? If not, the HarvestDrones will pass me by, and I will end up drugged for the next few days. And how much to take? He said this was enough for a two-hundred-pound male. If I take too much, it will kill me. I need to take just enough to knock me out, and have enough Dust in my system so that the HarvestDrone's scanner can pick it up. But not so much that I am incapacitated for too long. I need to be awake before they process me inside the facility.

I dump more than half of the Dust into a bottle of water and shake it well. I peer around to make sure no one is around. The last thing I need is to be picked up by a Lazurite patrol or worse. Here goes nothing. I double-check that my backpack with the serum is secure and that my scourge is hidden behind my back, and guzzle it down. It is tasteless. Probably by design, meant to look and feel benign. Ironic that what has enslaved us—what has killed us—just might save us.

I immediately feel light-headed. Woozy. I lay down in a patch of tall grass before I pass out. I have positioned myself between The Middle and the protocol facility. This is the path the HarvestDrones take for drop-off. I want to be sure they pick me up. If not, I don't have a plan B. My heart rate slows. So does my breathing. When I close my eyes, I am in a dream state: I can see Asher and Silas. Playing in the ocean as I watch, my feet wiggling in the soft sand. The winds are stagnant, and the clouds have disappeared, giving the shimmering sun a chance to finally show off its splendor. A perfect day with the ones I love. Is this what it feels like to be on the Dust?

Is this why so many people are hooked? Addicted to a manufactured and counterfeit happiness.

Suddenly, I am overtaken with terror and cannot move. I see Asher and Silas hovering inside a harvesting tube or *womb*, floating in the pink gel-like substance. They scream, but I cannot hear them. I bang on the glass cylinders and scream back. Then, the entire room begins to fill with the womb-like material. I am slowly drowning. Suffocating. The Dust is now revealing its true colors. Fraudulent and unearned euphoria always leads to despair. Things slowly go dark. I try to speak, but the words have no sound—my vision blurs. I cannot hear. I have no senses, yet I can feel everything around me. Have I taken too much? Not enough?

Then, I am out.

I don't see the HarvestDrone's long plastic tube an hour later, vacuuming me up. I am still out when it deposits me inside the protocol facility. When I finally come to, I am lying on what looks like a hospital bed. My backpack with the serum is resting on a table in the corner. So is my scourge. My vision is blurry, and my head is killing me. I try to sit up, but can't. I am already strapped to the bed.

Am I too late? Did I take too much Dust and not wake up in time? Now what?

The door swings open, and two scientists stroll in. I close my eyes and feign that I'm still incapacitated. They unstrap me and transfer my limp body to a gurney. I am to be transferred to a harvesting tube in preparation for LifeCell extraction. Now is the time to make my move. I have no idea how many guards are outside, but seeing how they struggled and strained to lift me, I'm confident I can take them.

"She's cute," one of them says.

"She looks familiar. But cute nonetheless," the other replies.

As flattered as I am, they are both about to receive the wrath of mama bear. Before they can wheel me to the door, I open my eyes and roll off the gurney, landing on one of the scientist's feet. From the ground, I quickly slam my elbow into the side of his knee. He goes down with a surprised yelp. The other, a coward, sprints towards the door. Before he can get there, I kick the gurney, which barrels into him. He is slammed against the door but is quickly back on his feet, reaching for the handle. Still dazed and a little off balance, I sidestep to the table to snatch my scourge. I rear back and snap it at his ankle. The electric current takes him to the ground.

Then, an arm is around my chest, and a needle is about to be jabbed into my neck.

The other scientist tries to hold me steady while plunging whatever is in that needle into my jugular. I grab his wrist with both hands and turn the needle around. With his kneecap broken, he only has one leg for leverage. I use my entire lower body to force his hand back towards him, effectively plunging the needle into his neck. His eyes roll back, and he drops to the ground with a thud.

I place my hands on my knees in an attempt to catch my breath. Coming off the Dust has left me wobbly and disoriented. Not to mention anxious and fidgety. My mouth is dry, and I just now realize how parched I am. I scan the room for water and find none.

Licking my dry lips, I slide on the backpack, roll up my scourge, and gently open the door.

Boots clap on the tile floor. I retreat back into the room and softly shut the door. A Lazurite guard marches past. I exhale and try it again. This time, the hallway is clear. I try to get my bearings and remember where my son and brother are being housed. I recognize the processing room, as they call it. *Processing*. A sterile term for what is essentially a concentration camp. Now I remember. Eleazar and Silas's cylinders are in the back, on the other side of the facility. I pass row after row of glass cylinders, trying not to look at the lifeless faces entombed inside.

Another guard turns the corner, and I duck into one of the rows. He will have a visual on me before I can run to the other side. I squeeze between two cylinders and hope he doesn't see me as he walks by. The hairs stand on the back of my neck; I'm inches away from the comatose bodies waiting to have their LifeCells harvested. They look alive and dead at the same time. Their eyes are melancholic, their mouths partially open, as if trying to say something. I exhale as the guard passes.

But then, the clacking of his boots stops. He turns around and makes his way into my row. I scrunch back against the glass, trying not to be seen. But I am exposed. In a few more steps, he will see me. I have to make my move before he does. I reach behind my back and unhook my scourge, silently turning it on. Just as he enters my line of sight, I crack my weapon. Its long, pulsating tentacle wraps around his neck. I pull him in. He slams against the glass and crashes to the ground. I cringe at how loud that was, but I had no choice.

"You!" To my left, at the end of the row, a guard spots me and dashes in my direction.

I exit the row and dart towards my son and brother. From another row emerge two more guards who join the chase. They are not elites, but they are armed. I'm not as fast as I used to be and only have a fifty-foot head start.

"Stop!" one of them yells, firing his plasma rifle.

I turn a corner, and in front of me is a stout guard riding an ElectroScooter. I whip my scourge at his ankle and yank him off the scooter. It ghost-rides into the wall. Before he can get up, I'm on the scooter and motoring towards the back. Plasma whizzes by me.

Then I make it.

Eleazar and Silas, side by side. My brother. My son. One will die, and one will live. I rifle through my backpack and pull out the two serum vials and a needle. I can hear the guards running in my direction. My hands shake, and in haste, I drop the needle. It rolls underneath one of the cylinders.

"C'mon!"

I scramble to my knees, both hands pawing for the needle. With my fingertips, I am barely able to roll it back in my hands. I fill the needle with the serum from the first vial and inject it into the tube that feeds my Silas inside the cylinder. I do the same for Eleazar.

That's it. It's done.

For them, protocol has now been rendered ineffective. I am sad for just a moment; there is a finality now. My brother can never return. He is finally truly dead. Perhaps he can now be at peace.

Before I can ponder further, I see the ElectroNet shoot toward me from the corner of my eye. It looks like a flying spider web.

All I can do is smile. It doesn't matter what happens to me now, for I have saved my son.

At least for now.

CHAPTER ELEVEN

Cephas

CEPHAS GROANS AS HE bounces around on the stretcher. His men have carried him for miles as they reach the outskirts of Zion West, near the arena. Thirsty, he licks his lips. He grimaces at the metallic, briny taste of blood mixed with dirt and sweat. He breathes in the spicy scents of late fall: woodsmoke and nutmeg, combined with the musty aroma of damp soil and decaying leaves.

"He's awake," Adam says.

"Glad to see you're still alive. You're heavy, Cephas," Eve tells him with a sideways smile.

Cephas grunts; he opens his cracked and bloodstained lips and blinks away the blur in his vision. "Where are we?"

"Almost there."

"And their army?"

Adam tries to hide his disappointment. "Just ahead."

"Size?" Cephas barely manages a whisper.

"Bigger than expected," Eve informs him. "It's not just Lazurites. It's some of Percival's army as well."

Jethro and Red Beard trudge towards them. "What kind of war did you get us into? They got us outnumbered three to one."

"Is that all?" Cephas still retains his sense of humor.

Jethro shakes his head. "You Drecks are crazy. But it's my kind of crazy. What's the plan?"

Cephas wheezes while managing to sit up. "Crazy? You ain't seen nothing yet."

Adam and Eve exchange a knowing glance. Adam sighs. "I'm afraid to ask."

Cephas coughs uncontrollably before wiping blood from his lips. "We surrender."

"Surrender?" they reply, practically in unison.

"Yes."

Jethro spits. "We didn't come all this way to back down. I thought you Drecks had more sand than this."

Eve grabs Cephas's dirty hand. "He's right. Maybe you aren't thinking straight. Why come all this way to capitulate? We can take them; we still have some fight left in us."

Adam says, "Perhaps a bit more rest. Think it over."

Cephas doesn't appreciate being patronized. He closes his eyes, fighting back the pain. "There's no time for rest! Look, the absolute best place for the nuke is under their barracks. It's directly in the middle of where his armies stage, and adjacent to his new cloning facility. It will give us the most leverage."

Adam's tone is now flustered. "How are we going to get in there? And what does that have to do with surrendering?"

Cephas manages to smile. He even pauses for effect. "They are going to put it there for us."

Eve lifts her hands. "Do enlighten us."

Cephas coughs uncontrollably for a good minute before composing himself. "It's Lazurite protocol to store their weapons next to the barracks.

We surrender, and the first thing they will do is take our arms and artillery and bring them to the barracks for storage."

Adam interjects, "And if they don't? Or discover the nuke, then what? We have given up for nothing, leaving Asher and Sarai high and dry."

Cephas wipes more blood from his lips. "We are outnumbered three to one. Those are normal Dreck odds; I get it. And you know I hate to surrender. But we don't have the element of surprise this time. Nor do we have a frozen lake to lure them onto or a ravine to trap them in. Neither Legion nor the Sons of Levi are coming to our aid. Their arms are superior to ours. We can't win this one straight up. This is our best shot. Fighting them head-on is suicide."

Jethro and Red Beard exchange glances. "Think I'm starting to second-guess our trip."

"What if they decide to kill us anyway?" Eve asks astutely.

"Hey, we have LifeCells; we are a commodity to them, which makes us somewhat valuable."

Jethro frowns. "But I was itching for a fight. But what you say makes sense."

"Look, this isn't just my call. We all need to make this decision. It's the best idea I have at the moment, that is all."

Everyone warily nods in agreement.

Cephas pulls out the remote detonator for the nuke. "Someone has to stay behind with this. Surely, they will search us for weapons, and if they find the detonator, the nuke is useless to us."

Adam grabs it and hands it to Eve. "Take it."

She shakes her head. "I'm not staying behind where it's safe. You take it."

Adam pleads, "Please, Eve. If things don't go as planned, I want you to survive. Live on. Carry out the oath we took at Eden. Take it. Please."

She reluctantly receives the detonator. "I'll blow it if I need to. Don't think I won't."

"I know you will. That is why you have it."

Cephas grits his teeth in pain. "You'll need to be out of sight but close enough for the detonator to work."

Adam unfurls a map and points at a clearing. "Here is where we will surrender." He turns to Eve. "And here is where you can hide out. This tree line just above us."

"Hide the nuke in the crate with the MREs and OatBars," Cephas orders them. "And make some white flags."

"On it."

Cephas dives into another coughing fit, blood spewing into his rag. His wheezing is getting worse. They all stare at him, concerned.

"What are you all looking at? I may be injured, but I'm not a corpse. Not yet."

They sheepishly turn away.

An hour later, they are gathered and have everything ready. Cephas lies down on a stretcher, his breathing shallow. He watches Adam say goodbye to Eve behind two oak trees. Before departing, he watches them kiss. Then, Eve slaps Adam on the shoulder. "Now, get outta here."

Adam approaches Cephas, who can tell that his look is melancholic. He tries to reassure him. "You'll see her again, son."

"I know," he feigns confidence.

"You belong together, right? I mean, c'mon, Adam and Eve."

Adam smiles. "Fighting for your life and out come the dad jokes."

"Do me a favor, Adam. I want you to tell Asher for me that—"

"No, don't do that. Don't say that. You'll be here to tell him yourself. Hang in there."

"Listen to me, Adam. I was trying to be strong back there, but the truth of the matter is that I am a corpse. It's just a matter of time. I need you to tell Asher that I am proud of him. That he has become the leader I never could—the father I never knew how to be. That his father is smiling down at him. And that this country is lucky to have him."

"I will, Cephas. I will."

It takes them another hour to reach the clearing. Cephas's front men march, waving a multitude of white flags. The Lazurites are staged in a U-formation, with dozens of HeliDrones above them. A Lazurite commander and a contingent of men ride their jeeps to the front of Cephas's army. The commander is tall with long blond hair, your prototypical Lazurite. He exits the Jeep, and his red sashes flap in the wind.

"Help me up," Cephas says.

Adam pulls him from the stretcher. With great pain, Cephas limps over to face the commander. "We are here to surrender peacefully and unconditionally."

"If this is a trick, know we have you surrounded," the commander says smugly.

"No trick," Cephas wheezes.

The commander scoffs, "Since when do Drecks surrender?"

"Like you said, we are surrounded. And obviously outnumbered. We may be stubborn, but we're not stupid."

"Have your men lay down their arms."

"Set your weapons down!" Cephas orders.

They obey.

"The mighty Cephas, how far you have fallen. You don't look so well, old man," the commander says, bleeding arrogance.

"Death will soon find us all."

The commander smirks. "No, it won't." He then turns to his men. "Gather all their weapons and supplies and bring them to the barracks."

"Yes, sir," the Lazurite to his right replies.

"And I want this entire army searched thoroughly."

Cephas watches as his army is frisked and patted down. The Lazurite soldiers collect their weapons and ferry them towards the barracks. He notices how young many of them are—and, he hopes, impressionable. Some feel dreary; he can tell they don't want to be here. Many are conscripts, which is also good.

Adam nudges Cephas and whispers, "Look. They are opening the nuke crate."

A tense moment as the soldiers pry the top off the wooden crate. They rifle through its contents, picking up MREs and OatBars. "Just food."

Cephas and Adam exhale.

Cephas nods towards the arena in the distance. "I only hope Asher can pull it off one more time. I hope that Lucas and Neriah didn't die for nothing."

Asher

We have four to their three. Two more Lazurites, and then all we have left is Apex. My plan is going well—too well. Apex has yet to engage. What is he doing? Whatever it is, it has me nervous. Apex pushes his last two Lazurites towards us. They reluctantly obey. We ready our weapons.

"Let's finish this," I tell my men.

We charge full speed towards them. They nervously peer back at Apex, then start their charge. And then a cracking sound. I can feel a chill emerge from the ground and climb up my legs. To my left, Tobias slips and falls. I try to stop, but can't. Instead, I glide toward the Lazurites. I peer down, and inexplicably, the arena floor has transformed into a sheet of ice. The crowd gasps in surprise.

I glance up and see Renatus's smug smile. He pats his Canonization Architect, Jokim, on the back and mouths, "Well done."

In front of me, Legion has lost his footing, and he slides uncontrollably towards Apex. Before Legion can regain his balance, Apex boots him in the other direction, sending him slipping and sliding until he crashes into me. We manage to find purchase again, somewhat. I toss my ricochet at a Lazurite, but before releasing it, I must duck an incoming spear. Legion grabs me by the arm and spins me in a circle.

"What are you doing, Legion!?"

"You set them up; I'll knock them down." He releases my arm, and the momentum sends me sliding into the Lazurite in front of us. I take him out at the knees. I don't particularly like being used as a bowling ball, but in this case, it works. I stun him with my ricochet and then finish him with his own spear. In the corner, Tobias struggles with the last remaining soldier. In any other context, it would almost be humorous—watching us slip and slide around like uncoordinated and untrained gladiators.

Apex still watches, arms folded, tapping his foot against the now-icy floor. His not engaging is making us anxious and surely making Renatus nervous. I think he is trying to simultaneously make the point that he can take us on alone, and that Renatus doesn't control him.

Legion and I skate over to help Tobias. Then, the opposite sensation engulfs my legs.

Heat.

Then steam.

The ice is melting—and fast. After less than a minute, we are swimming in a massive pool. My feet can't touch the bottom. The audience's amazement is audible. Indeed, they are getting their money's worth. I remember my first Canonization and hope I don't have to fight another shark.

"Help!" Tobias pleads. "I can't swim."

Legion and I swim to his location. The Lazurite is pushing Tobias's head underwater. Legion pulls the Lazurite off and forces him under. I swim in front of Tobias and then turn my back.

"Grab onto me!"

He wraps his arms around my neck, and in his panic, I am being swamped. "Easy, Tobias. Calm down. You're choking me. I got you. Just calm down."

Legion pops to the surface. The last remaining Lazurite floats next to him. I swivel my head, and no longer spot Apex. Now, panic engulfs me.

"You see Apex?"

Legion, treading water, shakes his head.

"What about Max?" I ask, referring to our last remaining Dreck. We nervously scan the arena. He has also vanished. Anxiety and confusion set in.

"Where'd they go? I don't understand." Tobias's panic meter rises again as his bear hug around me grows tighter. I'm unsure how long I can hold us both above the water. His fingers clutch my chest, and his nails dig into my skin. "Easy, Tobias."

"Maybe Apex can't swim either," Legion suggests hopefully.

"Unlikely."

Then, a body emerges in the water, in front of us, and it floats lifelessly by. It's Max.

"What is happening?" Tobias cries out in horror.

But I know what is happening. Suddenly, Tobias is gone from my back. Sucked down underwater or pulled down, more likely.

"Tobias!" I yell. I fill my lungs and dip my head underwater. About fifteen feet down, Apex holds Tobias down. I swim towards him and try to pull Apex off of him. Underwater, with no leverage, and with his size, it's no use. He punches me in the gut, expelling all the oxygen from my lungs. I swim to the top and gasp for air.

It's no use. Tobias is gone.

As quickly as it arrived, the water begins to drain from the arena. Apex stands stoic, while dead bodies litter his feet. The water glistens off his pulsating muscles. He isn't even breathing heavily. We stiffen as the onlookers go quiet. His savage countenance is enough to extinguish any residual chatter from the crowd. I peer down at Tobias's lifeless body, but there is no time to mourn—another senseless death in these barbarous games.

Apex, Legion, and I are all that is left. And I have no doubt this is how he wanted it—how everyone watching wanted it. I can hear my heartbeat, feel my pulse. Legion squeezes the water from his hair and cracks his massive knuckles. It sounds like tree branches breaking. Apex's lips curl up towards his ears. That aloof look has disappeared. He peers at his hands as if impressed by the carnage they can cause.

"Now I'm ready."

Sarai

I awake in handcuffs. My head throbs. I must have landed on it when the ElectroNet took me out. But it's okay. The deed is done. My son can't be harvested for his LifeCell. Four Lazurites escort me down a dim hallway. They march with purpose, like robots. The clacking of their boots against the cold concrete floors is not helping my headache.

"Where are you taking me?" I ask.

One of them grumbles. "No speaking."

"Where are we?"

"I said, no speaking."

Then I hear loud cheering and the stomping of feet above me. I am under the arena. My husband is up there fighting for his life. And here I am, so close, yet I can do nothing to help him. As always, we are separated because of my father. But I can sense it, feel it even: today it ends. One way or another, this entire saga of war, suffering, hope, and love. It ends today. Knowing this, a wave of inexplicable peace comes over me.

We turn a corner, and I am pushed up a flight of stairs. Then another. We are now inside the Coliseum, about halfway up. I am then led to my father's Sultan's Suite.

They escort me to a chair next to Renatus. He is intently watching the battle below. Sitting to his left is Czar Percival.

"Good to see you again, Sultana," Percival says derisively.

It takes everything in my power not to jump up and punch him.

"Daughter, you remember the Czar, don't you? The one you tried to convince to turn against me?"

Looks like my father has offered him protocol in exchange for his help. "I never forget a weasel, especially a short one."

"Daughter, oh daughter, what have you been up to?" It's a rhetorical question, he knows.

I peer down at the arena below me. I am jolted by what I see—flabbergasted even. Water drains from the arena. I see dead bodies float past Apex's knees. To my relief, Asher and Legion are not among the bodies.

Asher is gassed. He is tired. I can physically feel my heart ache watching him. I want to look away, but I can't.

Renatus's upper lip twitches in ire. "Ingesting Dust so you could be picked up by a HarvestDrone and sneak into my facility. Then, injecting my son and yours with a so-called anti-protocol serum. Clever daughter. Very clever. But all for naught, I'm afraid. You see, Boaz was a Trojan Horse. Your serum is nothing more than a placebo. You can't end protocol, my daughter. It was destined to be. Something like that doesn't go back into a box."

I don't tell him that he is wrong. At least not yet. I glance over to Percival and can tell he is concerned. If LifeCells are rendered unusable, that affects him as well. That is the reason he is here.

"I am one step ahead of you. I always have been, Sarai. Your Asher, your Defiance. Cephas. You rely on hope. Rely on faith. You trust. None of which wins wars."

I peer at him, and for the first time, I do not hate him. I feel sorry for him. I pity him. "Without those, what is victory worth?"

"Everything." He is serious, sober. He speaks as if this isn't something he wants, but it's something he has to do. I don't know which is worse. "Soon, Asher will be dead. You will see it with your own eyes. Cephas and your Defiance have surrendered. Your friends from Eden are no more. And after today, Eleazar will return to me."

"I wouldn't be so confident."

"Like you, daughter, I have faith."

"Confidence and faith are not the same thing."

Renatus leans in; I can smell his foul breath. "You think because you have love that you are entitled to win? That you are righteous?"

I peer at him with pity. "What do you know about love?"

"You can ask your brother that question when I bring him back."

What he doesn't understand is that because we have love, we have already won.

The door to the suite opens, and in stumble Cephas and Adam, pushed by two guards. Cephas is bleeding from his back. His lips are blood-stained. He wheezes.

"Cephas! Are you okay?"

He struggles to pull himself up into a chair. "Fine, dear." He manages to find his sarcastic tone. "And how are you? Enjoying the games?"

"What happened?" I ask Adam.

"He was shot on the way here."

It pains me to see the great Cephas, the leader of The Defiance, the man who helped my husband become the man he is, in such bad shape. For the first time, I notice how old he looks. Years of wear and tear have caught up with him. This past year has significantly deteriorated him, as it has all of us. We age and come closer to death, but my father is able to steer clear of it.

Renatus, strangely acting as a host, pours them both wine. Cephas flicks his from the table; the glass shatters at his feet.

Renatus shrugs. "I forgot, you no longer drink."

Then, Cephas finally sees Percival. With great pain, he launches himself from his seat and lands a massive right hook on Percival's small jaw.

Percival falls out of his chair. "That's for Neriah."

Two elites drag Cephas back to his chair. Percival pulls out a dagger.

"Wait. You will have your chance. Later," Renatus tells him.

Cephas's voice is raspy, dry. "What are we doing up here, Renatus?"

"I wanted you to witness this. Best seats in the house to watch the destruction of your beloved Asher. And the final downfall of The Defiance."

"You're a monster."

The crowd cheers as Apex raises his arms and flexes, putting on a show. "Not according to them."

Cephas snarls, his eyes bloodshot. "They'll figure it out one day, Renatus. The real you. The purpose of these games. One day, they'll open their eyes and wade through all the distractions. Discover the truth. Then you will be no more."

"I give them what they want. No more, no less." Renatus stands, as do I.

Asher picks up a ricochet and a sword. Legion grabs a StunClub. They race towards Apex, who gathers no weapons.

My father, always greedy for death and at the same time greedy for everlasting life, wrings his hands. "Ready for the end?"

Asher

I wonder why Apex is just standing there. Both Legion and I are coming at him at a pretty good clip. I hurl my ricochet at him. He bats it away effortlessly. I am ahead of Legion. When I arrive at Apex's position, I leap in the air and swing my voltaic sword down toward his skull; he blocks it with his voltage-absorbing arm plate. He swings his other arm sideways like a hammer into my gut. I fly backward toward Legion, who ducks to avoid me. The crowd cheers.

Legion, a little off-balance, swings his StunClub. Apex turns to the side, just avoiding it. He lets Legion's momentum send him flying right past. Apex turns and boots him in the back.

"You're getting old, brother. Old and slow."

Legion slides on the dirt. He pulls himself up. Blood smears his knees and elbows as he wipes the dust from his face.

I find a scourge on the ground and whip it at Apex's leg. It wraps around his ankle. I pull. He won't budge. Now what? He kicks his leg back, ripping the scourge from my hand just as Legion punches him from behind.

Apex hits the ground, then rolls back to his feet. "Good brother. That had some juice."

I charge him again. He backhands me in the chest. My knees buckle; the wind leaves my lungs. My ribs are cracked, for sure. Through teary eyes and blurry vision, I watch them run dynamically at each other. Their heels spew dust and mud into the air. The crowd hushes in eager anticipation of the collision about to come, like a train about to crash into a tank. They both go airborne as I still struggle to fill my lungs. Simultaneously, they both land a mighty fist. The crack sounds like tree branches snapping. The force sends them both backward, landing on the ground.

Apex is up first. Legion spits two teeth before Apex grabs him by the neck, lifts him, and runs him into the wall. He squeezes his throat while Legion gasps for air.

"It's not too late, Legion. Tap out and join me. There is still time for you—still time for repentance. Let's stop fighting each other. Rejoin Zion. We will defeat this little man, this nuisance. Then we can rule together."

Legion says nothing.

"I'll take your silence as a no."

I have to do something fast. Then, a four-foot section of the arena floor opens, and an ElectroCycle is elevated to the surface. Four in total are spread throughout the Coliseum. Weapons are still scattered about. I grab what's closest to me—a voltaic mace—and then hop onto the bike.

Apex sees me coming from the corner of his eye and releases his vice-like grip on Legion's throat. He scoops up a spear and jumps onto his own cycle.

We motor straight towards one another. He holds his spear in front of him, almost as if we are jousting. I twirl my mace above me and let out a primal battle howl. As we get closer, it's obvious his spear will reach me before I can utilize my weapon on him. As he is about to spear me, I hurl my mace at his front tire. The chain and ball of spikes wrap around his tire and flip his cycle into the air. Apex goes airborne over me, momentarily blocking out the sun.

Fifty feet behind me, he finally lands on the arena floor with a massive thud, creating a two-foot-deep indentation. I cycle to Legion, who is still gasping for air.

"You all right?"

"We need a plan," he grunts.

"It's hard to plan when we don't know what's coming. This arena is too unpredictable. As is your brother."

"I think you just made him mad."

Apex stands and brushes himself off. He stretches out his fingers and cracks his neck.

"I think he might be indestructible."

Legion points to Renatus. "If he were, Renatus wouldn't be so concerned." I peer up and spot Renatus standing. He is yelling at Apex, "Finish this already!"

Apex ignores him and marches towards us. I stand side by side with Legion; we steel ourselves for what is about to come. I ask my friend, "How do you wanna do this?"

Legion turns to me. "You go low, I'll go high."

"That's your plan?"

"You have a better one?"

"I'll go low."

Before Apex reaches us, about fifty platforms rise from the arena floor. They are four feet off the ground and have a circumference large enough to hold a single person, perhaps a little more.

"Now what?" I ask.

Legion starts collecting weapons. "I'm guessing we should get on one."

He's not wrong. A black, murky substance pours from two pipes on both sides of the arena. It looks like dark, steaming blood.

"That's hot oil." I shout the obvious, and scoop some weapons up. In minutes, the entire arena is covered in the bubbling dark substance.

I stand on one of the platforms. To my right, Legion does the same. Apex has found one of his own. If that's not bad enough, the platforms rock back and forth, forcing us to keep our balance.

"This is intolerable," Legion growls.

God-given imagination and creativity were meant for the greater good. Ironically, Zion, a society claiming to be intellectually and physically superior to all others, uses them for evil in what can only be described as preposterous and grotesque. Some of the most educated people in this crowd—the ones yearning for our blood—will go home tonight and speak of morality to their children, and brag about how civilized they are compared to us Drecks. How does one lift such a veil? I guess calling them educated is being generous. Since they were children, Lazurite schools have been impressing upon them that they are superior, almost godlike.

"Asher!" Legion stirs me awake from my internal philosophizing. "He's coming."

Apex jumps from platform to platform, making his way in our direction. The distance between the platforms makes it a problematic jump, at least for an ordinary-sized man. Which is calculated, I'm sure. I hurl my ricochet at him. He ducks it, and it returns to me. In return, he fires a spear at me. It is coming in low. I jump, and it sails past me, underneath my feet. I land on the platform, which tilts to and fro; I try to keep my balance. The spear hits just underneath one of the platforms in the corner. Its electrical system shorts out, and the platform disappears into the burning oil.

Just as I find my balance, Apex is flying through the air. He lands on my platform; I have to bear hug him to keep myself from falling in. His mighty arm crashes into my chest, sending me flying to Legion's platform. Legion catches me, but we are both off balance. Before we both fall, I quickly jump to the platform behind us, but don't quite make it. Where are my Air Jordans when I need them? My hands are able to grab the rim of the platform. I'm older, but my grip strength is still intact. The tips of my toes nick the hot oil. I lift my knees and pull myself up. The front of my boots is melted off, exposing my burnt toes.

Just as I gain my bearings, a sword flies by my peripherals. It lodges in Legion's right shoulder. He grunts and drops to one knee, his platform tilting.

"Legion!" I yell.

He looks at me and grimaces. "It's okay. Heart's on the other side."

It won't take long for Apex to overpower us at this rate. He raises his fists and again plays to the raucous crowd. He is in no rush, but Renatus is not so patient. I see him mouth the words, "Finish them."

I have an idea and whisper, "Get him to jump to your platform."

Legion whispers back, "Are you crazy?"

"Just do it. But be sure you leave it before he lands."

"This sounds like another one of your crazy Dreckish ideas."

"It is."

With the sword still stuck in his shoulder, he turns to me. "This is the last time I play along."

I smile back. "It could very well be."

Legion asks, "What time is it?"

"Why? You have somewhere to be?" I look up at the sun. "It's probably around three."

"Ya know, if it weren't for you, I would be sipping tea about right now, feeding Buttons his afternoon treat."

"That's no way for a man like you to go out."

"I guess you're right." Legion sighs and turns back to Apex. He slaps his chest. "Is that all you got, brother? Is that all you got?!"

Apex's eyes narrow. "I'm glad to have finally woken you."

"I'm waiting." Legion eggs him on, hands in the air.

Apex exhales a primordial howl and leaps from his platform.

"Now!" I yell to Legion.

Just as Legion jumps towards my platform, I toss my ricochet at the electrical circuits under the platform that Apex is aiming to land on. They spark and fizzle. Apex's eyes go wide as he registers what is happening. Legion lands on my platform, almost pushing me off. Apex lands on his just as it sinks into the blistering oil. He tries to jump from it, but it's too late. He makes it halfway to ours before splashing into the oil. We turn our heads, not wanting to watch. Ear-piercing bestial shrieks emanate from Apex, until he is finally buried under the gurgling oil.

Gasps from the crowd.

Then, dead silence.

I peer up at the Sultan Suite. Then I see Sarai, and my heart skips a beat. She is standing, leaning towards me. Cephas and Adam are with her.

Renatus cannot hide his fury. I can see him tremble from here. He exits the suite.

I turn to Legion. "We did it. We won."

Oil drains from the stadium. A gate slides open, and Renatus emerges, escorted by thirty elites.

"Are you sure?" Legion asks.

I look up to Sarai. She gives me a nod. "The plan is in place."

"Now what?"

"Now it's up to Renatus."

Asher

Blood drips onto the arena floor from the blade still impaled in Legion's shoulder. We stand defiantly as Renatus marches up to us, his platoon of elites surrounding us. Is he going to kill us now for defying him? For killing his beloved Apex?

He seethes as he talks through his teeth. "I thought we had an understanding."

"Things have changed," I tell him. The confidence in my tone has shaken him. He circles us.

"Your disobedience has forced my hand. What is to stop me from slaughtering your entire army, which is surrounded just outside this arena? What is to prevent me from sending a nuclear warhead to every Reservation in The Middle? You and Legion shall watch The Defiance's final annihilation. Then you'll go on to your permanent home in The Mountain."

"The surrender was my call," I inform him. "There was a nuclear warhead left at NORAD that is now operable. Your men have unknowingly placed it in the barracks. You nuke us, we nuke you. You and your entire army obliterated. Along with The Mountain."

"You're lying!" His tone is now feral. He paces as if he's about to lose it. This is the first time I've seen him sweat.

"Try me."

"You would kill yourselves and your entire army along with ours?"

"Yes. But our souls are prepared. You? Last time I checked, you can't perform protocol on dust and ash."

His tone devious, his question rhetorical. "So now what, Asher? Where do we go from here?"

"We won. Let us go. Unless you want to break the rules of The Canonization—your own rules—in front of everyone here, everyone watching. What do you think the people will do when they find out this is rigged? If they lose faith in your precious Canonization, they will lose faith in you."

He laughs. Uncontrollably for a minute. He even hunches over and grabs his belly. "You did well, Asher. You and Legion did well. You never cease to amaze—besting Apex like you did." He slaps me on the shoulder like an old friend or a mentor. "One hell of a Canonization. One for the ages. But it's not over yet."

"Apex is dead. We won. What else is there?" But I know.

He waves his hands in the air and does a little dance. "Why, the rematch everyone has been waiting for, of course." He then yells to the crowd. "Who wants to see a rematch? Legion versus Asher! Ten years in the making. But this time to the death!" They roar and chant our names. "Just listen to them, Asher. Give the people what they want, and you, too, can have power."

"No," I tell him simply.

"No?" He points to the Sultan's suite, where four elites have their blades pressed against Sarai, Cephas, and Adam's throats. "You fight, or they die."

I hadn't planned for this, but my answer remains the same. "No."

"Are you sure you want to be responsible for their deaths?"

"The difference between us is that we are willing to die for what we believe in, where you would only kill for yours."

"Very well then." Renatus turns and saunters back toward the gate. With his back facing us, he yells, "Feel free to wave goodbye to them."

I turn to Legion. "I won't fight you." He ignores me and yells at Renatus. "We will fight."

"Legion. No."

"Shut it, Asher." He raises his voice as Renatus makes his way back. "We will fight. To the death."

Renatus pumps his fist. "That's the spirit, Legion. Once a warrior, always a warrior. I knew you still had it in you." He slaps the sword's handle, still protruding from Legion's shoulder. Legion grimaces in pain. "You sure you're up for it?"

Legion takes a deep breath and pulls the sword out of his shoulder. He stabs it into the ground. It waves back and forth. "You keep your word." He points to Sarai. "They live."

"Of course." Renatus turns, his tone sing-song. "Make sure one of you dies this time."

Minutes later, Renatus is back in his suite. Drones drop a smattering of weapons, littering the arena. The crowd rubs their hands, excited about the encore of bloodshed.

I lean in and whisper, "I won't kill you, Legion."

He smiles. "Like you could." Then he grimaces. "Nor will I you. Just put on a show, buy some time."

"Time for what?" I ask him.

"Who knows? Maybe a miracle?"

Our plan with the serum and the nuke was to save Silas. Save The Middle and our army. It was to prevent future harvesting. To render protocol ineffective. It didn't include saving us. I will fight Legion. Make it look good for Renatus.

Then, I will fall on my sword.

He has sacrificed enough.

"Let it begin!" Renatus bellows.

Legion grabs a voltaic sword and a dagger. I pick up the closest thing to me: a spear. He comes at me, mightily swinging his sword. It looks ferocious. The bloodthirsty mob loves it. But he is purposely telegraphing his moves, allowing me to block each blow with my spear. I swing my spear at him; he ducks and boots me in the chest. I somersault backward. That hurt. He shrugs as if to say sorry.

I hurl my spear at him, purposely aiming a tad high. He dodges it and sprints towards me. Blood is oozing from his shoulder now. I scramble to my left and pick up a sword as well. We duel vigorously, putting on a show with several near misses. He knocks the sword from my hand, and I duck his swing. He chases me across the arena until I swipe a ricochet from the floor and fling it in his direction. It nicks the armor on his left leg, and he trips mid-stride. He is on one knee; he is bleeding sweat, heaving for oxygen. He grabs his injured shoulder. It's worse than he lets on. But he is up again and charges. The crowd chants his name. It's almost nostalgic for them. Many here grew up watching Legion slaughter contestant after contestant.

We do this dance for another ten minutes or so. It has been long enough. It's time for Legion to win. It's time to give Renatus his loser. I let him push me into a corner. We are chest to chest. I reach into his belt and pull out the dagger. Legion instinctively grabs it. The crowd cannot see what is happening with our hands. I see his surprise when I turn the dagger and point it toward my chest. Time slows down. I peer up and see Sarai watching me. A solitary tear rolls down her cheek. She knows what I'm about to do. And she knows I have to do it. Besides, I would want her last memory of me to be one of sacrifice. What good will I be to her and my son if, years from now, protocol has turned me into another Renatus?

I mouth the words to my bride: *I'm sorry*.

She mouths back: *I know.*

But Legion has other plans.

"No, Asher."

He turns the blade towards him.

"What are you doing, Legion?" I whisper.

He begins to press the dagger into his chest. I try, but I'm not strong enough to stop him.

"Don't, Legion. Stop. You have done enough!"

"Asher. You have a child. A wife. It is you, and only you, who can defeat Renatus. Reunite this country."

"Don't do it, Legion. Please. Let me do something good while there's still good left in me."

"That's nonsense, Asher. You're the most worthy and honorable man I know."

"Please, Legion."

"I am not a leader of men. You have your purpose. I have mine."

I can't watch. My eyes close when Legion plunges the dagger into his heart. I scream as he drops to his knees. "No! No, Legion!"

He spits up blood. Grabs my hand. "Tell Renatus... tell him I am free."

Chapter Twelve

Sarai

I WEEP FOR LEGION, but am relieved Asher is still alive.

My father, not so much. He stands, his body quivering in anger. From here, at least to us, it is obvious that Legion gave himself up. I have lost count of the people who have sacrificed themselves for us and our cause. My arms slacken. I stare at my hands. Legion has once again become our savior. It's always the ones you least expect. It must pain my father greatly to have lost Legion to our side. Now the question is, will my father hold up his end of the bargain?

Renatus grabs an elite guard and slams him against the wall. "Bring Asher to holding cell fourteen underneath the arena." He points to us. "And them too."

"Right away, my Sultan."

Percival stands. "What does this mean, Renatus?"

"Nothing. Just wait here."

Percival looks confused. "Is something wrong?"

Renatus ignores him. As he escorts me, I whisper, "I hope you didn't come all this way for protocol."

Minutes later, we follow Renatus through the maze of tunnels underneath the arena. Eight elites escort us. Cephas, panting and losing blood, collapses to the floor.

"Cephas!"

"I'm fine," he lies.

"Get up!" an elite orders, kicking him in the ribs.

Adam and I gingerly lift Cephas by his arms and help him down the hallway. We turn the corner, and there is my Asher. He is chained to a cement wall inside a holding cell. A guard unlocks the cell door, and we all enter. We help Cephas sit on a concrete bench in the corner, and I rush into Asher's arms.

"You okay?"

Two elites rip me away at my father's command. Asher turns to Cephas. "What happened, Uncle?"

He waves him off. "It's a scratch, Nephew."

Renatus strolls towards Asher. "I hate to break up this little family reunion." He grabs Asher by the throat. I try to charge him, but two elites immediately hold me down. Renatus's eyes are like an inferno as he chokes Asher. "I told you to fight to the death."

"That is what we did." Asher's words barely manage to come out.

"You think I'm a fool? You staged it! Legion killed himself."

"What does it matter?!" I yell at my father through tears.

"It's the only thing that matters! You cowards dishonored yourselves and The Canonization. It is an insult to Zion and me." He releases his hands from Asher's neck and points to Cephas, Adam, and me. "You three will be exterminated today. And as for Silas? Well, he will bring life to my Eleazar. And you will watch it all." He turns back to Asher. "You and Legion will head to The Mountain until next year's Canonization."

I eye my father with a mix of fury and pity. "You can do whatever you like with us. But your beloved son, your *wounded prince*—my brother—cannot be saved. Nor can my son be harvested. Protocol is now dead."

"My daughter, we went over this already. Your serum is fake. Boaz gave you the wrong information. You band of Drecks are far too trusting."

Adam stands. "Well, good thing I'm not a Dreck."

Renatus eyes him, suspicious. "You shall die as one."

Adam is calm, his tone confident. "You see, our problem was testing the serum. How do we do that without taking an innocent life? Then your boy Boaz tried to escape. He killed one of our guards before they fired back, killing him. So, we tested it on the guard using Boaz's LifeCell. But when protocol worked, we knew the serum Boaz gave us was wrong."

Renatus's lips curl towards his feet. Adam paces like a professor explaining something to his students. "So now, we had a guard who had Boaz's LifeCell... and with that, his *memories*."

I interject. "And with his memories, we had just enough technical knowledge of protocol to figure out how to reverse the serum."

Renatus's voice is hollow, shocked. He presses his fist to his mouth and says slightly. "You lie."

Asher says, "It's over, Renatus. Eleazar is gone. Forever. Soon, everyone will be protocol-resistant. Second Life is over. The Wall will come down, and Zion will die. The abomination of protocol is no longer. The age of man wielding God's power has ended. You are finished."

Renatus unsheathes his dagger and presses it against Asher's neck. "AND. SO. ARE. YOU!"

Asher keeps Renatus's gaze. "Protocol is no more; do with me what you will."

Asher's neck begins to bleed as Renatus pushes his dagger even harder. "You have taken everything away from me. First, my daughter, then Legion, and now Apex. I will not let you take my son."

"It's too late, Renatus, it's done."

Renatus paces, slapping his shiny forehead.

"You don't have to do this, Renatus. We can work something out. Let us go and surrender your army. You weren't always like this. Your intentions were once good. You can return to that. Help us put this country back together."

Renatus bites his tongue and lifts his hands, tightening into claw-like formations. His lips quiver, and his breathing becomes sporadic as he moves back towards Asher's throat.

Is this it? Is this where he kills my husband? Does it end here for us? And what will he do with him if he can't harvest Silas? My father is too far gone to be rational. Pleading with him doesn't work. Is there anything more I can do or say?

Yes.

I know my father. He is my blood. I know what makes him tick. "Coward," I say softly.

Renatus turns toward me. "What was that, daughter?"

My voice is calm, still low. "Asher is chained to the wall. Is that how he dies? Will the legend of Asher the Traitor or Asher the Liberator be that he once again won the Canonization? And instead of being rewarded, you stabbed him in the back in a dark room where no one could witness your cowardliness? You will only make him a martyr. A Dreck who defied Zion. A Dreck no Lazurite could defeat. Not even Legion. Not even Apex."

I can see my father's wheels spinning. I am getting to him. He is all about pride. All about legacy. I continue, "How will they remember Renatus, ruler of Zion? Will it be that he was able to do what no one else could? Will it be you who finally vanquishes Asher? Or will you be known as Renatus the Dastard?"

"I know what you are doing, Sarai." His tone turns frenzied, crazed. "And I think it's a fantastic idea!"

I see Asher's look go from surprised to hopeful.

Renatus continues, "Yes. Yes, I will slay Asher with my own hand, and they will love me for it. Thank you, daughter. You just saved this Canonization." He turns to an elite and points to Asher. "See to it that he is fed and cleaned up. And let the people leaving the coliseum know we are about to have an encore."

The elite asks, "What about the rest of them?"

"Let them watch. Then we will kill them."

He leaves the room, and I rush to embrace Asher. "Does it ever end?"

He pulls me tight and whispers, "If I lose, take Silas and go far away from here. Never come back."

"But how?" I ask, not wanting to entertain the idea of him losing.

"Use the nuke as leverage."

"I'm not going anywhere. You won't lose."

"I don't know how much I have left in me, Sarai."

I pull him in tighter. "One more battle, my love. One more fight, and then it's over."

The guards separate us and drag Asher to the door.

Our eyes lock for what might be the last time. We have been given one last chance. Once again, it's all on his shoulders. Shoulders I desperately wish I could unburden. But the weight is heavy on me also. I have to watch my husband kill my father.

Or my father kill my husband.

Asher

I once again stand in the middle of the arena. It's becoming my second home. Spectators are filing back into the coliseum and returning to their seats. There is an aura of muted astonishment from the crowd that borders on anxiety as they wonder if the rumor is true. Is Renatus really going to grace the arena and fight me? I am starting to wonder what the catch is. I am the more skilled fighter—or, the more experienced, at least. Is he really that crazy, or is there some other ruse that guarantees his victory? It doesn't matter now; that is out of my control.

I am unable to summon the usual adrenaline surge I get before a battle. I am empty, my reserves depleted. Exhausted would be an understatement. Sarai's words ring in my head: *One more battle. One more fight. Then it's all over.*

Instead of drums, I hear loud horns and trumpets. A victorious and uplifting ballad is played as Renatus enters the arena to a standing ovation. Smoke wafts and twirls at his heels as if he is being introduced by heavenly clouds, like an archangel. The trumpets reinforce that image. The mob eats it up. Isn't that always the way? The devil will appear in sheep's clothing—an angel just slightly askew.

Renatus's exoarmor is bright red, whereas mine is standard-issue black. The red and white sashes tied to his arms and legs flutter in the breeze. I prefer the trumpets over the drums—an odd thing to ponder right before a death match.

Renatus raises his hands to quiet the crowd. "I may be your ruler, but I'm not above getting my hands dirty. Asher has proved himself a mighty adversary, reaching legendary status. His accolades include defeating the mighty brothers, Apex and Legion. Some are beginning to think he cannot be killed—that he may even be a Lazurite. I'm here today to dispel those myths!"

As the mob's jubilation grows in tenor, he approaches me. "I could get used to this."

"Don't," I reply.

"After all these years, it's finally come to this—just you and I, Asher. How does it feel to know that your bride and your uncle are going to watch you die?"

I don't take the bait. I need to settle myself. Concentrate. "So it's really just you and me? Pure and simple? No drones? No burning oil? No lions or tigers? No sharks?"

He nods. "Just your skill against mine."

His confidence worries me, but when is he not overconfident?

"It's a shame, Asher. You would have made a great prince of Zion. You would have been a great son."

"I already am a son. I already have a father."

"And you are about to join him."

Then, drones drop a new batch of weapons onto the arena floor: Stun-Clubs, ricochets, scourges, and plasma shields. Oddly, we are only fighting with plasma and pulse weapons—no swords, spears, or daggers. I grab a shield and StunClub, then clip a ricochet and scourge to my belt. Renatus does the same. I peer up and take one last look at Sarai and my uncle. Then I charge, furiously swinging my StunClub. With his plasma shield, he blocks blow after blow. He is quicker than I expected. Agile and light on his feet. In my haste, I leave him an opening. He tags me on the side with his club. Its initial shock sends me to the ground, but I roll to the left and am back on my feet. His movements and fluidity tell me he practices with these weapons.

I fling my ricochet, which he also blocks. But he doesn't see me whip my scourge at him simultaneously. It wraps around his left ankle, and I pull him to the ground. He rolls to the left three times, untwisting the scourge from his ankle, and is back on his feet.

"Asher, Vanquisher of Giants, you're so predictable."

He hurls his ricochet at me, and I sling my scourge at it. It wraps around the metal boomerang while still in flight. I swing my electric whip around and redirect it. Now, at twice the speed, the ricochet barrels towards Renatus. He barely has time to hold up his shield to block it, but the force is too great. It knocks his plasma shield out of his hand, sending it rolling across the arena.

He has a momentary look of shock now that he is without his shield, unprotected. I take advantage and go on the attack. He is able to block most of my club strikes, until I finally land a direct hit to the head. He falls to the ground with a thump. I lean down and check his pulse to be sure.

He is gone. Finally gone.

I exhale and turn my back, wondering what will happen next. I hear the murmurs of the crowd first. Then I feel something knifing into the rear of my shoulder, just between my armor. I hit the ground, roll back up, and turn. There is Renatus, covertly sheathing his dagger.

He is alive. But how?

But of course. That is why he was so confident. That is why we are dueling with plasma weapons only. He is secretly wearing a LifePack underneath his armor. Instead of losing his head with a sword, he can come back to life with these weapons, without anyone knowing.

"You can't kill me!" he yells, riling up the crowd. I also hear the roars of his army just outside the coliseum as they watch on a giant HoloTube, along with my army.

He is living up to his legend of invincibility. That he is a deity. Once again, the lyrical, ringing sounds of the trumpets are unleashed. Smoke is blown into the arena. The question is: how many LifeCells are in his pack? How many times do I have to kill him? And with the fresh wound in my back, it hurts to move my right arm. I was naive to think this was going to be a fair fight.

He comes at me now using both his scourge and club. I block what I can. I gasp, trying to catch my breath. The stabbing pain in my back intensifies. The multiple shocks to my system are beginning to add up. His club hits me again. I hemorrhage sweat, and my vision blurs. I drop to my knees. He hammers away at my shield. Salty blood trickles from my mouth. My eyes sting, and my nose is crushed.

He pauses. "You're a bloody Dreck, Asher. You didn't actually think you would win, did you?"

I dig deep, but there is nothing left. Cephas once told me that the point of life is to die empty, to give everything. I have.

He pounds me again with his club; I barely have enough strength to lift my shield and block it. I close my eyes and think about Legion. I think about what Renatus has done to my Sarai. My son. My Uncle. My parents. Jude.

A sudden surge of energy jolts me up, buoyed by my uncle's words, my father's actions, and my love for Sarai. This startles Renatus. With rising intensity, I furiously attack him, pounding his shield until he can no longer hold it.

Rage has taken over.

I hit him in the arm so hard I can hear his bones crack. Next is his leg. That, too, breaks at the ankle. He folds to the ground. I am on top of him as he unsheathes his dagger, but I easily wrestle it away.

I slide it between his back and exoarmor—and cut the tube connected to his LifePack.

For the first time, I see actual fear in his eyes. I place the tip of the dagger at his throat. His timbre is full of panic. "Don't. Don't do it, Asher. You don't have to do this! We can work something out. You can have your son."

"It's too late for that."

Renatus's eyes go wide; he clenches his fists. "Listen to me, Asher, I loved you. I loved you like a son. I was prepared to give everything to you. I still can. You and my daughter can have the keys to the kingdom. You don't have to do this. We are family, Asher."

"Now you're on your last life. No longer a Lazurite. How does it feel to be mortal?"

I am about to press on the dagger.

"Wait! Stop!" It's Sarai.

"Sarai! What are you doing down here?"

Renatus's elites can see the writing on the wall. They instinctively follow power. They have been obeying Renatus out of fear. They don't even try to stop her as she runs to me.

"Don't, Asher. It's not worth it."

"It's the only way to end this, Sarai. Once and for all. The only way to finally get out of this nightmare. As long as he's alive, there will never be peace. We will never be free. I know he's your father. But we need justice."

"And he will receive it. We will let him stand trial and expose him to the world. But this doesn't look like justice. This looks more like revenge."

My fists clench around the dagger. "This is the only way out."

"No, all this does is make him a martyr in his own arena."

"It's the only way."

She steps closer. "No, Asher. Love is the only way out."

Then behind her, limping and wheezing, is Cephas. "She's right, Nephew. Let it go, son. Let it go."

Asher

She's right.

So is Cephas.

If I can't remain true to who I am, then Renatus will have taken everything from me. The crowd is deathly quiet, speechless at the events they are now witnessing. My flesh wants to drive my dagger into his larynx. What I do next will live on in the history books and televised replays. One day, my son will watch it. My grandchildren will read about it.

"Let it go, Nephew," Cephas repeats.

My hands shake, my head throbs. The battle for my mind rages. But one takes over: my father. Silas. Silas the Peacemaker. His persona is bigger than all the other LifeCells inside of me combined. He is the one good thing to emerge from receiving protocol. I can hear his voice. I am unsure what he is saying, but I know it's him. It's more of a feeling than words.

I do what he would have done. Sarai looks at me and nods.

I rise from my knees, removing the dagger from Renatus's throat. Not only did she save him, but she saved me. I embrace Sarai. The crowd simultaneously exhales and begins to chant new monikers for me: "Asher the Charitable. Asher the Forgiving. Asher, King of Zion."

I'll take the first two, but I don't want to be king of anything.

From his knees, Renatus points to his elite guards. "Arrest him! Arrest Asher the Traitor!" They ignore him. "Kill him, or I'll have you put to death!"

"Detain him!" Sarai orders. The guards stand frozen for a moment, unsure what to do or who to support. She marches towards them, her tone unwavering. "Renatus is finished. We have won. Just listen to this crowd. It's time to choose a side."

"I will kill your family," Renatus threatens.

Sarai assures them, "You will be protected. So will your family. You will be treated fairly. Now detain him."

A tense moment. Then, "Yes, my Sultana."

We exhale as they grab Renatus and lift him to his knees, but our moment is short-lived. Adam rushes into the arena, his voice urgent. "We have a problem. The Lazurite army is preparing to take up arms and storm the coliseum."

Cephas trudges closer. "Show's not over, I'm afraid."

Sarai grabs my shoulders. "You must convince them otherwise. They are still watching on the HoloTube." She winks. "You have one last speech in you, don't ya?"

I need to clear my head. All I can think about is drinking a gallon of water and sleeping for a week. I can see the Lazurite army and my army on the giant HoloTube screen below the Sultan's suite. They are starting to stir and ready their arms. A mob mentality is brewing. I have one chance to stop it.

"Wait!" I yell. "Who do you think Renatus is? What do you think he is? A god? A brave and selfless leader?" I bend down and rip off Renatus's exoarmor, exposing the LifePack on his back. "See this! Do you see this? Does this look like courage to you? You know what's inside this pack, don't you?" I point to the remaining LifeCells floating inside. "These were once human lives: my relatives and yours. When did you become a society obsessed with death? Why do you feed off one another's suffering?"

Renatus shouts, "Don't listen to him! He is a traitor. A Dreck! I am your Sultan. Storm this arena and rescue me."

I think about having him gagged, but the more he speaks, the more the words dig his own grave.

"Do you hear me? Enter this arena and kill these Drecks. Now! The first hundred Lazurites to do so will be given eternal life!"

I respond, "And he will kill your brethren to do so! Renatus cares nothing for you. Everything he has done has been for his benefit. You have been blinded by it in the name of entertainment."

I gesture to the arena floor. "How is this entertainment? Do you let your children watch? No. Why is that? I want to see the world through their eyes. Let's look forward to the day they marry and have their own children... not the day they are sent to an arena to satisfy the bloodlust of a corrupt and immoral society. Open your eyes to what Zion really is and how it has enslaved you. The veil is so thick that you cannot see through it. I understand; it almost happened to me. I, too, was once caught in its web."

I stop for a moment to catch my breath. But I need to continue while I still have their attention. I understand how delicate the situation is. One wrong move or word, and everything can descend into chaos. "You have two armies facing each other right now. Lazurites and Drecks. But not too long ago, you were brothers and sisters. You aren't as different as you think you are. I know this from experience. I am a Dreck who lived as a Zion prince and married a Lazurite!" Some laughter from the crowds. The tiniest bit of humor has cut the tension. Sometimes that's all it takes. "Let's lay down the sword. Peace has been fragile for too long."

I suddenly realize I still have a death grip on the dagger. With a bit of fanfare, I drop it. "It's time to start over. It's time to forgive. Let's tear down this Wall, not only the physical one but the one that stands between Dreck and Lazurite. In fact, let's be neither. Let's lose the labels. I say it's time to unify again as one country. We can once again be called Americans. Let's dispel the notion that one life isn't enough. Eternal life on a fallen earth isn't freedom; it's a prison." I hold out my arms. "If none of that sounds appealing to you, then come take me now; do as you wish." I fall to my knees. "I can fight no more."

Silence. Both armies outside the coliseum are frozen in place. Did my words resonate enough to cut through the ignorant and barbarous mob? We are about to discover just how deep and compelling Renatus's spell is. Can Zion's seduction be broken? I look to Sarai, then Cephas; we collectively hold our breath.

Then, a glorious sound. The clunking noise of PlasmaRifles hitting the ground. The two armies converge—the shaking of hands and small talk.

A final resignation falls upon Renatus's face. His last hope of being saved is now dashed.

I practically fall into Sarai's arms. "Is it over? Is it really over?"

Tears of joy overcome her. "Yes. You did it."

"We did it."

"Let's go get our son."

I don't see it. My back is to him. Renatus slides one of his arms free and swipes a dagger from one of his elite guards. Or maybe the guard let him? Doesn't matter. He rears back, aiming the dagger at my back.

Before I know what is happening, Sarai shoves me out of the way and flings her own knife at Renatus. It slices through the air and sinks into his heart. At first, shock crosses his face. As Renatus stares at his daughter, his countenance changes. Now his face practically radiates with pride. In some sick and twisted manner, he almost appreciates that it was her. Renatus rears his blood-stained teeth, drops his dagger, and flops to the ground. Dust rises from the arena floor as if Demons are leaving his body. She has saved me.

Again.

I peer up at my bride and realize that Renatus isn't the only one whose heart was pierced by that dagger. Yes, he was evil incarnate. Yes, he was about to kill me, and yes, he deserved it. But her father's death is by her own hand. I am not going to pretend to know what that might feel like. All I can do is hold her.

"Now it's over," Sarai says.

It's hard to believe those words. It has been so long since we have had a clean slate, a chance at a new beginning, I almost don't know what to do. Even so, I would be a fool not to embrace this, make the most of it.

Moments later, ten Lazurite elites enter the arena and approach us. I tense up. But they all fall to one knee. "Asher the Liberator, we pledge allegiance to you."

I wave my hand upwards. "Stand. Stand up, soldiers. There will be no more of this. No more pledging allegiance to one man or government. We will be free. We will vote. Your leaders will serve you as intended, not the other way around."

They stand. One of them nods towards Renatus's body. "What should we do with him, sir?"

For Sarai's sake as well as the crowds, I want his image gone as soon as possible. "Get him out of the arena, as quickly as you can."

Sarai points towards the Suite of Sultans. "And Czar Percival. Arrest him."

We watch as they drag Renatus's limp body from the arena.

But my joy is temporary as Cephas collapses to the ground. "Cephas!"

We rush over. I bend down and yell, "Get a medic! Get a Doctor!"

His voice raspy and ragged. "No. No, Asher. It's time."

"Don't talk that way, Uncle. You're gonna make it. Medic!"

He grabs my collar and pulls me close. "Listen to me, Nephew. My job here on earth is finished. Don't shed tears for me. I am about to start a new life. Remember, Asher, nothing in this world is permanent. Everything eventually turns to dust and ash. I'm going home, Nephew. I'm going home. Home to my bride."

"C'mon, Cephas, not yet! I need you; this country needs you!"

He pulls a tattered, blood-stained Bible from his coat and hands it to me. "Take this." He then looks to Sarai and says, "Seems to me you have everything you need, Nephew. There is nothing more this old man can teach you."

And before any medical help can arrive, his eyes close.

My uncle. My rock. The leader of The Defiance. The man who overcame his scars and demons and taught me about faith. The man who could one moment fight a grizzly bear, and the next help a recovering addict. It was his rough edges that helped sand and shape me into the man I am now. My father may have molded me, but he polished me.

That man is gone.

Asher

It's been a month since our victory at the Canonization. Everyone inside The Mountain has been liberated, including our Silas. He stands between Sarai and me, holding our hands. I am inspired by his resilience and self-lessness. I have no doubt Silas will live up to his namesake.

Smoke still emanates from inside The Mountain. Protocol and every-thing related have been destroyed, as have the drug factories. We have dispatched multiple crews to clean up the trash that was dumped into The Middle for decades. Our anti-protocol serum is now being mass-produced, just in case someone decides to resurrect second-life technology. We have a lot to celebrate.

But today, we mourn. Today is a day of funerals for those friends and heroes we have lost:

Cephas.

Legion.

Eleazar.

Kenan.

Neriah.

Hagar.

Lucas.

And so many others.

As the many caskets are lowered simultaneously into the ground, a haunting voice ascends. In a show of solidarity, five Drecks and five Lazu-rites sing a passive version of Hallelujah. I cannot help but shed a tear at their angelic voices. But it's not the song that has Sarai sobbing. It is the size of Eleazar's casket. Smaller than any casket should ever be.

I have once again been asked to speak. I trudge to where the dirt is being piled on top of the caskets. For a moment, God shoos away the dark clouds and lets the sun shine upon our faces.

"We have won a great victory for freedom, but today is proof that it doesn't come without sacrifice. We have lost so many throughout the years, and today, we celebrate, honor, and mourn just a few who have given so much. They were many things to many people. An uncle. A warrior. A brother. A friend. A mother. A confidant. A son. They were one of these things and all of these things. We could not have won this war without them. We would not be the people we are without them. I would not be standing here without them.

"I take solace in the fact that they have finally been given rest. Evil grows in the silent complacency of those who consider themselves righteous. It's not enough to just be a good person and abstain from wickedness. Sometimes you have to give more. And sometimes everything, as each one of these brave souls did. We will always remember them. We will never forget them. There will never be anyone like them. They are with God now, and there is nothing that man can do to take that away. So whenever you need an uncle, a warrior, a brother, a friend, a mother, a confidant, or a son, remember the names: Cephas. Legion. Eleazar. Kenan. Neriah. Hagar. Lucas."

We spend the next several hours reminiscing. Drecks and Lazurites. The Sitkans and the children from the Sons of Levi. We tell old stories and some new ones.

As the sun fades and the winds pick up, Adam and Eve approach us. "Well, we are off."

"Where to?" I ask.

Adam smiles at Eve. "After a hundred and thirty years, I think it's time for a honeymoon."

Eve nudges him. "And it better be good."

Adam grabs my arm and pulls me in for a hug. "I don't know how to thank you." He turns to Sarai. "Both of you. If it weren't for your uncle, we would still be frozen in time, waiting for the apocalypse. And you made me realize something."

"What's that?"

"Well, I thought what I was doing at Eden was important. Don't get me wrong, it was, and I believed in it. But what we did here, what you did for this country. This was more important. I guess what I'm trying to say is it's hard to make a difference when you're sleeping—or frozen, in our case."

Eve adds, "Better to prevent an apocalypse than try to rebuild after one."

"We couldn't have done it without you," Sarai tells them. She grabs Eve's hand. "It's about time we get to write our own ending."

Eve points to Timothy, who is running around with his friends. "Take care of him while we're gone. When we get back, we are going to officially adopt him."

"Of course," Sarai tells them.

I say, "Hey, I don't think I ever caught your real names."

"I'm Naomi," Eve states, then she turns to Adam and smiles, "And his name is—"

"Adam will do just fine," Adam interrupts.

"Godspeed to you, Naomi and *Adam*." I then hand Eve Cephas's tattered and blood-stained Bible. "And this one, you'll want to finish."

Before they leave, Adam turns to me. "And you? What will you do now?"

I smile at Sarai. "I think... I think I want to be Asher again."

Sarai

The ocean is calm, as if expecting my arrival. I man my father's thirty-foot fishing vessel off the coast of Pt. Reyes. The sun is just beginning to melt into the frigid, blue Pacific. I am alone; this is the way I wanted it. Asher offered to come, but I told him to stay back with Silas. This is between Renatus and me.

I cut the engine and let the boat slowly drift. I am the only one out here on the placid sea. My father lies in a simple pine box coffin near the bow of the boat. We decided that the best way for him not to be martyred was to destroy the coliseum and commit his body to the sea. This way, his remaining supporters could not visit his place of death or honor him at a place of burial.

I open a side door near the bow and slowly push the wooden casket into the cobalt water. It makes a small splash before starting its descent into the cold depths. I close my eyes, aim my face towards what is left of the sinking sun. The further my father's casket sinks, the more peace I feel. I have come to accept the fact that my father was evil, that I didn't grow up with parents who loved or cared for me. I even have forgiveness in my heart—not for him, but for me. I can no longer drink the bitter poison of unforgiveness. The further he plummets towards the darkness, the more I bathe in the light and the more I am released from the burden of resentment and anger.

I open my eyes and dwell on the irony: that my father is now buried in the same unforgiving ocean that claimed my brother. These icy waters remain indifferent and aloof to my pain. They didn't force Eleazar to swim in them, but they also let him drown. I no longer blame the Pacific, nor am I afraid of it. It just is. It was just reacting to our decisions. It gives me some comfort that one day I will see my brother again. He is in heaven now, no longer *wounded*.

I turn the boat around and head back to port as the horizon swallows the last of the sunlight. For the first time in as long as I can remember, I am optimistic about our future. The wall dividing our country, the wall dividing our family, has been torn down. To my left, a pod of dolphins slices through the salty water. I think one is smiling at me.

I smile back.

Asher

It has been almost a week, and most of the swelling has disappeared. I peer in the mirror, and for a moment, I am shocked. I have lived with Amos's face for so long that I have forgotten what I look like. I rub my fingers across my face.

My face.

I am fully Asher again. The Sculptor took great care to bring me back. The scarring is barely perceptible. Sarai said I didn't have to go through with it. That she loved me regardless, but I could no longer don the face of my enemy. It was the final remnant of a time I want to forget.

I walk outside and turn towards the morning sun with a smile. Magnificent hues of orange and purple cascade through the retreating clouds. I close my eyes and let my face absorb the shimmering glory.

"Glad to have you back," one of my soldiers tells me.

"Glad to be back."

"This way." He escorts me to a HeliDrone. "And, sir, permission to speak freely?"

"Always."

"I never liked Amos's face on you."

"That makes two of us."

A few hours later, we are nearing The Middle. I peer down and see a glorious sight: portions of The Wall coming down. And in every town we fly over, I see our nation's flag rise once again. I am told that the entirety of The Wall should be down and deactivated before our reunification ceremony next week. There, we will re-ratify the Constitution, and add an amendment abolishing protocol forever. But, before that, there is one more thing I need to do.

The drone lands in a clearing next to two others. I jump off and practically sprint up the hill. I am more nervous than I thought I would be. It's not Sarai so much as it is my son. Amos's face is the only one Silas has ever known.

When I reach the top, I see them below. Sarai and Silas play tag in the tall grass. Behind them is our Weeping Willow—still charred and black, but green strands are beginning to emerge. Like our nation, a rebirth from the ashes. I am almost down when they spot me. Sarai smiles. Silas backs up behind her.

"Who is that man?" he asks her.

"That's your father, Silas."

He looks up at her, bewildered.

"This is what he looks like, the real him."

I drop to one knee and hold out my arms. "Hey, buddy. What do you think?"

"You look old but not bad." I love his honesty as he hugs me, touching my face.

I rise and approach my wife. "And what about you?"

She grabs my chin. "This is the face I fell in love with."

"Hey, Dad!" Silas yells, holding a small tree branch.

"Toss it up."

He does, and I split it into two with my ricochet.

Silas smiles. "Yep, it's you."

Sarai grabs my hand. "It's kind of ironic. First, you had to convince me who you were, and now our son."

"Let's hope for the last time."

She grabs her scourge from her belt. "You ready?"

The three of us stroll to our Weeping Willow. A small hole has already been dug underneath it. An antique-looking chest sits on the ground. She opens the chest and places her scourge inside. I grab my ricochet, hesitant for a moment, then put it inside as well. Here is to the hope we never have to use these weapons again.

We lower the chest into the ground. Silas helps us kick dirt over it.

"Why did you bury them?" Silas asks.

Sarai stands. "The war is over. Now it's time for peace."

Peace.

That word has been like a phantom my entire life—a shadow I could never catch. But for the first time in a long while, I am optimistic. I still have headaches. I still live with the memories of those whose LifeCells live inside of me. There is still a daily battle for my mind. But when I have forgiven myself, those memories seem to disappear. When I accept the memories for what they are and do my best to honor those people's deaths through how I live my life, it makes it easier. I must never forget who I am. A child of God. Asher, son of Silas. Father to Silas.

We walk back up the hill, swinging Silas. The wind is at our backs, the sun upon our faces. I beam at Sarai. She winks back. I think about everything we have been through. We started with hope. We needed faith. But we ended with the greatest of all... love.

It's hard to be imprisoned behind a wall. Even harder when you fall. But now we must do the most difficult:

Rise.

Acknowledgements

First and foremost, I want to thank my readers for following Asher and Sarai to the completion of their journey. Once again, I would like to thank my beta readers: Nancy, Clint, Jessalynn, and many more. Your wisdom and support are appreciated more than you know. Your encouragement when, at times, I felt like giving up has pushed me to continue putting words on paper.

To my wife, Erica, who reminds me to find the courage to rise after I have fallen, and to my parents for supporting me in not giving up on this dream. To my editor, Salima Alikhan, thank you for your insight and patience. Perhaps one day, I'll figure out how to properly use a comma. To my cover designer, Natalia Junqueira, once again, you nailed it.

To my children, Noah, Madelynn, and Marshall: you have inspired me to follow my calling. I hope you do the same. Lastly, I want to thank God for making this possible. I could not do any of it without Him.

If you enjoyed this novel and are so inclined, any reviews would be greatly appreciated!

If you would like to stay informed on my upcoming novels and other news, feel free to subscribe to my mailing list:

https://www.BrianAlanPenn.com/#contact